WRITTEN BY: Dylan Collins Dunbar
EDITED BY: Mick Muggs, aka Lord Mugso
COVER DESIGN: Dylan Collins Dunbar
COVER PHOTO: J.A. Dunbar
BACK COVER PHOTO: Bryan Mitchell

jenniferwestwood.com/dylan

WOLF'S HYDE

BY DYLAN COLLINS DUNBAR

PROLOGUE

STALINGRAD

NOVEMBER, 1942

Erich Kaiser opened his eyes as he lay in the freezing snow near the city of Stalingrad. His ears still rang from the explosion. A Russian anti-tank round hit his Panzer IV shortly after it had run out of fuel and became immovable in the Russian terrain. Erich's commander had ordered him to crawl out and check the fuel reserve canisters when his Panzer exploded. The force of the blast tossed him ten yards through the air. Killing the remainder of the crew inside. Realizing this order saved his life, he lay there dazed, trying to regain his senses and figure out his next move.

Erich was part of the 4th Panzer Division, which was taxed with holding the outskirts of Stalingrad while Germany's 6th Army pushed to take the city. What started off in the German army's favor in the summer of 1942 was no longer going according to plan. The Germans were already feeling the harsh climate of the Russian Winter, with temperatures reaching forty below. They had also started to run out of supplies such as fuel, ammunition, and food. At the current moment, Hitler's forces were unprepared for the Russian offensive retaliation of Operation Uranus.

Erich lay there breathing, still dazed, watching his breath rise from his face in the frigid temperatures. He could hear explosions of more Russian anti-tank rounds decimating the remaining tanks in his division as they sat there like sitting ducks with no ability to return fire or retreat. He finally scrambled to his feet and saw the remnants of his Panzer tank, realizing then that he would still be inside if his commander hadn't ordered him to get out and check supplies.

As the sound of continuous gunfire filled the dense air, Erich looked around, trying to decide what to do. Plumes of black smoke billowed up into the gray skies as it began once again to snow. There were bodies of soldiers, both German and Russian, for as far as he could see. He was not mentally or physically prepared for this in any way. After all, Erich was just a Panzer tank radio operator. He wasn't much of a fighter, nor did he share the same beliefs of the Nazi party.

To his left, in the distance, he saw the tree line of the forest about ninety yards away from where he was standing. His need for self-preservation said to run and use those trees for cover. Taking in one last deep breath, he ran.

The wind howled, and the snow began to increase in intensity as he ran as hard as he could. An anti-tank round exploded off to his right, just far enough away that the blast knocked him over, sending him rolling. Another German soldier reached out and helped him to his feet. Just as he was about to thank the soldier, his savior's head exploded from a rifle round, sending bone and brain matter all over Erich's uniform and face. Shaken by what had just occurred, his survival instincts kicked in once more and, without hesitation, he began to run for his life.

He figured if he could just get to the forest, he could at least try to use the trees in his favor and go unseen as he fled. Possibly catch his breath, collect his wits, and try to figure out his position. There was another explosion off to his left while another Panzer tank returned fire, only to explode seconds later from another anti-tank round. He was so close he could hear the screams of the men inside as they burned alive in their iron tomb. His will to live was the only drive keeping him from lying down and giving up. He clenched his jaw and pressed on.

Bullets whizzed past his head as he ducked and zigzagged through the snow as the sounds of machine guns and explosions rang through the air. He spotted the shell of a burned-out German half-track that was still smoldering. He figured if he could just make it behind that, he could use it as cover till he made the tree line. When he got to the half-track, he collapsed behind it, resting his back against the immobilized metal carcass. He quickly patted himself down, checking for any holes. Other than some singed eyebrows, he seemed okay. A German Mauser was lying in the snow just in front of him. Snatching up the rifle, Erich checked the chamber, confirmed that it was loaded, and rose to his feet to start his fifty-yard dash for the cover of the birch trees. More explosions went off all around him as he climbed over his fallen comrades with only one single thought: survival.

Erich made it to the trees and ran another 100 yards before diving behind a spruce tree. He took a moment to gather his thoughts. All he could think of was how he never wanted to be a part of this war in the first place. Being well into middle age, he was quite older than the average German soldier and was thrown into Hitler's war against his will. He was a well-educated man who lived in Berlin before the war. A scholar who spoke ten languages, including Russian, Japanese, and English. This was the main reason he was drafted and placed in a

Panzer division as a radio operator. Most of his days prior were filled with reading books, drinking wine, and laughing. But ever since that madman took leadership of his country, he was forced into servitude against his will. With his heart thundering against his chest, he tried to block out the sounds of war behind him and take in the beauty of the surrounding birch trees and falling snow. This simple act helped calm his nerves and gather the mental fortitude to continue.

Erich had walked for a little over three hours now in a direction he hoped was west. The snow kept falling, and he figured that might work in his favor. Possibly the fresh snowfall would help to cover his tracks so the Red Army wouldn't be able to follow. He figured he had two choices, and that was to try to walk back to German-occupied territory or lie down and freeze to death. Dying was not high on his list, so he kept walking, knowing he would probably freeze to death anyway. He had to at least try.

Within an hour, Erich had lost feeling in his feet and his hands were beginning to ache. He stopped for a few minutes and removed his gloves to check his hands. He noticed some of his fingers had begun developing blue blisters and he could tell that frostbite was starting to set in. Like most of the 6th Army, he was ill-equipped to handle this weather and knew he was not going to last much longer if he didn't find shelter or warmth soon.

Trying not to think about how he was already going to lose his toes and possibly his feet, he just pushed on. He had wrapped a scarf around his face and ears, but it was no longer effective at keeping the freezing temperatures out.

He was starting to show signs of severe hypothermia and having a hard time remembering where he was or what he was doing. Confused, he was positive that he was beginning to hallucinate. Something seemed to sprint through the trees off in the distance, keeping up a steady pace with him. He just chalked this up to the delirium from hypothermia. By now his will had started to dwindle and he thought he caught the smell of an open campfire somewhere off in the distance. Just when he thought this was his hysteria taking over, he came into a clearing where he found a lone man sitting on a log by a raging fire. Erich prayed that what he saw was real. Hopeful that the man was friendly, he walked towards the small camp seeking some rest and warmth.

The gypsy sat quietly and content in front of his fire, cooking a meal on a spit over the open flames. The snow had ceased falling and the man's long black beard was covered with frozen chunks of snow and ice. He wore a long bear-skin shawl over his shoulders and a fur-covered ushanka hat on his head. His long black hair fell down his chest from underneath his hat framing his beard over his tattered dark clothes which were a mix match of German and Russian uniforms. The gypsy looked up from the food he was preparing and noticed the German soldier walking toward him in the distance. He could tell that Erich was emaciated, and it was clear he was already in the beginning stages of death. The soldier spoke out in Russian as he peacefully approached the fire.

"Please, may I join you?" Erich leaned on his rifle in exhaustion. "I mean you no harm. I barely have enough life in me to stand let alone hurt you."

There was a long pause of silence. The gypsy took a large bite off a shank of meat and began slowly chewing. Making eye contact with Erich the entire time, he waited until he swallowed before speaking.

"Yes comrade, join me." He pointed towards the tree stump on the other side of the roaring fire for the soldier to sit. Erich carefully laid down his Mauser in the snow next to him and sat down on the stump with a sense of defeat. His host stood up and walked over to him with a fur blanket and draped it over Erich's shoulders.

"Here, that will help a little," he said as he walked back to his seat across the fire.

"My name is Erich Kaiser and I am of Germany's 6th Army," he said through chattering teeth. "I was a tank radio operator for the 4th Panzer division and we ran out of fuel during the Soviet offensive strike back near Stalingrad. Once I stepped outside to check our fuel reserves, an anti-tank round hit us dead on. Destroying my Panzer along with its crew and commander."

The German noticed that there was a large elk or moose carcass to the gypsy's right, which he assumed was what the man was cooking over the fire. The aromas reminded him of back home in Germany before the war started.

"Would you like some sbiten?" the gypsy asked Erich.

"What is sbiten?" he asked.

The gypsy explained to him that sbiten was a Russian mulled wine that contained cinnamon, mint, ginger and daisy and that he was more than welcome to have some. He then offered to share some of the elk he was cooking over the fire. Erich graciously accepted. The Russian reached down and stirred the sweet liquid in a pot, which was resting near the hot coals. The steam and smells of the mulled wine were rejuvenating as he ladled it into a copper mug and walked it over to his frozen guest.

Erich took note that the man did not appear to be armed and he also noticed he was barefoot in the snow. They both sat in silence as Erich gripped his mug as tightly as he could and took in the smells that wafted up at him, filling his nostrils. He drank deep and tried to collect what wits he had left, for he knew he was dying.

"My name is Nikolia Sergeev," the gypsy said, finally breaking the silence. "You are safe here, comrade, for this forest belongs to me and the Soviet Army will not venture into these woods. So please rest yourself. I could use the company."

Erich sat relieved, still shaking uncontrollably from the cold, sipping his hot beverage as he listened to the man speak.

"I have to say that I am very impressed, comrade, for that was a long trek through harsh climate and terrain. Yet your will and determination brought you to me. I believe this was fate, little one," the gypsy said. As the firelight danced across the surrounding trees, Erich looked up and noticed the stars were shining brightly in the night sky.

"I must admit, it is very beautiful out here," Erich said.

"Da it is. I have resided here for a good portion of my life and the wonders never cease to amaze me," Nikolia responded.

Erich wondered if this was real, or a delusion caused by hypothermia. The two men spoke for what felt like hours. They discussed everything from classic literature to their favorite classical music while enjoying more mulled wine and fire-roasted elk meat. It was like the two of them had known each other for years. Even on the verge of death, Erich was somewhat at peace for the first time in months.

"Do you know how far it is to occupied German territory?" Erich asked.

"I'm afraid I do not. I do not concern myself with the wars of man and I do not leave these woods very often. I am just a simple man from simpler times," the gypsy responded.

The German nodded in agreement as he tried to warm his hands through his gloves by the fire, wishing he were back home by his own fire.

"Let me see your hands," Nikolia said.

Erich began to peel his gloves off. Revealing tattered black fingers. He grimaced in pain as the gloves peeled off small strips of blackened skin. They both knew that the freezing temperatures had already taken their toll on the German soldier's appendages and that the damage was now more than superficial. Erich stated that he couldn't feel his feet and that the numbness was all the way up his shins now.

"I can fix this for you if you let me," the gypsy said with an empathetic look on his face. "I can cure you of all your ailments and make you feel young again. With this I can make you feel strong and powerful like bear and swift and tenacious like wolf. I can provide you with a gift that makes it so you will never grow old or get sick again. You will be like new."

As the man spoke, Erich noticed something strange about him. His demeanor somehow darkened and there was something about his eyes that now glowed yellow in the firelight. His gut was now telling him that Nikolia was something more than just a man.

What do I have to lose? My choices are to either die right here or walk as far as I can, only to surely die elsewhere, he pondered to himself.

"At this point, my friend, I would take anything you had to offer seeing how I will not likely live to see the sunrise," Erich said. "I fear that once I close my eyes, I will never open them again."

As the German soldier finished his sentence, Nikolia leaped through the fire at him. The gypsy's mouth was now full of rows of impossibly sharp teeth and his eyes were yellow and rimmed with red, like a demon from the depths of Erich's worst nightmare.

PART I
"HIT ME MAC..."

CHAPTER ONE

Mac's bar sat nestled on the west side of Detroit where it had been a staple of neighborhood dive bars since the early 1960s. It was a hodgepodge of eclectic tastes, unique mismatched furniture, and folk art. Having been a former chicken coop in the early 1920s, then a house of ill repute after that. Finally, by the 1960s, it was changed over to a bar by Mac's father, Mac Senior.

Inside, the bar wasn't much to look at. Its small dark, and dingy ambiance was accentuated by crooked floors, wobbly bar stools and poor ventilation. The highlight of Mac's was its giant twenty-foot cherry wood saloon-style bar that ran the length of the north wall of the establishment. It also contained a single scuffed-up pool table and a rustic jukebox that didn't play anything newer than 1972. The smell in the badly lit Irish Pub was a mixture of twenty-five years of cigarette smoke, stale beer, and hopelessness.

There were not a lot of people in the bar on this Saturday afternoon. Not that there usually was for Mac's Bar. On any given day you might find one or two college kids, some Vietnam vets, or the local drunks drinking their problems away. It sat in a rough part of town and for Detroit in the 1980s, that was saying a lot. Mac's wasn't exactly the safest place for your normal suburbanite to call home but it had an alluring charm to it that made it home for society's forgotten and unwanted. Those who were trying to get away from something or someone in their life.

Daniel Methric sat quietly at the bar nursing his Black Label beer and listening to the black man next to him ramble on about work, his kid, and the life he could have had. Mac was behind the bar shaking his head listening to the man blabber on and on as he began to put clean pint glasses away. Daniel slumped and rubbed the bridge of his nose with his thumb and forefinger.

"Hit me Mac," he said with a heavy sigh.

Mac turned around and took the bottle of Kessler's Whiskey from the shelf and topped off Daniel's glass. Daniel kicked it back and let out a long exhale as he looked out the window and noticed that it was still a torrential downpour.

"When is this shit gonna stop, Mac?" he asked.

"Supposed to rain all week, from what I hear," Mac replied.

"Can't see shit through your windows. Maybe someday you should possibly clean them?" Daniel suggested.

Mac just shrugged and went back to wiping down glasses.

"Right…" Daniel muttered. "Why would he wanna do that?"

Daniel was a middle-aged man who appeared to be in his early forties. His hair was about shoulder length with what used to be dark brown but now streaked with gray. His face was covered with a light dusting of gray stubble, and his lean frame made him appear wiry and spry. He wore blue jeans and black Adidas high-tops. Under a light denim jacket that had a patch on its left breast that read "I Love NY", sat an old, ratty Kiss t-shirt.

He was Mac's best regular and would stop in four or five days a week. Each day was the same to him; he would order a few cans of Black Label beer and a couple shots of bottom-shelf whiskey and then stumble out the door. So it was a typical stormy Saturday afternoon for him and nothing was out of the ordinary.

The blabbering black man in the wrinkled business suit to Daniel's right was Stanley Hawkins. A used car salesman from Albuquerque, New Mexico. He was a portly, short black man in his late thirties that was the kind of man who looked like he ate a pound of bacon every morning followed up by a carton of Newports and a fifth of gin.

"Her name was… I mean is, Julia Ann," Stanley corrected himself as he showed Daniel the same old tattered photograph of the eight-year-old girl that he always did.

"Today is her twentieth birthday and I haven't seen her since this photo was taken," he said. "I think she moved to Santa Fe with her mother Sharon around 1978. I remember this photo like it was yesterday. God, I miss her," said Stanley with a sense of regret.

Daniel sighed. *Every time it was the same sad story with Stanley. Blah blah blah, my kid this and my kid that,* he thought.

All he did was bitch and bitch and bitch. I used to be someone; I had a good life, so on and so forth. It was always the same for Daniel. He couldn't remember for the life of him the last time he saw Stanley, and he wasn't complaining. It was like he was being punished by having to listen to this man day in and day out.

Daniel couldn't remember much on any given day and his memory was always blotchy at best. He would typically forget where he was or how he got there and could never really remember why he was like this. He couldn't even think of when it started happening to him.

As Stanley went on and on about his hardships, Daniel sank into deep thought, trying to remember what happened five nights ago. All he could remember was getting blackout drunk at Mac's and stumbling home to his apartment. The next thing he knew, it was three days later. No recollection of the prior three days. Daniel downed a shot as the door to Mac's blew open, letting in rain and a large gust of wind.

"Aww man. I just put those there," complained Mac as cocktail napkins flew everywhere.

At the door stood a black man wearing a hooded rain poncho soaked to the bones and seeking refuge from the cold, wet weather. The rain continued to hammer away at the city sidewalks outside. The thunder clapped and the lightning lit up the sky as the man entered, keeping his hood on and covering the details of his face. He walked over to Mac's antique bar and pointed to the bar stool to Daniels' left.

"This seat taken?" the man said in a hoarse voice.

Daniel grunted in compliance, seeming to remain indifferent to whether or not the man sat down or not.

An entire freaking empty bar and these two dweebs decide to sit next to me, Daniel thought to himself.

The man took a seat and sat still for a minute, staring forward. Then turned on his barstool towards Daniel and removed his hood. To Daniels' horror, the man was missing his right eye as well as half of his face. It gave the impression that someone had forcefully thrown him into a wood chipper with his face taking the brunt of it. His poncho was still wet from the outside and Daniel realized it was spattered with congealed blood.

"Hello Daniel," the man said, as his voice seemed to gurgle softly.

"JESUS CHRIST!" Daniel screamed and fell off his stool.

Daniel quickly crab-walked away from the stranger, then rolled over and began to evacuate the contents of his stomach all over Mac's linoleum floor. He swore he caught a quick glimpse of a wedding ring sparkle in his bile.

"Aww man, what the hell! I just cleaned that floor last week," Mac yelled.

As Daniel finished heaving all the beer and whiskey he had drank the past two hours, he realized the man was gone. Daniel quickly shot up from the floor, pointed at the empty barstool and shouted hysterically to the other two. "He was right there! Right there!"

Mac and Stanley both looked at Daniel with surprise and confusion and then they both turned to look at each other with a raised eyebrow.

"I have no idea what you're talking about, buddy. One minute you were nodding off and the next you're on my floor puking all over my place," Mac said.

"Yeah, I think you might have had enough for today," said Stanley.

Daniel brushed himself off, threw down a twenty-dollar bill to cover his tab, and thought that maybe he had fallen asleep and had a startling nightmare.

No, it was way too real for him to think it was just a dream. Mac and Stanley both looked at Daniel, glanced at each other, then back at Daniel. The room was completely silent except for Daniel's heavy breathing.

"Dude, I swear he was right there. He walked in ... sat down... and he had no face…no face!" His hysteria continued to grow.

"Easy, buddy. It's just the three of us in here," Stanley said.

"He looked like a freaking zombie! I swear it was real. I know I'm crazy but I'm not that crazy," Daniel said as he began to pace the floor.

Stanley nodded, "Ahhhhhh. One of those. Yeah, that happens to people like you, Daniel. We have been over this before, buddy."

"What the hell are you talking about?" Daniel replied. "One of those, what?"

"Hey, you gonna clean this up?" Mac interrupted.

Daniel dusted his palms off like he had had enough and slowly backed his way toward the door and continued out into the rain.

"I guess that's a no, huh?" Mac called out from inside the bar as the door closed.

Daniel stood outside Mac's door in bewilderment and confusion, not believing what had just happened as the rain pounded away at him. Stranger and stranger things had been happening to him lately, and he didn't know why.

What the hell just happened in there? he thought to himself.

Less than a year ago, Daniel moved from Columbus, Ohio to Detroit, Michigan. His memory of his time in Ohio was spotty at best. He did, however, recall liking life in a college town. What he remembered was that he enjoyed the mix match of culture. He enjoyed the record stores, the food, and the nightlife. It was a much different place than Detroit was. There was an old saying in Detroit that said, "Detroit eats its young," and Daniel quickly learned how that saying came to be. He didn't have any friends here in the city, and the people he met always ended up being very confrontational. It was a tough city, and you had to have a chip on your shoulder to get by.

To make things worse, he never could remember why he moved here in the first place. He just woke up one day and he was in his apartment. All his stuff was there, but for the life of him, he could not remember what happened that led to the move. Why was this happening to him? A small voice from behind him broke his train of thought.

"Hi," a child called out.

Daniel slowly turned around to find a little blonde girl no older than the age of six wearing a Hello Kitty raincoat, matching galoshes, and holding an umbrella.

"You gonna get it right this time, mister?" She placed a hand on her hip as if trying to be an adult.

"What?" he asked as a flummoxed look came across his face. "Who the heck are you and what are you doing out here in the rain?"

Despite the thunderstorm, this was not a place for a little girl to be carelessly walking around without her parents. She was more than likely to be kidnapped or something worse.

The little girl looked annoyed at Daniel and sighed, "I said, are you gonna get it right this time?"

Daniel still looked at the child without knowing how to respond.

"I hope you do cuz this place sucks," the girl said with a frown.

She quickly turned and took off down the sidewalk. The little girl splashed in every puddle she came across and giggled. Daniel pulled up his collar on his jacket and started to walk. Not sure how to process the past ten minutes of his life. That's when it began to speak to him.

You are weak... Pathetic, a deep voice inside Daniel's head called out.

Shut up, he thought to himself.

Weak, the voice answered.

"Fuck off," Daniel said out loud. "Get out of my head and leave me alone!"

Sopping wet, Daniel kept walking away from Mac's.

You are nothing but a petulant child, the voice said.

I'm full-blown bat-shit crazy, Daniel thought.

Eventually, you will be gone completely, Daniel. It bellowed from inside his skull.

Daniel rubbed his temples with his middle and forefingers, ignoring the fact that he was drenched. He had gotten used to hearing this voice in his head for some time now. It was always annoying and condescending. Most times he could block it out, but as of late, it had become far more vocal. As he continued this dark inner monologue, he stopped and realized he had already walked a mile since he left Mac's place. The rain began to let up, and the sun started to peek through the clouds. He stopped at a street corner and took in the warmth of the sun on his face.

Don't! the voice said as he started to take a step forward.

Dooooont! it began to scream.

"Fuck it." Daniel exhaled and stepped off the curb.

And that's when the garbage truck plowed over Daniel Methric...

CHAPTER TWO

FLAGGSTAFF
JULY, 1985

Barbara Chee stood outside the hotel Monte Vista in downtown Flagstaff waiting for her boyfriend Patrick Nelson to pick her up. Her boyfriend had planned a camping trip in the Coconino National Forest with their friends, Emily Riggs and Samantha Murtah. The twenty-four-year-old impatiently paced back and forth, constantly checking her watch and waiting for her partner to arrive. The hotel sat on the corner of San Francisco St. and East Aspen Ave. With its three stories, seventy-three rooms, and a tall neon sign atop made it one of the city's landmarks. The hotel was built in 1927 and was known to have a slew of famous guests who stayed there, from John Wayne to Humphrey Bogart. The Monte Vista was also a filming location for the classic movie Casablanca and was even rumored to be haunted. Though Barbara had yet to find any validity to the hauntings, she did enjoy pretending it was true.

It was a beautiful Friday afternoon in July 1985, and Barbara had just gotten off work. She had been working as a bartender at one of the bars inside the hotel for a little over a year now. For the time being, she deemed it a less desirable but honest job. Patrick had planned to pick her up after her shift, with his jeep packed and ready to go. Then they would head out to the Coconino National Forest and meet up with their friends. The next four days would be under the stars and away from civilization and, most importantly, people.

The weather was a comfortable seventy-four degrees, with puffy pillowy clouds filling the blue sky like floating hot air balloons. Barbara looked at her watch again and took in a deep breath and exhaled loudly to shake off the day's work of dealing with smug hotel guests and drunken day drinkers. She wore her favorite Motorhead tank top, torn blue jeans, and her hiking boots.

Growing up, her peers had considered Barbara a tomboy. She always played with the boys and did "boy" things at an early age. As a child, she was always more interested in climbing trees, camping, and being outdoors more than playing with Barbie dolls and Easy Bake Ovens. This all probably had something to do with the fact that she was raised by her father, Tanaka.

Tanaka Chee worked for the Coconino County Sheriff's Department for over ten years. Barbara's mother died when she was nine in a horrible car crash off I-40 out near Williams, Arizona. The driver of an eighteen-wheeler fell asleep and forced her car off the road at seventy miles an hour and into an embankment. Paramedics found her dead at the scene when they arrived. The twisted, horrible mess of her 1968 Mercury Cougar was unrecognizable. Barbara's father was devastated and vowed to raise his daughter as well-rounded as he could, making it so she could take care of herself when he was gone.

Her father was from the Navajo Nation and her mother, Caitlin, was of Irish and Welsh descent. Her parents had met in the early 1960s when Tanaka still lived on the Navajo reservation and her mother was still in college. He insisted on giving his daughter a white man's name because in the 1960s it was difficult being Native American, let alone a woman.

Barbara looked at her watch and grumbled because Patrick was running late as usual and, as much as she loved him, this habit drove her nuts. She ran her fingers through her jet black hair and pulled it back into a ponytail as she daydreamed about her brief vacation. The next four days were going to be a much-needed relief from her eighteen-day streak of slinging beers and pouring shots for ungrateful people. She imagined herself kicking back in a folding chair and sipping on a cold beer with her best friends.

She pulled a cigarette pack out of the back pocket of her jeans. After smacking it a few times in the palm of her left hand, she pulled open the top and took out a smoke. Just as the cigarette went into her mouth and she reached for her lighter, Patrick came screeching around the corner of Avery Avenue in his 1982 Jeep Scrambler. The Jeep slid to a halt while he leaned over and opened the passenger door.

"Pardon me but do you have any Grey Poupon?" the man asked, as if he were some sort of aristocrat.

Barbara looked up over the top of her aviator sunglasses at the man with sandy blond hair, and without blinking or looking away, lit her cigarette, then slid her lighter back into her pocket.

"You're late. I said pick me up at 4 pm." She glanced at her watch. "It's now 4:30 and the last thing I wanna do is have to wait around at my job after already being here all day."

Patrick gave her his saddest puppy dog eyes. "Sorry babe, how can I ever make it up to you?"

She squinted her eyes at him and jumped into the front passenger seat of his Scrambler.

"You better think of something, shit-ass," Barbara said as she closed the passenger door. Patrick put the vehicle in gear and drove towards the Coconino National Forest for their four-day getaway.

The Scrambler clipped along at seventy-five miles per hour down I-17 south while the ponderosa pines of northern Arizona zipped by. They could see the San Francisco Peaks mountain range along the horizon in the distance behind them.

"This view never gets old," she said, looking over her shoulder.

"Do you know why they are named the San Francisco Peaks?" he asked.

"No. Actually, I have always wondered," she replied.

"Spanish friars named them around 1629. They started a Spanish Mission in a Hopi Indian Village about sixty-five miles south of Flagstaff, in honor of St Francis. So they gave them the name San Francisco to honor St. Francis of Assisi, the founder of their order." He replied with a proud smile.

"Soooo… nothing to do with California?" she asked.

"No ma'am, this would have been a good 147 years before California was even a state," he said as he gripped the steering wheel.

"Wow," she said. "They teach you this at NAU, or are you just full of useless information?"

Patrick chuckled, "Yeah."

"Which is it, Poindexter?" demanded Barbara.

"Both," he responded with a laugh.

Patrick was enrolled at Northern Arizona University for their Park Ranger Training. He was born and raised in Coconino County and could not think of any other place he would want to spend the rest of his life.

Though Patrick hadn't traveled much over his mere twenty-five years on earth, he never actually thought to bother when there was all this beauty here in northern Arizona. He seriously couldn't think of anywhere on earth that could top the red rocks of Sedona and the surrounding rim country. Patrick was also very familiar with the land, so he figured he would become a Forest Ranger. He dreamed of spending his days out in the wilderness among the giant pines and wildlife. He only had a couple of weeks left before he completed his seventeen-week course of training. Then all he had to do was apply and see what happened. He was hoping to stay near Flagstaff unless he could find work down in Sedona, which he knew was more than likely not going to happen. There was a long line of people going for that position. As the wind blew Barbara's black hair, Dire Straits's latest release played "So Far Away from You" on the Jeep's cassette player as they cruised along at a leisurely pace.

"Man, this is such a good record," said Patrick.

"Did you remember to pack the coffee?" Barbara asked.

"Oh yeah, for sure. It's in the milk crate with the camping cookware right behind your seat," he answered.

"Good, cuz I'd have to kick your ass if you didn't," she said.

Barbara always thought that northern Arizona summers had the perfect weather. It's one reason she stayed after high school and didn't look to leave for college. The second reason she stayed was her father. Barbara had a very close relationship with him and he meant the world to her. Her father never remarried after her mother died and he did everything he could to make sure that she was clothed, fed, and happy as she grew up. He was always calm and collected around her, never raising his voice. He wasn't too strict with her growing up, but he was such a good father that she never really had any desire to act out or rebel. Plus, he was the one person who was always there for her no matter what was thrown her way.

In Arizona, the Bureau of Land Management allowed you to pretty much camp anywhere you wanted in the national forests. As long as you were in a designated camping zone, all you had to do was pull off the road and drive through the forest anywhere you liked. You could just stop your car under any tree and set up a tent. Then it was just you, nature and some of the most amazing star gazing you could do. There were no "campsites" per se, it was more like camping areas. There were no bathrooms or running water, so it was 100% rustic. You were smart to bring a shovel to dig a hole for your bathroom needs and you needed to make sure you didn't burn the forest down with your campfire if the season was too dry. Other than that, you were pretty much on your own. Just you, the ponderosas, and the rest of nature. No people, televisions, telephones or customers.

This was going to be perfect, she thought to herself as she put her feet up on the dash and enjoyed the rest of the drive.

Patrick spotted their exit, "This is us. Here we go," and turned off the interstate.

They pulled into a gas station that was located just off I-17. This gas station had a country store attached to it and was their usual last stop for gas, refreshments, and snack supplies before entering the forest. Patrick circled the parking lot and pulled up next to one of the gas pumps.

"The girls are bringing the food, but we need to bring the beer. So run in and grab two cases of Coors and I'll top the tank off," he said.

"You got it. Um, should I get some snacks too?" she asked.

"Hell yeah," Patrick replied, "Surprise me."

She hopped out of the passenger seat of the Jeep and walked across the parking lot as Patrick got out and began to operate the gas pump.

The old gray-haired man behind the counter had skin that looked like a cross between a leather chair and an alligator's hide. He sat there buried in his Reader's Digest and sipping on a hot cup of mud that passed as coffee. He was reading an article titled "Junk in the Trunk and Other Problems by Andy Rooney". The noise of bells clattered as the door opened, causing him to look up.

"Afternoon," she said, "Where's the Coors?"

The man just grunted and thumbed to his left towards the coolers and went back to his Reader's Digest.

"Thanks," she said.

The country store was pretty basic and had a very limited supply of items and useless odds and ends. Overpriced canned goods, marshmallows, and packs of stale hot dog buns lined the shelves as she hurried passed. She stood in front of the beer cooler's glass doors and could have sworn she heard angels beginning to sing.

As Patrick stood outside pumping gas into the jeep, he looked up at the sky and noticed that it was now completely blue and cloudless. This excited Patrick because it meant it was going to be a super clear night for stargazing. He wiped his hands on his chinos and looked at his Swiss Army watch and it read 5:37 pm. They had about a twenty-minute drive into the forest before they got to their usual spot where they were meeting Emily and Samantha. After that, they would have the remaining three hours to get their campsite together and the tent up before sundown. It was going to be nothing but a folding chair, some rad tunes, and ice-cold beer.

Patrick smiled at the fact he was about to spend the next four days camping with nothing to do but waste time and relax.

"What could go wrong?" he muttered to himself.

Barbara set two cases of Coors Banquet stubbies, a bag of Funions, and a bag of Hot Chips on the counter.

"Will this be all?" the old man asked, annoyingly.

"Yup, that's it," she replied.

"That will be $10 for the gas, $20 for the beer, and $5 for the chips".

As she dug into her back pocket for money, she noticed next to the cash register was an old Halloween poster of Elvira and what looked like a man in a horrible wolf-man costume wearing a hat. The poster said "I love a man with a hairy chest" and depicted Elvira standing in the arms of the Coors Beer Wolf. The Beer Wolf was a goofy-looking suit with googly eyes and a Coors trucker hat. She chuckled, then pulled out her money and handed it to the man. He didn't even say a word, just took her exact change and placed it in the cash register. He then closed the register and went back to reading his periodical.

"Ummm, can I get a bag for these chips?" she asked.

"Ma'am, aren't they already in bags?" he replied.

"Yeah no shit Sherlock, but I kinda have my hands full here with all this beer and would like to not smash my chips," she said in frustration.

The old man sighed and leaned over below the counter to dig for bags. Just as he leaned down, Barbara noticed a row of local and national newspapers behind the counter. Some headlines read; Yankees retire Roger Maris. More animal attacks in Northern Arizona, death toll now reaching six. Another read; Death toll now caps off at six. Is a serial killer on the loose? One read something about a cancerous growth discovered in President Reagan's colon.

As she was lost in thought, Barbara jumped and let out a little yelp as the sound of the old man shaking open a paper bag caught her off guard. He just looked at her and furrowed his brow.

"Sorry," she said, "long day."

The old man nodded in approval and began placing her salty snacks into the paper bag. She graciously accepted the bag folded the top over and clamped it in her teeth to hold it in her mouth. Then grabbed each case of beer in each hand and walked towards the door.

"Full Moon tonight," the old man said. "I'd be careful if you're staying out in the forest."

Barbara stopped for a second. Without turning around, she rolled her eyes. Quickly she nodded in acknowledgment and continued out the front door. Patrick heard Barbara's muffled cry for help from behind him as he was hanging up the gas pump. He turned around to find her struggling to carry two cases of beer and holding a brown grocery bag in her mouth. She gave him a pathetic look as she pandered for his help. Patrick quickly hurried to her aid and grabbed the beer from her, which she gladly gave him, removed the bag from her mouth, and said, "Thanks." Then gave him a peck on the cheek and skipped off. Her hair flopped purposely back and forth as she moved. He watched her butt in her tight jeans as she skipped off and shook his head back to reality. Patrick walked over and placed the cases of beer in the back of his Scrambler along with the camping supplies. Then he hurried around the truck hopped in the driver's seat and buckled his seat belt.

"It's 106 miles to Chicago. We got a full tank of gas, half a pack of cigarettes. It's dark... and we're wearing sunglasses," Patrick said.

"Hit it," Barbara replied. Patrick sped off, kicking up dust and gravel as they tore out of the parking lot.

This happens every time, Sam," Emily cursed as she flailed her arms in the air.

Emily and her partner Samantha bickered like an old married couple as they tried putting their tent up.

"What?" Sam replied, "I'll just go find some sticks and whittle them down and we can use them for stakes. I mean, we only need four more."

Emily's OCD could not allow her to sleep in a tent that was not properly set up. This meant that all the tent stakes had to be present and in the ground before she would even enter.

"Argh!" Emily said and stomped away to tend to the fire pit.

"Love you!!" Sam called out to her as she stormed off.

Samantha Murtaugh was a twenty-six-year-old black woman who was as forgetful as she was stubborn. The two of them had been dating for three years now and they both moved to Flagstaff from Phoenix to get to a more "progressive" environment. Samantha wore a pair of camouflage army pants that came over her hiking boots and a red flannel shirt. Her hair was in dreadlocks and tied back, draping down to the middle of her back. Emily was younger than Sam by almost a year but was taller than her by two inches. She wore blue jeans, a plain white v-neck, and hiking boots. Her hair was short and spiky because she wanted to look like Bridgette Nielsen from the movie Rocky IV. Their friends thought they made the perfect couple. A good yin and yang of each other. One, insanely organized and reserved, the other carefree and to the wind.

They had met Barbara and Patrick about two years prior at a concert in Flagstaff and have been close friends ever since. Spending most of their free time together camping, hiking, skiing, and all the other outdoorsman activities people do in the area.

Sam was a volunteer tour guide at Walnut Canyon National Monument. She was tasked with taking groups and families down to the ancient cliff dwelling and showing them how people lived around 1100 AD. She would take groups down the mile-round-trip trail that descended 185 feet. It was more than 240 steps. The real challenge, however, was the 7,000 ft elevation that made the hike strenuous for those who were not prepared for it. It was a fun job that was only two or three days a week, but it helped keep Sam in shape and gave her some pocket money.

Emily was the breadwinner and had her own real estate office in downtown Flagstaff. Emily was very successful and recently sold a few of the higher-end houses in the Flagstaff surrounding area. Sam always caved in to Emily's needs because she never liked to be referred to as a freeloader, but never really wanted to find a nine-to-five job.

Emily began stacking firewood into the fire pit she had created before the tent argument. While Sam was still out searching for sticks, she heard Barbara catcalling from the passenger side of Patrick's Scrambler. They now darted through the pines towards their campsite.

"WOOOOOOO! YEAAAAHHHH! Looking good, mama!" she called out the window as the Jeep slid to a stop next to Sam and Emily's blue Subaru Brat. "Let the party begin," Barbara said as she jumped out of the passenger seat, pulled her jam box out of the back, put in Phil Collins "No Jacket Required," and pressed play.

"It's montage time!" said Patrick as he started unpacking his Jeep.

CHAPTER THREE

IT took them all about two hours to get everything just right at their site which included two tents, some folding chairs, a couple coolers, some stacks of firewood and a folding table piled with dishes and supplies. Patrick reached his hand into the ice-filled cooler and pulled out a Coors stubby. He twisted off the cap and plopped down in his folding chair for a victory beverage, and flicked his beer cap into the fire pit.

"Ahhhh… and we still have forty-five minutes of daylight to spare," he said, taking a long pull.

Barbara sat down next to him and flipped open her copy of the latest Rolling Stone Magazine, which had John Travolta and Jamie Lee Curtis on the cover. Barbara leaned over and kissed Patrick on the cheek and said: "Thank you, honey, I needed this." Patrick grunted and nodded as he stared off into the pine trees, trying to clear his head and enjoy his beer.

"Who's hungry?" Sam asked as Emily began lighting the fire.

"I've whittled a couple of sticks for hot dogs and I made my homemade potato salad for a side dish," Samantha said.

"That sounds rad. I'm starving," Barbara said.

Emily got the fire roaring while Samantha began prepping the food for their meal. Once the fire was ready, they all grabbed a stick and began roasting their wieners. Barbara was transfixed on the sky as the sun set and the fire orange glow seemed to engulf everything around them.

"It's perfect here," Patrick said as he noticed the look on Barbara's face taking in the sunset.

Barbara snapped to, remembering her trip to the country store earlier.

"Hey you guys hear about this wild animal or whatever that has killed six people already?" she asked.

"Yeah, I read about that," Sam replied.

"I saw one headline suggesting a serial killer may be on the loose," Emily said.

"I read somewhere that they think it's possibly a rogue mountain lion," said Sam.

Patrick sighed heavily in response. "A mountain lion will not kill like that and there are no reported fatal mountain lion attacks in our state's history, so I highly doubt it's a mountain lion,".

"Maybe a grizzly bear then?" Emily said.

"The grizzly bear was pretty much wiped out in northern Arizona by 1935. There have been no sightings since," said Patrick. "All we have are black bears here and they might be agitated since its mating season, but it's not likely and not in their nature to fatally attack a human let alone six of them," he continued.

"Then what do you think it is Ranger Rick?" Sam asked.

"I don't know, but it is usually the simplest explanation. I think it has something to do with some crazed crackhead out there killing people and trying to make it look like an animal. Or he believes he or she is an animal himself," said Patrick.

"Oh, it's a he," Barbara cut in. "Women don't kill people like that."

"I hope," Patrick said. Looking at her, he raised an eyebrow.

They all looked at each other in silence, and then all began to laugh at once.

"So you guys think we will be safe, right?" Barbara asked everyone.

"Yes," Patrick said. "It's a big forest and besides, I have my rifle with me just in case and I will keep it in the tent next to us at night."

Patrick carried his dad's old Winchester Model 70, 30-06 bolt-action rifle in his jeep wherever he went. He liked to say it was his "Oh shit!" gun. Even though he knew the habits of the wildlife that were indigenous to this area, he always felt you could never be too careful. "Besides, I'd be more worried about getting bit by a rattlesnake than some crazy guy out in the woods or some rogue animal," he said.

"Okay great. Now I'm paranoid about snakes. Thanks, dude," Sam said.

They finished cooking up their hot dogs and piled their paper plates up with food. They were all in a moment of complete serenity as all four of them began to stuff their faces by campfire light as the stars and moon began to shine brightly above.

"God, would you look at that?" Samantha pointed up towards the sky and the Milky Way.

The stars and solar system were noticeably visible throughout the night sky. Its bright belt of stars and planets split the night in half right above their heads with a kaleidoscope of purples, blues, oranges, and greens. If you watched long enough, you could see a lone falling star die out across the night sky.

"Yeah, pretty intense, isn't it?" Patrick replied. "Plus a full moon. I mean, could you ask for a better night sky?"

Barbara began to feel the buzz of the five beers she had drank after they ate dinner and looked at her watch. It read 11:45 pm.

"Whelp, I'm freaking beat, and it's been a long day. I'm heading in for the night. Don't let me ruin your guys' party. You stay up as long as you want, babe," she said to Patrick as she stood up and downed the last of her beer. Then she belched, pardoned herself, and tossed the bottle into the fire. "Make sure we tie up the garbage before bed. We don't want any unwanted visitors tonight," Barbara said as she wobbled towards her tent.

"I'll be there within the next half hour, honey. Get the sleeping bag warm for me," Patrick said as she stumbled off.

Barbara unzipped her blue Coleman tent, climbed inside, turned on her camping lantern, and let out a huge sigh. She changed into her sleeping sweats and climbed into the down-feather sleeping bag. Then she turned off the lamp and was sound asleep, snoring in a matter of minutes.

A noise coming from behind the tent startled Barbara out of a deep sleep. To her, it sounded like the shuffling noise of someone walking and rustling through the bushes. Thud… drag… thud… drag… She looked at her watch with sleepy eyes and noticed it said 1:14 am.

"Patrick," she whispered, "Wake up."

She then turned over and realized he was not there. She could hear what sounded like moaning from behind the tent. Her heart was racing as someone, or something pushed against the back of the tent. Feeling its way around the canvas.

"They're coming to get you, Barbara," Patrick said in his spookiest voice. "They're coming to get you, Barbara."

"Patrick, you asshole," she called out as she turned on the camping lamp inside the tent.

Just then, Patrick burst out laughing.

"You're lucky I didn't shoot you with your rifle, you shit-ass!" she spat.

Patrick couldn't stop laughing as he unzipped the tent and walked in, holding his hands up.

"Don't shoot. Don't shoot," he pleaded, "I'm unarmed."

Patrick was only wearing a pair of gym shorts and flip-flops.

"That wasn't funny, dude," she said.

Patrick zipped the tent closed and climbed into their sleeping bag as Barbara turned out the lamp.

"Seriously, man, don't ever do that," she said, clearly annoyed.

"What? Not a George A. Romero fan?" Patrick asked.

"Well, yes, but still. What the fuck were you doing out there?" she demanded.

"Sorry I had to p..."

Before he could finish his sentence, they both heard a nightmarish howl that made the hairs on the back of their necks stand straight and their faces go pale.

"Jesus, what was that?" she said. "That sounded way, way too close for me."

"Yeah," Patrick said, "I honestly have no idea what that was. It sounded like a wolf, but way more pissed off. Wolves don't sound like that."

They both lay perfectly still inside their tent, listening for any sounds of movement. They heard nothing. The forest was dead silent. Almost too silent, Patrick thought. Nothing made a sound around them and they just lay there listening to their own heartbeats. They both wondered if their imaginations were running away from them.

"Okay," he whispered. "I don't hear anything."

Then it howled again. This time, it was closer and seemed angrier.

"Saaaaammmm… Emily," Patrick called to the tent next to them. "Did you hear that?"

"Yeah, what the fuck was that?" Samantha responded from inside their tent.

There came a snarl and a huff that sounded like it was right in front of them. Twigs snapped and broke as something heavy walked by their tents. After waiting a few moments in complete silence, Patrick turned to Barbara.

"I have no idea what that was, but I think I should stoke the fire and get it going again to ward off anything that might be out there," he said loudly enough for their friends to hear.

"Okay yeah. That's a smart move," Sam and Emily agreed.

Patrick quickly slipped on his hiking boots, put on his flannel, took up his flashlight, and his bolt-action rifle, then exited the tent.

"Be careful," Barbara whispered, gripping her sleeping bag tight to her chest as Patrick left the tent and zipped it behind him.

"I will," he responded as he turned on his flashlight and looked around the campsite.

Patrick was happy to find that they had forgotten to put out the fire due to the amount of adult beverages they went through. "Oh thank god," he said to himself as he walked over to the glowing coals still burning in the bottom of the fire. Patrick then quickly started to toss a few logs onto the embers and poked them with his fire stick to get them going as fast as he could. He even bent down to blow on them to speed up the situation. As soon as he started blowing, the dry logs caught fire. He tossed another log on and figured he would check the perimeter of the campsite. The fire instantly lit up the area, causing the trees encircling their campsite to glow from the flickering orange light.

Just as Patrick started to check his surroundings, he noticed how bright the full moon was and how his field of vision through the forest was pretty decent for having to adjust after getting the fire going again. Patrick had his rifle slung over his shoulder and held his flashlight in his hand. He shined it back and forth towards the forest, where he thought he heard the noises coming from earlier. That's when his heart sank and his face went instantly white.

SCREEEEEECCCCCHHH!

The sound came from where they parked the cars just behind Sam and Emily. The girls seemed to scream at the same time in reaction to the noise.

"I just pissed myself," Emily whispered as she and Samantha held each other tight.

Patrick quietly removed the rifle from his shoulder and began to walk toward the cars. He was purposely ignoring the women's whispers as he slowly stepped towards his jeep. Once he got close, he saw right away that the hood of his Scrambler was destroyed. Four huge gouges were dug deep in the metal and through the brown paint. They didn't just go through the paint but through the metal, about seven inches wide in total.

"What the hell did that?! Freddy Krueger?" he whispered.

He slowly spun around in a circle, pointing his rifle in all directions. He saw nothing, heard nothing, and it was still way too quiet. It was like even nature was terrified to make any sound at all.

Something is definitely here, he thought to himself.

The moonlight and his imagination began to play tricks on him. Through the trees off in the distance he thought he saw something circling the camp. There was a low growl and a chuff from behind him, back by the fire pit. As if some predator was warning him, this was its territory.

He slowly turned around towards the noise and saw nothing. Quickly spinning to his left and right holding his flashlight while gripping his rifle so the light was shining in his direct line of fire. Still, he saw nothing and all he heard were the quiet whimpers of the girls coming from inside their tents. He heard it again, but this time off to his right, away from the camp. He turned and caught a set of yellow eyes blazing at him from about twenty yards in some tall evergreen shrubs.

Jesus, he thought as a chill ran through his body.

The eyes were way too animal to be human and way too human to be animal. Then, just like that, they were gone. Keeping his attention on the underbrush in front of him, he side-stepped around Emily and Samantha's tent and towards Barbara's. The sound of sticks breaking from behind the tents caught his attention as something moved from that direction.

It's fucking with us, he thought. *What the fuck kind of animal fucks with you? he thought.*

While trying not to panic and keep his cool, he inhaled a deep breath and began to frantically check his surroundings. Then he heard a loud pop and a hiss. Followed by another, and then another.

Patrick knew exactly what the sound was. Whatever this thing was that stalked them had just slashed their tires.

"Fuck," Patrick whispered.

He raised the barrel of the Winchester to the sky and fired a warning shot into the air. All three of the girls yelped at the same time. As the noise echoed, he noticed the forest did not make a sound. Not even the sound of a rabbit scurrying away.

"That was me! I just fired a shot to scare this thing off," he said.

After the sound of the gunshot died off, the forest was dead quiet again. Patrick's heart was racing faster than it ever had before. He didn't know if he was gonna have a heart attack or shit his pants. As the beads of sweat started to come down his forehead into his eyes, he calmly called out to the girls, doing his best impression of a cool and level-headed person.

"I want all of you to quickly get dressed and get out of your tents. Then get into one of the cars and lock the doors," he said.

The girls didn't hesitate or question. They began getting their stuff together post haste. Trying not to panic, Barbara put on her hiking boots.

A slow tearing noise came from behind her at the back of the tent. She slowly turned around to see a black, scythe-like claw slice its way through. Inching its way down like it was unzipping the back wall of canvas.

"Patrick! It's trying to get in the tent!" Barbara spat.

Right when she screamed, the claw stopped and retracted through the slit. Patrick heard her and ran between the tents and waved his rifle and light. He then saw the tear in the canvas.

"It's gone. You okay?" he asked as he peeked through the hole.

She quickly nodded back to him, acknowledging she was unharmed.

He grabbed her hand. "Let's get the hell out of here while we can," Patrick ordered.

Emily and Sam were just getting out of their tent when Patrick came back around Barbara's and helped her out of the zipper. Just as Barbara exited her tent, Patrick noticed a horrible, musky scent.

"You smell that?" Barbara asked.

"Yeah, I do. It's almost burning my eyes," he said.

"God, it's horrible," Emily said from behind them.

Just as they gathered to get their bearings and tried to steady their breathing, it came at them.

With a snarl and a flash of silver and gray fur, a huge beast leaped from behind Samantha and Emily. Emily was knocked to the ground as it tackled Samantha. The force knocked Sam through the air and she and the beast both rolled across the forest floor and through the fire pit. Hot sparks and glowing cinders spewed everywhere. Once they stopped rolling, the beast dragged her off, kicking and screaming. The two disappeared into the forest in front of them and out of view through the darkness. Then Sam's cries for help came to an abrupt stop. This all occurred so quickly that none of them could register what had just happened. The remaining three stood there speechless and shocked that Sam was there one minute and now she wasn't.

"Samantha!" Emily screamed. Barbara and Patrick lifted her off the ground and dragged her towards the cars.

"Run!" Patrick yelled as they dragged Emily wailing at the loss of her partner.

"We gotta get the fuck out of here... Now!" Barbara yelled

As they rounded the tents, they tried for Patrick's jeep first. Hoping the noise he heard earlier wasn't his tires.

"Shit!" he belted.

Three of his four tires on the Scrambler had been slashed.

"It's fucking with us. How is it fucking with us?" he babbled.

"What kinda of animal slashes tires?" Barbara questioned.

"I don't know!" Patrick snapped.

"Samantha!" Emily kept screaming hysterically towards where Sam was last seen.

Patrick noticed that Emily's Brat remained unharmed.

"Emily!" he called out, "Keys!"

Barbara shook Emily to bring her back to reality. "Do. You. Have. Your keys?" she yelled.

"We have to get out of here… Now!" Patrick called out.

"Yes yes. Hold on. Fuck!" Emily said as she dug into her front pocket, pulled out the keys to her Brat and handed them to Barbara with shaking hands.

"Here Patrick!" She tossed the keys to him carefully so he wouldn't drop them.

He quickly ran to the passenger door and opened it for them.

"Get in!" He cried out as he motioned them inside the passenger door.

Without hesitation, they both jumped in, slammed the door, and pressed down the door lock. Patrick raced around the front of the Brat and over to the driver's door. Barbara was already leaning over and opening it for him. Patrick handed Barbara his rifle and jumped in the driver's seat. He quickly stuck the key in the ignition and on the first try, the Subaru cranked over and came to life.

Patrick flipped on the headlights, and that's when they saw what it looked like. Standing a mere ten meters in front of them, basking in the glow of the headlights. It stood on two legs like a man but had the head of a wolf. The monster must have been easily over seven feet tall, not including the ears that were sticking straight up from the top of its head. The creature's silver and gray-colored fur was spattered and covered with Sam's blood. Its chest heaved as it breathed and seemed to boil over with rage. Yellow, red-veined eyes glared at them with such hate and malice that it made their skin crawl and hearts race uncontrollably.

"Oh my God! That's all Sam's blood, isn't it?" Emily cried, just as Patrick threw the Subaru into reverse.

"No unwanted visitors, eh?" Patrick mumbled under his breath.

The beast opened its maw, let out a roar, and whipped Sam's entire left arm through the air at their windshield. Her appendage impacted the passenger side with such force, causing the shatterproof glass to spiderweb with a wet crunch. Patrick floored the Brat in reverse and cranked the steering wheel hard. It spat a cloud of rocks and dust in front of them, blocking their view of the creature. Patrick quickly spun the Subaru around, threw it in first gear, and dumped the clutch as he tried to put his right foot through the floorboard. With tires spinning, they headed back towards the road. They sped along the forest floor as pine needles and branches shot past them.

"I think we made it!" Patrick said.

Just when he turned to his right and looked at Barbara, the beast rammed itself into the driver's side of the Brat. The blow had the force of a freight train shattering the side window, sending glass shards all over Patrick and the two girls. The Brat fishtailed from the inertia and spun the small truck around. They ended up smashing its rear passenger quarter panel into a massive tree trunk. The sudden blow rendered everyone inside unconscious.

CHAPTER FOUR

IT circled the Subaru Brat on all fours without making a sound, sniffing at the air and taking in the scents of its prey. Silently, it moved through the trees, being extra careful not to be seen. It waited for its opponents to make the next move. Then it would continue this little game of cat and mouse. The beast grew more excited at the thought of chasing them some more.

Its superior senses could hear them still breathing and they did not carry the scent of death yet. So it knew there was still some fight in them, for it was enjoying this far too much. To the beast, fear made the meat of its victims taste so much better and its hatred for man was so great that it loved nothing more than tormenting its prey. It relished the thought of feasting on their organs or just tearing them to shreds. It had not made up its mind yet about what it was going to do. Sometimes it ate and sometimes its rage was so intense it just tore them apart and scattered the pieces. Either way, it liked to take its time and was in no hurry whatsoever to end tonight's "feastivities"...

The beast arrived in the Coconino National Forest about a month ago, turning it into its killing field. The local authorities were only aware of six people it had killed in the last month, but there were many more than that. Coconino County had a lot of unsolved missing persons cases. It was a very large forest and there were still a lot of secrets yet to be found.

Northern Arizona itself was full of those looking to not be found as well as transients that were passing through on their way to California. This was perfect for the beast. It led to unsuspecting people wandering too far out into the woods after dark or careless campers that were never seen again. Since the majority of the area allowed for dispersed camping, there was no real record of who went where. No reservations or way to track who came in or out of the forest. It was just first come first serve and you could go days without seeing anyone or anyone seeing you. When it finally saw movement from inside the vehicle, it crouched down and sat perfectly still while it waited to see what these mice would do next.

When Barbara came to, she was still wedged between the front two seats of the Subaru. Emily was to her right with her head against the dashboard and Patrick was sprawled against the steering wheel. She was still dazed as she reached down to Emily, trying to make sure she was okay.

"Emily..." Barbara said, "Wake up Emily."

Emily groaned as she leaned back in the passenger seat with a small cut above her right eye, but otherwise okay. Just as she turned to Patrick, he shot awake, choked for a breath, then immediately gripped the keys in the ignition and cranked. The engine took a minute, but it finally started as its 1.6 liter gasped for fuel and air. He slammed the gearshift into first gear and the Brat peeled out and shot forward.

"Everyone okay?" Patrick asked as he maneuvered the small pickup in and around the tall pine trees.

"I think my wrist might be sprained and, well… I peed myself… again," said Emily.

"I just have a goose egg on the back of my head and a splitting headache," Barbara stated.

Patrick kept the pedal down and made it to the dirt road. The Subaru leaped out of the forest as Patrick cut the wheel in a fury of gravel and flying dust. It had been a while since the road they used had been graded so a maximum speed of thirty-five was about all they could do without losing control.

"Why didn't it kill us?" Emily asked.

"Cuz it's fucking with us, Emily," said Patrick. "It wants us to run for some reason. That's why it didn't mess up your car back there and only mine. It seems to want to chase us."

"What kind of animal does that?" Barbara spat.

"I have no idea," said Patrick, as he maneuvered the small truck down the gravel road. The Subaru washboarded as Emily looked out her side window and saw it off in the distance, keeping pace with them as they clicked along.

"It's right there! Through the trees!" she screamed.

"Go faster!" Barbara barked.

Patrick pressed the accelerator down more but was hesitant to go above forty-five miles an hour. Even though the Brat was made for this sort of driving, it was just stupid for him to make it all this way just to get in a car accident due to driving too fast on a dirt road.

"It's gone," said Emily.

"Gone?" Barbara asked.

"Where the fuck did it go!" Patrick responded while cranking the wheel to the left, just barely making a sharp corner. As soon as they came barreling around the turn, there it was. Patrick slammed on the brakes to see it there on all fours in the center of the road, looking right at them.

"Hit it! Hit it!" Barbara cried out.

Patrick floored it, heading straight for the beast. It stood up on its two rear legs, opening its arms as if to give them a giant bear hug, and braced itself for impact.

They all jolted forward inside the truck cab as the Subaru made a complete stop as if they slammed into the side of a house. The force tossed Barbara onto the passenger floor. The eight-foot behemoth more or less caught the front of the car in his grip and leaned towards them, blood and drool dripping from its gums. It focused solely on Patrick as he tried to floor it, shifting gears, only to have the rear tires spin in the loose dirt. Patrick finally caused the truck to stall after letting the clutch out too fast, and it sputtered to a halt. When the dust settled, it just stood there looking at Patrick, heaving its chest in and out with anger as it watched him intensely. It began to drool even more at the thought of tasting their flesh and devouring their organs. Without moving his head or taking his eyes off the monster in front of them, Patrick began to instruct the girls on what was going to happen next.

"Barbara remember that farm we passed on the way in? It can't be more than a mile or two up this road," he said. "Emily, I want you to open the door and for both of you to start running as fast as you can and do not look back, no matter what."

The passenger door flew open, and the beast was instantly distracted, unlocking its eyes from Patrick. Right when it looked towards the fleeing women, Patrick laid on the horn. That seemed to get the monster's attention and seriously aggravate it. The beast covered its ears and let out a painful howl. Then raised its fists in the air and started bashing and clawing at the hood of the Brat hoping to make the sound stop.

Patrick kept on the horn as the other two ran for their lives. As the beast smashed away at the front of the car, Patrick slowly opened his driver's door, keeping the horn down as he crept. Staying low, he slid out, still keeping on the horn, and inched his rifle towards him with his free hand.

"Shit. Did I chamber the next round or not? God, I hope I did. Shit," he whispered.

In one smooth motion, Patrick let his hand off the horn and got out of the vehicle, raising the rifle into a shooter's stance. With the stock of the Winchester against his shoulder, he quickly aimed at the beast's face and pulled the trigger.

CLICK...

Patrick's screams reached the girls, and they knew exactly what had happened. "No," Barbara muttered and collapsed to the forest floor as soon as she heard his frantic scream. Emily quickly stopped, turned around helped her friend up, and begged her to run.

"We have to just keep going," she pleaded to Barbara.

With their hearts racing and their legs weak, they found the will to continue. Just as Barbara took Emily's hand and began to stand up, the beast came out of the dark leaping onto Emily from behind, and closed its jaws around the back of her head, crushing it like a melon. With blood spraying everywhere, it ferociously began to tear Emily apart.

Barbara was so close that arterial spray showered all over her as it tore Emily's head free. Standing there blinking in shock, her inner survival instinct kicked in, "The gun!" she gasped, as she turned and ran as fast as she could. She was now doubling back to Emily's Subaru.

One half of her brain telling her she was a moron and the other half cheering her on. She ducked under branches and leaped over bushes, running with everything she had left. Barbara figured if she could just grab the gun and follow the road, she would have a better chance, especially since it seemed preoccupied with Emily.

The headlights became visible about thirty yards in front of her. She reached the truck, ran around the driver's side and collapsed at the site of Patrick. His head was torn off and was nowhere to be seen and the entire side of the blue Subaru was bathed in his blood. Within seconds, her adrenaline snapped her out of it and she noticed the rifle was gone. Without even reacting, Barbara jumped up and began to run.

"I told you that was a stupid idea," she told herself out loud.

The only thing she was thinking now was that she was gonna live, get the police, army, or whoever she could, and have them come back, hunt, and kill whatever this thing was. She kept on running as her chest began to burn and her legs began to fill up with lactic acid. Barbara must have run for a good mile straight before realizing she was completely spent. She slowed down and stopped, leaning over with her hands placed on her thighs, breathing heavily, wondering how much farther this farm was.

"Fuck!" she screamed in anger.

She stood up and opened her arms wide and began yelling.

"Alright! Here I am! Come and get me asshole!"

She bent back down to catch her breath.

"Fuck it," she muttered in-between wheezes. "I'm done. I'm done running. Fuck it." She gasped, "You can just have me assho…"

She heard a branch snap behind her and she slowly turned around with her eyes closed, knowing exactly what she was going to see. She opened her eyes to find the beast standing not more than twelve meters from her, holding Patrick's dad's rifle.

"Well?" Barbara called out. Her voice was now hoarse. "Well Asshole. We gonna kiss or fight?"

It tilted its head while it looked at her like a dog would when trying to hear something better. It then tossed the rifle on the ground at her feet. Barbara saw it land about a meter away from her in the gravel. She looked at it in disbelief and looked back up at the monster.

"You gotta be shitting me. You are fucking with us. You've been God damn fucking with us the entire time."

It began to chuff as its shoulders went up and down. It was laughing at her. Her jaw dropped as she realized what it was doing. Without hesitation, she lunged for the rifle, brought it up, and chambered a round by working the bolt action. Just as she brought the gun up to pull the trigger, the beast was gone.

Barbara looked around her perimeter, aiming the Winchester in every direction, trying to steady her breath. She tried to remember how many shots she had heard tonight. She could only remember hearing the one warning shot Patrick fired while she was still in the tent. *Four left,* she thought to herself as she turned and began to jog.

Now she was ready for it, but she had to keep moving. She had to get to this farmhouse and hope someone there could help her. Slowly and as quietly as she could, she started to walk, listening and frantically looking all around her as she moved. She noticed the forest was still just as quiet as it was earlier in the night. Realizing it must have been because of this thing and how nature seemed to know when an apex predator was in the area.

Trying to regain her strength, she now walked in a slow creep. She waved her rifle around in every direction. A branch snapped to her right, causing her to turn to look. Without stopping, she continued to creep. She noticed it was right next to her, just past the tree line, stalking her. The beast walked on all fours, using its front arms to pull itself along like a primate does. The moonlight above caused the beast's yellow eyes to glow at her through the darkness. She didn't take her eyes off it as she continued to sidestep up the road, pointing the rifle at it.

"So big boy. Is this what we call a Mexican standoff?" she said through gritted teeth.

It slowly walked next to her, staying in the shadows of the trees and out of the moonlight. It looked right at her as she looked at it and knew she was aiming a rifle at him. He could tell by her smell she did not have the silver needed to harm him. He made sure she could see him and kept her eyes on him as they walked in unison. She was a brave one, and he loved it. He couldn't remember the last time someone tried to fight back, let alone put up a fight. The wolf snorted at the thought of this hunt coming to an end.

"I know what you are now," she called out to him. "The Yee Naaldlooshii."

The sound of that name made it let out a low growl.

"Yeah, you don't like that name, do ya, big boy?" She said it once more, "Yee Naaldlooshii."

It growled once again and then stopped in its tracks. Barbara also stopped, against her better judgment. She slowly lined up the iron sights and squeezed the trigger on the old rifle. Just as the beast rose to its two legs, she fired, nailing the beast center mass. She saw it jerk back, but it began to walk towards her unfazed. Fluently working the bolt of the rifle, she fired again, hitting her target again in the chest. It just jerked from the bullet's impact and kept walking. She worked the bolt as it cleared the tree line and she paused. Now she got a good look at it under the moonlight.

The Yee Naaldlooshii was huge. Its haunches looked like those of a bodybuilder. A massive chest and imposing shoulders topped its long torso. Muscular arms that almost seemed too long for its body ended in huge hands, sporting long fingers tipped with black, blood-covered claws. Its maw hung open while blood mixed with saliva dripped from its gums and contained enormous teeth. Its silver and gray fur was matted with a mix of wet and congealed blood.

The closer it got to her, the more she could smell its aroma of musk and copper. Its yellow eyes bore two holes through her as she stood motionless. *Yee Naaldlooshii,* she thought to herself as she took a deep breath and slowly drew a bead on the monster's face. It was now about five meters away and she could hear its breathing. She calmed her nerves and slowly exhaled, just like her father taught her, and then squeezed the trigger on the Winchester. The rifle barked as the 30-06 round flew down the barrel, through the air, and struck the beast in its right eye. It rolled back in pain, letting out a roar as it grabbed at its eye and turned away.

"That's right, tough guy. How does that feel?" she said, quickly slamming another round into the chamber.

The Yee Naaldlooshii started to chuff as it slowly turned its head back towards her. Its right eye was gone as blood dripped down its face, mingling with all her friend's dried gore caked to the beast's fur. Barbara's face went white as she realized the beast was unfazed except for the missing eye. Barbara finally realized it was over. There was no making it out of there tonight. She had nothing left in the tank and her will to fight had fled. Deep down she knew she was out of options and she debated putting the rifle under her chin.

"Fuck it," she said, and she raised the rifle, this time aiming at the creature's groin, and squeezed off her last round. The beast let out a howl as it grabbed at its crotch area and fell to one knee in pain.

"Felt that, didn't you, asshole?!" she spat.

Pulling back the bolt one last time she double-checked if it was out of bullets. Finally, she realized it didn't matter because she had no idea how to kill this monster. It rose to its feet and towered over her now. She tossed the rifle on the ground just as it had done to her earlier in this macabre game of tag. The beast looked down at the rifle, then up at Barbara, and cocked its head in confusion.

There seemed to be a look of disappointment on the beast's face as she stood defiantly in front of it, breathing heavily. Tears began to run down her face. All she could think of was when she was a child playing in the yard with her mom and dad and how happy they were together. Back when life was much simpler and they were a family.

"I'll see you soon, Mom," she said to herself and spat in the monster's face.

The last thing Barbara saw before everything went black was the Yee Naaldlooshii's jaws lunging towards her.

CHAPTER FIVE

DETROIT

MAY, 1987

Daniel slowly opened his eyes as the light stung his corneas. He could hear the sounds of machines beeping and realized he was in a hospital bed. Stanley sat in the chair in the far corner of the room working a crossword puzzle.

"Man, what's a six-letter word for your mother's daughter?" Stanley asked.

"What? Where the hell am I? What are you doing here, Stanley? I mean, what am I doing here?" Daniel frantically asked.

Stanley pointed his pen straight at Daniel and said, "Sister…" and went back to his crossword.

"The last thing I remember is drinking with you at Mac's and then now I'm here," said Daniel.

Stanley responded with, "Five across, a four-letter word for Lobo?" Then, with a pop of his mouth and a pistol finger point said, "Wolf."

Daniel, realizing Stanley was no help, looked around the room. He noticed he was in a single room with one bed, which made him feel a little better. To the right was the door, and he could see hospital personnel walking back and forth outside his room. To his left was a dirty window framed by sun-faded yellow curtains with blue flowers. There was a TV mounted in the corner above where Stanley sat. One of the fluorescent bulbs flickered as it tried to indicate it was ready to be replaced.

The afternoon sunlight came through the curtains and left Daniel a bit relieved to know it was daylight. Daniel noticed that there were no cards, flowers, or any sign of anyone's sympathy sitting on the table next to him. For a brief minute, this made him sad. He only had Stanley, who wasn't being much help at the moment. Daniel had just relocated in the late fall of 1986 and didn't have any friends outside of the people he met at Mac's bar or work. He didn't meet many being a bag boy in inner-city Detroit.

He had just renewed a six-month lease for his tiny one-bedroom apartment. It was located a couple of blocks from Mac's on the west side. He had gotten by with various odd jobs here and there and currently bagged groceries and stocked shelves a couple of days a week at a local market for $3.50 an hour.

"What's an eight-letter word for anteater?" Stanley asked.

Daniel closed his eyes and concentrated as hard as he could to piece together the events that led him to this situation. Stanley smacked his forehead with the palm of his hand. "Duh, aardvark."

Daniel grew incredibly impatient, "Why am I here, Stanley?"

Stanley looked up from his crossword and said, "What? All this?" As he pointed to the hospital bed. "If I had to guess, you messed up again."

"Messed up?" Daniel asked.

"Yeah, bud, you haven't gotten it right yet. Which is pretty clear with you being … well... alive and all," Stanley said.

Daniel laid his head back on the pillow and sighed as he looked at the ceiling tile, baffled and confused. He looked down and saw that he was in a spica cast from the waist down. The cast covered his belly button and ran down both his legs with a brace in the center to help keep them apart and keep him immobilized. There was a hole in the cast between his legs, so he was able to use a bedpan.

Right then, a short, robust lady with dark brown skin glided through the door, wearing a nurse's uniform and a huge smile. Daniel was instantly annoyed at the sight of someone so bubbly. Especially when he was still trying to decipher where he was.

"Hi there, sugar, my name is Nurse Evans. You gave us all quite a scare," she said. "We thought you would be a goner when the EMS brought you in here."

"Here?" Daniel asked in return.

"Why, you're at Henry Ford Hospital and you arrived yesterday in the late afternoon," the nurse said.

Daniel pondered for a bit and asked. "Why? I can't remember anything other than being at Mac's bar around noon and after that, I must have blacked out."

The nurse tilted her head and frowned as she tried to help replay the events from once he got to the hospital. "Hun, they said you stepped in front of a moving garbage truck. You came in with two broken legs, a crushed hip and a skull fracture. You were covered head to toe in blood and barely breathing. I'm beyond surprised you're still alive, let alone talking to me right now."

Daniel felt his head and noticed the bandages and gauze wrapped around it. "How did I? I mean what? I don't understand. I don't remember any of that."

Nurse Evans checked his IV and pulled out a blood pressure cuff.

"Here honey, give me your arm and let's see what this says." She slipped the cuff over his arm and latched the velcro, tightened the valve, and began vigorously pumping away at the bulb. She put the stethoscope earpieces in her ears, and slipped the diaphragm under the cuff. She listened as she slowly released the valve. "110/70. That's pretty perfect for a man who was run over yesterday."

Daniel looked at the nurse, perplexed, and said, "I feel great. Like seriously, never better. I am starving, though."

The nurse frowned at him and shook her head. "This makes no dang sense at all. I know that Dr. Fraser would like to run a few more tests and keep you a few more nights. Let me bring you some water and some food." She smiled and leaned over to adjust his pillows to make him comfortable. He noticed the smell of cocoa butter on her and found it soothing.

"Okay, I guess," Daniel responded, "and yeah, food would be great."

The Nurse glanced at his chart and then clipped it back on the footboard. "Be right back in two shakes of a bunny's tail." She turned and hurried out of the room.

"What's a six-letter word for affliction?" Stanley asked from his corner of the room.

"Shut up Stanley," Daniel replied as he let his head fall back onto his pillow.

"Cursed!" Stanley shouted as if saying AHA and began scratching at his crossword excitedly.

Daniel devoured four plates of hospital food and drank at least two gallons of water. He had no idea what he was eating, but it was apparently some kind of protein, a potato, and some sort of green vegetable that could have possibly been beans.

The Doctor came in and reviewed his X-rays with him. He showed him that he did have two broken patellas, two shattered tibias, a fractured fibula in his right leg, and a compound fracture in his right femur that required surgery. The doctor continued to show him that the coxal bone on his right hip had been crushed and needed to be surgically put back together with a plate and some nuts and bolts. The doctor showed the images of his skull and fracture at his parietal bone. Dr. Fraser explained to Daniel that he had never seen anyone with this much damage to themselves be awake, speaking and so lucid the next day. Daniel tried to explain to the doctor that he couldn't remember anything after leaving Mac's Bar. The doctor explained to him that he wasn't surprised at the loss of memory with the kind of head trauma he received.

So Daniel agreed to stay as long as the Doctor wanted him to and figured he didn't have a choice because he had nowhere else to be at the moment. Daniel did, however, leave out the part about not being able to remember certain parts of his life and figured he would save that for another time. He just wanted to see how things played out first. He did notice that Stanley was gone and he couldn't remember seeing him leave, but there had been a lot of nurses and doctors in and out of his room all day. So he settled in and got cozy and sipped on his Vernors through a straw and noticed the TV in the upper corner of the room.

"Oh man a color Zenith," he said out loud and started searching around his nightstand for the remote.

He eventually found the black remote, pointed it towards the television, and pressed the red power button as it clicked on. He flipped past some game show he didn't recognize, the Home Shopping Network, and an episode of The Fall Guy, which briefly caught his attention before he settled for the evening news.

An anchorman named Bill Bonds was wrapping up a segment about something to do with Cabbage Patch dolls and choking hazards before it went to a commercial. Daniel never really watched a lot of TV. Back at his apartment, he only had a twelve-inch black-and-white TV with a crappy rabbit ear antenna that never really got any stations in all that well. He didn't mind watching the commercials because it was in wondrous Technicolor. Bill Bonds came back on the television set with a serious look on his face and began to start his next story.

"Still no leads on the four people found dead on the west side of Detroit six days ago. Police still do not have any information, nor are they revealing much about the case other than that the four people were brutally murdered. We have an eyewitness from the scene." The TV changed to a shot of a street corner where an elderly black lady holding her calico cat. She stood in a bathrobe with her hair a mess.

"Yes sir, I was taking my garbage out late that night and I heard such a ruckus. It sounded like a few gunshots and some screaming coming from the alley behind the RadioShack over there," she said and pointed across the street.

"What did you do next, ma'am?" the male reporter asked.

"I almost shit myself, that's what I did. You hear gunshots around here, you don't go looking around or asking questions. You run the fuck back inside. Which is exactly what I did. I will tell you one thing though. After I closed the door and locked it, I heard a noise that will haunt me forever and I have not been able to sleep since," she stated.

"What did you hear, ma'am?" the reporter asked.

The lady hesitated for a minute as if trying to decide whether she should say this on live television. "A howl," she said, "The most frightening noise I have ever heard in my life. That is NOT something you hear around here."

The reporter looked at the old woman like she was off her meds.

"You heard a howl?" he asked.

"Yes," the lady said. "I know it sounds crazy but I know what I heard. It was the sound of something evil and mad as hell. You are not going to find me out after dark ever again."

The reporter finished the interview by turning to the camera and saying, "Okay… back to you, Bill."

The anchorman shuffled a few papers in front of him looked at the camera with a stern look and said, "Horrible news, just horrible news. Kinda reminds us of what happened in Memphis last summer. Well, when we come back, a North Sea oil platform explodes, killing over 100 people. Thanks for tuning in Detroit. We'll be back after these messages."

Daniel figured that was enough for tonight. He turned off the TV, closed his eyes, and was soon sound sleep.

CHAPTER SIX

COCONINO COUNTY

JULY, 1985

Sheriff Tanaka Chee got the call that they found Emily Rigg's Subaru on the old dirt road down from Bull Flanagan's sheep ranch. His deputy sheriff also told him they found the body of what they believed to be Patrick Nelson. It had been two days since his daughter and friends should have returned from their camping trip in the Coconino National Forest. Tanaka floored his 1981 Police issue Chevy Silverado down Interstate 17 South.

"Goddammit Babs, where are you?" he said to himself as the V8 engine screamed and the sirens blared.

Tanaka had been the sheriff of Coconino County for almost eight years now. He was going to be up for reelection soon and he couldn't imagine doing anything else in life. He also couldn't think or fathom a life without his daughter, either. Babs was his entire world and reminded him of her late mother. A hundred things went through his head as he blasted down the interstate.

Why didn't I try harder to talk her out of going? he thought. "Why didn't I try harder?"

Tanaka had been working on this case for the past month and knew more than he allowed the press or the public to know. As far as the public was concerned, there had been only six murders twenty-nine days ago. Tanaka still had close ties to the Navajo Nation and was aware of similar cases they had on the reservation. Over the course of the three days, there were numerous missing person reports in both Coconino County as well as the nearby reservation. If he had to speculate, his number was around fifteen total that were either found dead or missing. His men only recovered six bodies.

The past month had been the darkest time of his entire career in law enforcement. The media only cared about the white victims and stayed out of the local tribal and reservation affairs. Each victim's remains showed signs of a wild animal violently attacking and ravaging them. The bodies remained in such a gruesome state that it was hard to determine exactly how they died.

The first of the six victims they found was a thirty-two-year-old single woman named Casandra Stockwell. The woman had been torn apart while walking her two Yorkshire terriers. Everyone knew Casandra because she worked at the favorite local diner in downtown Flagstaff. Her neighbors filed a missing persons report when they found her two Yorkshires alone on her front porch, which was something Cassandra never did.

The second and third victims were a married couple, John and Kelly Hockersack and their fate was even worse. What was left of John was found in the back of their three-acre lot that backed up to the forest. His upper torso was twenty yards from the back porch where his left leg was found. An empty pump action Remington 12-gauge lay at his side, surrounded by spent shells. They found one of his arms from the elbow down on the roof of their 1200 square foot ranch. His head and face looked like it had been a chew toy for a grizzly bear or Siberian tiger. John's wife Kelly was found inside their shed behind the house. Her husband apparently tried to lock her in to keep her safe. That plan failed horribly. The padlock was busted, and the shed doors were ripped off their hinges and lay in the yard in front of the small structure. Kelly's face was crushed and mauled and her chest cavity was torn open. They later discovered that her liver and heart were missing completely.

The fourth victim was Marcus O'Riley, a fifty-two-year-old banker who had gone out mountain biking in the Coconino Forest one night and never returned home. He suffered a similar fate. The man's chest cavity was ripped open and his liver and heart were removed. Where it gets even worse is how his head had been pummeled or stomped to a pulp, leaving hardly anything left to identify. The coroner's report indicated that his head had been crushed post-mortem.

The fifth and sixth victims' remains belonged to NAU college students, Margaret Rose and Shirley Oscarson. Police found their car abandoned off I-40 east and their bodies were both found 200 yards to the south in the forest among the pine trees and underbrush. It appeared their car broke down and something or someone spooked and chased them into the woods. The sheriff's department found the bodies days later by reports of the amount of buzzards circling above seen from the highway.

Tanaka read all the reports and the one thing that each victim had in common was that they found animal hairs on each. The sheriff had the coroner send the hairs off to NAU's zoology department to see if they could do a DNA test and possibly identify the species. They were still waiting for a response. Other than this shred of evidence, Tanaka had no other leads or any theories yet. The victims were in no relation, there really wasn't any motive, no smoking gun and they all just seemed to be in the wrong place at the wrong time. One possibility was maybe there was a killer who was targeting people at random and using his pet grizzly bear to do the heavy lifting.

Tanaka did not believe that theory. He couldn't think of any wild animals that would do this by nature. They were all ravaged with such force and savagery that no animal he knew of was capable of doing this, trained or not.

What kind of animal would throw an arm on top of someone's roof, bust shed doors off their hinges, or stomp a man's head to mush? It just wasn't possible, he thought.

None of the crime scenes were in any areas where they could see any animal tracks or footprints to help them narrow their search. This was not the normal habit of a mountain lion or any other big cat that he knew of. There was no circus in town or escaped zoo animals. Flagstaff didn't even have a zoo. Now with his daughter Barbara missing, his mind went wild with fear and insane possibilities.

Deputy Sheriff Mark Winston had already closed the old road off and placed Deputy McFerrin on the road to keep people from coming down and driving through the crime scene. Jennifer McFerrin was a rookie deputy who had only been on the job for two weeks before this incident.

"You apparently started at the right time, eh, Officer McFerrin?" Mark said.

"Yeah, sorry I lost my lunch back there. I actually knew Patrick from high school," she said.

"Yeah, that's horrible. I don't know what to say," he replied. "For now, if you could just stay here and keep your radio on, we don't want anyone coming down this road and contaminating our scene,"

She looked around. "I really don't think anyone will be coming, Officer Winston."

Mark took a pouch of Redman long cut out of the breast pocket of his uniform, opened it, and placed a huge wad in his mouth with his forefinger and thumb.

"You would think that, but this place will be crawling with news vans once word gets out. Those slimeballs have been listening to their police scanners lately and seem to be everywhere we are when we least expect them." He then spat in the gravel.

"Here comes Sheriff Chee. Do we have any idea where his daughter is? If Patrick is back there?" she asked.

"No… and I fear the worst," Mark said as he waited for the sheriff to pull up.

Tanaka pulled his truck up next to Officer McFerrin's patrol car and leaned out the window to hear what they had to say.

"Afternoon Sheriff. It's about half a mile up the road that way." Mark said pointing in the opposite direction of the patrol car. "Ole Bull Flannagan discovered the scene this morning while out with his tractor grading the road when he called me. Bull didn't say much. Just that I had to get here right away. I have the coroner and forensics on their way now and they should be here in about twenty minutes," said Mark.

"Good. Any signs of Barbara?" Tanaka asked.

With a sympathetic look, the deputy sheriff replied by shaking his head no.

"Well, hop in Mark and let's go see what we have," the sheriff said.

Mark walked around Tanaka's Silverado, opened the passenger door, spat before he climbed in, then slammed the truck door shut.

"Is it bad?" the sheriff asked.

Mark just nodded and looked at him grimly. He explained to the sheriff as they drove towards the crime scene. He already ran the plates on the Subaru Brat just to make sure and it came back registered to Emily Riggs. They sat in silence as they drove the rest of the way.

They arrived at the crime scene where Mark's patrol car was parked. "I've got Deputy Basterson down the road about a half mile, blocking it from that direction, though I doubt anyone will be coming along. No one drives down this old road," Mark said.

Tanaka put the pickup in park, stepped out of the driver's door and surveyed the surroundings. Tanaka was not a tall man standing only five foot six and weighed about 152 lbs. He was, however, in great shape for his age, let alone anyone twenty years younger. At the age of fifty-one, he was still able to outpace most of the younger deputies in their twenties. He had a pronounced jawline and a slender face with Navajo features. The sheriff wore a cowboy hat and his black and gray hair hung down on either shoulder in two long braids. The men wore the standard Coconino County tan and brown sheriff's department uniforms, and both men wore leather cowboy boots.

Mark got out of the passenger side, walked around the truck, and stood next to Tanaka. The barrel-chested man towered over the sheriff at a height of six-three and had an easy 100 lbs on the man. Mark used to lift weights in his twenties and thirties and was at one point super lean, but now age and gravity had caught up to the fifty-eight-year-old man. Mark had been told recently that he resembled an older Biff Tannen, a character from the movie Back To The Future that had recently come out at the theaters this past year. Tanaka removed his hat and took a blue bandana out of his back pocket to wipe his brow. Mark stood next to him and pointed towards the road in front of them.

"It looks like the Brat came out of the brush about 100 yards down the road just around that corner." The sheriff put his hat back on, stuffed his bandana in his back pocket and started to walk towards the wreckage of Emily's car.

The Brat looked like it had been attacked by a can opener. "Yáadilá óolyé," Tanaka said in Navajo as he bent down to look at the claw marks that ran through the demolished hood. The front hood was gouged, crushed, and smashed inward.

"What in tarnation you think did that?" Mark asked.

Tanaka just shook his head and kept examining the small truck. The windshield spider-webbed on the passenger side and the small rectangular grill was busted apart. Both the passenger side and driver side doors were wide open. The driver's side door had been caved in like something had rammed it full tilt and the side window was shattered. The smell of antifreeze and death filled the air, causing Tanaka to remove his bandanna once more and place it over his mouth and nose.

"Patrick's body is on the driver's side and if I had to guess, he was driving," Mark gestured in the driver's direction.

The sheriff walked around the open door and saw Patrick's body lying there on his back with his arms out at his side. "Jesus, where the hell is his head, Mark?"

Mark just shrugged, "Don't know. Haven't found it yet."

Tanaka bent down to get a closer look at Patrick's body, making note of the blood spray that was all over the driver's side of the car and even on the rear wagon wheel rim. "Whatever got him, hit him hard and fast. Doesn't appear to be any other external damage to the body or sign of a struggle," Tanaka said as he stood up. Taking notice of the dried blood droplets across the roof of the Brat that was slightly caved in by something heavy.

"Looks like our suspect then leaped over the roof and headed in that direction," Tanaka said pointing towards the open passenger door.

He could barely make out another set of footprints around Patrick's remains. They were hard to see because of the condition the old road was in, but they were there. Tanaka walked around the back of the small pickup and saw that he was correct. There was another set of hiking boots that came out of the forest behind the Subaru and around to the driver's side. To him, they looked like about a size eight woman's boot.

"Babs," he said to himself.

Mark started to walk towards Tanaka when the sheriff told him to watch his step and to be careful not to disrupt any loose gravel because he found another set of tracks that could belong to his daughter or Emily. Mark halted without hesitation with his eyes open wide, then spat some chew on the ground.

Tanaka looked at him and sighed loudly. "Don't be a shit-ass."

"Sorry," Mark said as he daintily tiptoed towards him, trying not to mess the crime scene up even more.

"See that? Looks like someone, possibly Barbara or Emily, came running out of the forest here, stopped by Patrick's body, then went back that way," Tanaka said and pointed back down the road they had just come from.

The officers backtracked about 250 yards, following what they could of the second set of tracks. They came to where the tracks appeared to end, and they both stopped. The sheriff and deputy sheriff carefully looked around that area of road. They quickly noticed four spent 30-06 shells lying on the road.

"How in the hell did we miss this?" Mark said as he pointed down at the shells.

Tanaka heard him but was distracted by a third set of tracks that seemed to meet the ones they were following in the center of the road. It was clearly an animal paw print which resembled that of a wolf. These, however, were twelve inches long and about ten inches wide, with four symmetrical toes and evident claws. They were not that of a bear or a mountain lion, but Tanaka could tell it was definitely in the canine family.

"Hey Mark? Last night was a full moon, wasn't it?"

Mark walked over and looked down at the track and said, "Jesus' crackers. What made that?"

Tanaka asked him again, "Was it a full moon last night?" Mark looked up at Tanaka and raised an eyebrow.

"Yup," the deputy sheriff said with a slow nod.

Two white Ford Econoline vans broke their silence as they came towards them down the road from the direction of Flanagan's farm.

"Crime scene investigation is here," Mark said.

"Make sure they don't drive over all this," Tanaka motioned towards the ground. Both their radios chirped alive as Officer McFerrin came across the radio speaker.

"We've got the press incoming," she said.

"That was fast," Tanaka said to Mark.

Mark pulled his radio from his belt and pressed the talk button. "Do not let them near this. Shoot the bastards if you have to."

CHAPTER SEVEN

Tanaka walked deep into the forest following a hunch while Officer Winston stayed with the forensic team. After double-checking around the Subaru, he noticed more sets of footprints and some partial animal tracks that matched what they found back up the road. The pair of tracks appeared to come from the passenger door and off into the woods. If he had to guess, he figured two people fled while Patrick was being attacked. His first thought was that it had to be Barbara and Emily, who ran while Patrick tried to cause a diversion.

In Tanaka's gut, he knew they were no longer dealing with a man. Nor were they dealing with a man and his trained attack pet. He knew this was something very different.

His grandfather had told him stories as a young boy about a creature called a Yee Naaldlooshii, which was more commonly known as a skin-walker. A man or woman that was cursed to change into a beast by the light of the full moon. They were always stories that he never really believed as a child and thought it was just some made-up crap from over the years to keep kids in line. In all his years of law enforcement, Tanaka had never seen anything like this. Sure he had seen dead people or murder victims and even had to work with the FBI on a case involving serial murders back in the late 1970s. This made him no stranger to blood and gore; it came with the job.

Until now, everything he had worked on was pretty self-explanatory. Man gets angry, man murders other man, and it is usually that simple. In most cases, they would find the murder weapon and it was an open and shut case. These, however, were much different and far more malevolent.

When the smell hit him, he knew he was close. He hoped and prayed to the creator that it was not Barbara's body he was going to find. Pulling his blue bandana out of his back pocket, he covered his nose and mouth as he neared the source of the rotten smell. About thirty meters in front of him and close to 150 yards from the crime scene, he saw what he knew was a body.

Right away, he spotted Emily's blonde hair and his gut sank, but quietly he sighed in relief for the time being. Emily's body had been mutilated. Her head was severed and crushed. Her body was mangled and what was left of her lay on her stomach on the forest floor. Tanaka shooed off a few buzzards that had been feeding on her remains as he walked over to get a closer look. Emily's back was torn open and her spine was yanked out. If he had to guess, he would say her heart and liver were missing.

Pulling out his radio, he called it in, stating he had possibly found Emily Rigg's body but no sign of any others. The sheriff let them know that he was about 150 yards from the Brat and to send a team in while he waited.

Tanaka was an expert pathfinder and tracker, which is something he learned from his grandfather. He learned at an early age how to tell the difference between types of animal tracks and animal territorial patterns. This was like nothing he had ever seen before. Nothing, to his knowledge, killed this way. Especially anything that was native to the Coconino National Forest. This reminded him of a story he read about two male lions in Tsavo, Kenya that terrorized workers during the building of the Uganda-Mombasa Railway in East Africa in the late 1800s. The pair of lions were named "The Tsavo Man-Eaters" and were reportedly responsible for the deaths of over a hundred people. That, however, was in Africa and this was Arizona where there have not been any reported cases of lethal attacks of the much smaller indigenous mountain lion. Besides, Tanaka believed the tracks he found were canine and not those of a big cat.

As the sheriff examined the ground around Emily, he noticed that the forest was suddenly eerily quiet. No birds were chirping, no critters scampering and even the carrion feeders had stopped circling above. Other than the sound of the wind whistling through the trees, it was completely silent.

Too silent, he thought.

Tanaka had the sudden feeling he was no longer alone, and that he was being watched. He felt a faint chill shoot down his back as a man's voice called to him.

"Hello sheriff," a voice said from out in the distance.

Tanaka's blood froze. He put his hand on his Smith and Wesson Model 66.

"I see you found some of my work. I have to admit, last night was the most fun I have had in a long time," the male voice said.

Tanaka drew his .357 service revolver and scanned the trees as he turned in a 360-degree motion, trying to spot where the stranger was.

He must be hiding behind a tree, he thought.

Whoever was speaking to him was clearly trying to play some kind of game.

Am I losing it? he thought to himself.

"I am enjoying it here in Coconino County this time of year. I've traveled far and wide over the years and it is breathtaking up here. I really wish I discovered this area sooner. I think I'll stay a little longer," the mysterious voice said.

This time, the voice was coming from behind the sheriff. He spun around, aiming his revolver, and found nothing but pine trees and underbrush.

"You smell just like her, by the way. She would have made you proud. She put up quite a fight before I killed her," the voice said.

Tanaka knew he was talking about his daughter, Barbara. Tanaka kept scanning through the trees, trying to figure out if he was going crazy or if there was actually someone out there with him.

"I'll be seeing you, sheriff. I think I'll pay you all a visit later tonight," the man's voice said, then it stopped. Just like that, the forest went back to normal. He once again heard the birds chirping, and it felt peaceful again. Tanaka carefully continued scanning the area with his Smith and Wesson in hand.

Just then, his radio barked. "You there, sheriff?"

Tanaka was startled and almost discharged his firearm. He took a deep breath and pressed the call button on his radio.

"Go for Sheriff Chee."

IT had been several hours now since the forensic team arrived at the crime scene. They had bagged up Patrick's remains in a body bag and loaded them into one of the vans. A flatbed tow truck from a local towing company pulled up to remove the ravaged Subaru Brat. The Crime Scene Investigation team scooped up what little evidence they could find into small bags. They combed the surrounding area and tried to locate Patrick's head, but had no such luck. Deputy Sheriff Winston had found Patrick and Barbara's campsite by entering the woods about fifty yards from where Emily's Subaru had rejoined the dirt road.

Other deputies had arrived and were helping wrap up the crime scene, tow the Brat and keep the media hounds at bay. Mark found himself curious and walked back down the road toward where Officer Basterson was posted. He wanted to see if he could find where the car was coming from and if there were any signs of the sheriff's daughter. Tanaka had already found Emily and radioed it in and the Crime Scene investigation team was already out there with the sheriff gathering evidence. The deputy sheriff didn't have to look that hard to find the path the car made as it smashed and bashed its way through the woods.

He found the campsite in a circular clearing of pine trees. The deputy sheriff noted this would have been a great place to stargaze on a clear night. He checked the glove box of the Jeep Scrambler that was left unattended, noticing the three slashed tires. The registration papers said it belonged to Patrick Nelson.

Mark let out a big whistle as he noticed the massive claw marks on the hood of the jeep, nearly cutting his fingers as he ran his hand over the jagged metal. The fire pit had been knocked around, leaving burnt logs strewn all over as if someone had run right through the fire. Mark could see that there were traces of dried blood on the far end of the site. By the amount of dried blood, the deputy sheriff could tell something had been butchered, but there was no body left behind.

"God, I hope it wasn't Barbara," he said as he kneeled to inspect the area.

"Afternoon, officer," a voice came from behind him.

Mark drew his Colt Officer Revolver that was chambered in .38 caliber and turned around to find a man leaning against the brown Scrambler's front fender. He was a white male of average height and wore a blue hooded sweatshirt and matching sweatpants. He had the hood pulled up and a long light-brown beard, which contained streaks of gray, that came down his chest. The man's long greasy hair hung down past his shoulders and poked out of the sides of his hood. He looked like he hadn't bathed in some time. Mark noticed the man was not wearing any shoes and his feet were black with dirt and grime.

"You're disturbing my crime scene, mister, and I don't like that. Can you show me some identification and explain what exactly you're doing here?" Mark said.

"Oh, I'm sorry ... name's Norman Thatch... and there's a woman's arm over there, by the way," he said and pointed towards Samantha's remains.

Mark cocked the hammer on his Colt and spat a wad of Redman off to his left. "Okay, now talk. What are you doing here, Mr. Thatch? This is a police crime scene and you are not allowed here," the officer said sternly.

Is this the guy we are looking for? he thought to himself.

"Why, this is my forest. I could ask the same of you," Norman responded. "Don't you know the law of the jungle 101? The biggest and baddest takes possession of a territory by showing his dominance and staking claim to what he wants."

"You know I'm holding a gun, right?" Mark questioned the man's sanity.

The officer noticed something was very wrong with this man's eyes. They seemed to flash a yellow hue in a certain light. Mark felt there was something seriously wrong with this man. A person just doesn't walk into an obvious crime scene with a severed arm and be this cool and collected.

"Okay, enough of this shit. I'm taking you in for questioning and placing you under arrest for tampering with evidence!" Mark said as he pulled his handcuffs from his belt and walked towards the suspect.

"Sure thing Officer. Why I'm here to help in any way I can," the man said and put out his hands in a nonthreatening manner and smiled.

Mark placed the cuffs on him pulled his radio from his belt and called it in. The deputy sheriff then instructed the man to start walking slowly as they headed back towards the road.

"Worked here long, officer?" Norman asked playfully.

"You know I'm placing you under arrest for tampering with a crime scene?" Mark said.

"Of course. Whatever you need me to do, I am willing and able. Plus, I am looking forward to meeting this sheriff of yours, in person," the man said.

Who is this guy and why is he in northern Arizona? the deputy sheriff thought.

Later, Tanaka watched as the deputy sheriff placed the suspect in the back of his patrol car and closed the door. He wondered if this was the man he had heard talking to him earlier in the forest. Tanaka had not mentioned that to anyone else for fear that he was possibly letting the stress of this case and his missing daughter get to him. He walked over to the patrol car and instructed Mark to get him into an interrogation room as soon as possible because time was of the essence.

Tanaka turned and looked at the man in the back seat of the patrol car and the man returned his glance and smiled widely. It took everything he had not to bust out the window and strangle the man, but he kept calm. The sheriff made note of how perfectly white this man's teeth were for how dirty this vagabond looked.

"Mark," Tanaka said.

"Yeah?" he replied.

"Watch this one. I have a very, very bad feeling about this," Tanaka said.

"I do too, boss," Mark nodded. The deputy sheriff spit his chew on the ground then climbed in the driver's seat of his squad car and drove off.

CHAPTER EIGHT

Norman Thatch was confined to interrogation room four at the Coconino County Sheriff's Department. His hands were restrained by handcuffs to the table and gazing silently at the wall directly in front of him. He was still barefoot and wearing his blue sweatsuit. Deputy Sheriff Mark Winston stood in the observation room separated by the one-sided mirrored glass watching the suspect and waiting for Sheriff Tanaka to return. The deputy sheriff had brought the suspect in just over an hour ago.

He made sure they took his fingerprints so he would be in the system and left him there to wait in the room. Mark did not offer him anything to drink or eat, just instructed him to wait here and they would be with him for questioning shortly. Norman Thatch had not said a word since they last spoke at the campsite where they met. He had not spoken at all while in the back of the police car, nor did the deputy sheriff ask him any questions.

In the state of Arizona, tampering with a crime scene was only a class six felony. While this was the least serious felony under Arizona state law, it was still something. The sentence for this was a year and a half for first-timers and they knew they at least had him on this. Mark read the man his rights and placed him under arrest before he put him into the patrol car and took him in. Now they just needed to find out what he knew or how he was involved.

Until now, the Sheriff's department had no leads or suspects whatsoever concerning the previous six related murders. None of the previous crime scenes had led to them finding any prints or murder weapons. Forensics made a plaster cast of the large animal print they found and sent it off to NAU's Zoology Department in hopes they could identify what it came from or at least get them pointed in the right direction on what the hell was going on here.

Tanaka walked into the observation room with two steaming styrofoam cups of hot coffee and handed one to the deputy sheriff.

"Extra burnt with extra sugar just how you like it, Mark," the sheriff said.

Mark graciously took it from the sheriff. "Aww, you really do get me, don't you." Then he took a sip from the scalding brown tar.

"Has he said anything yet?" the sheriff asked.

Mark shook his head, no, and he sipped his coffee as they both watched Mr. Thatch from behind the glass. "He's taking advantage of the right to remain silent. Not made a sound since I placed him under arrest. No identification and his prints did not pull up any matches in our system," Mark said.

"I think he might know what happened or where Barbara is, so we have to make him talk as quickly as possible," the sheriff said. Just when Tanaka said his daughter's name, Norman Thatch turned his head towards the mirror.

"Oh hello again, sheriff."

Both officers glanced at each other and wondered how he just did that. The laminated safety glass was about seven millimeters thick and the room was sound-proofed. There was no way this man could hear what the two officers were talking about. Tanaka and the suspect seemed to make eye contact through the one-way mirrored glass.

"Why did he just say 'again?' Have you two seen each other before?" Mark asked Tanaka.

Tanaka shook his head no and recounted what had happened out in the forest when he discovered Emily's body and how he thought it was his mind playing tricks on him. Tanaka and Norman still held eye contact.

"Mark… Make sure you take the phone book with you. This bastard knows something about what's been going on over the last twenty-nine days and I don't care how you get the information out of him. The mayor's up my ass and is talking about the Feds getting involved."

Mark agreed, threw his empty cup in the trash can, and left the room. Tanaka kept his eyes locked on Mr. Thatch as he patiently waited for the interrogation to begin.

Officer Winston walked into the room carrying a thick yellow phone book and dropped it on the desk in front of Norman with a loud audible thud that echoed off the walls. Without flinching, the homeless man looked up at the officer and smiled.

"Well, Officer Winston, so nice to see you again. Please, won't you have a seat?" He gestured towards the metal chair on the opposite side of the table they cuffed him to.

Mark purposely pulled the chair out in a way that made the most noise possible. This seemed to make the man flinch as the chair screeched across the floor, but he continued to sit with his hands folded. The officer sat down rested his left hand on the phone book and slowly tapped his fingers.

"So, Mr. Thatch is it? If that is even your real name. Care to tell me what you were doing out in the forest at my crime scene earlier today?" Mark asked.

The man in question just sat there with a smile and looked at the interrogating officer.

"Okay then, is this how you want to do this? I was going to try to be Good Cop for a while but I guess not. Sooo… I'm going to hit you now." Mark stood up with the phone book in both hands and, in one quick motion, blasted Thatch on the right side of his head with it. The force would have sent the man to the floor if they had not handcuffed him to the table. Norman corrected himself and sat back upright in his chair as Officer Winston sat back down.

"I can do this all day and, in fact, I kind of enjoy it," Mark said with a smile and crossed his massive arms in front of him. He gave that statement a second to linger.

"Shall we try this again?" the officer pushed on.

"I have had a few names over the years, but yes, today you can call me Norman Thatch," the man replied.

"I notice there's a hint of an accent in your voice. Is it Dutch?" the officer asked.

"Ahhhh, look at the big brain on you, Officer Winston. It's German actually and I've been trying for years to get rid of it, but I just can't seem to. Vu know vat zey zay, vu can take zee German out of Germany, but vu can not take zee Germany out of zee German." The man chuckled and grinned.

"So what were you doing out there in the Coconino National Forest today?" the deputy sheriff asked. The man just gave the officer a blank stare and tilted his head to the left.

"I told you, Officer Winston. That is my forest now. I rarely stay in one place too long, but I have grown to like it for the brief time I've been here. Think I will stay another night. There are a few things that I need to tidy up. Then I will be on my way," the stranger said with a pleasant smile.

"Do you know anything about what happened to the four people that were camping at the site I found you at?" Mark asked.

"Of course I do. I killed them all. Ate some of them too, but you know it's all a bit of a blur. At some point, they all kinda look the same. Hard to keep track sometimes," the man said and shrugged his shoulders without care.

Mark turned to look at the glass through which the sheriff was observing the interrogation.

Tanaka quietly watched as he thought about everything that had just gone down in the past twenty-four hours. Deep down, he was boiling over with anger at what the man had just said. He envisioned himself bursting in with a pistol and whipping the man until he told him what they wanted to know.

Regardless of his personal feelings, he could sense that something was very off with this man named "Norman". He couldn't place it just yet, but his gut was telling him something bad was coming. Tanaka could tell that tonight was going to be a very long night.

Tanaka gave the glass a tap, signaling Mark to return to the observation room.

"What's up boss," Mark said as he entered the room.

"Take him to a holding cell. I don't think this is going to get us anywhere," Tanaka replied. "Let's let him stew for a couple of hours first. Then we will both question him. Possibly apply more pressure than just a phone book."

"There is seriously something not right with this guy," Mark said. "His eyes. Something about his eyes is like nothing I've ever seen before."

"I sense it too. I wanna get back and go over our notes from today before we come back at him," the sheriff replied.

Their conversation was interrupted by the man sitting in the interrogation room.

"What was her name?" Norman asked as he looked directly at Tanaka through the one-way glass.

Tanaka just furrowed his brow and watched the man intensely.

"You smell a lot like her, Sheriff. She was your daughter, wasn't she?" Thatch replied with a smile as he clicked his nails on the desk he was handcuffed to.

"The fuck?" Mark responded.

"Get him out of there now and get him to a cell," Tanaka ordered.

Mark and Tanaka sat in the sheriff's office, discussing the previous events. It had been a very long day for both of them and the exhaustion was written all over their faces. Mark was also worried about his friend's daughter. He had known Barbara since she was a teenager.

The sheriff was a minimalist and didn't believe in clutter or unnecessary belongings that didn't have an everyday function. His desk was always kept super neat and the only things that sat on his desktop were two framed photos; one being his wedding photo with his late wife Caitlin, the other of his daughter Barbara in hiking gear at Yosemite National Park.

A Panasonic electric typewriter, which he used from time to time, sat off to the side, taking up most of the room on his desk. The sheriff was not good with technology and didn't like to use computers, let alone know how to turn one on. He had only recently upgraded from an old Remington typewriter from the 1970s to this bulky big electrical monster that sat on his desk.

There wasn't much in the sheriff's office. Just a couple of filing cabinets and a small bookshelf that held various law books. The walls were mostly bare except for a piece of Native American art and a circular clock that made an audible ticking noise from the minute hand. The clock read 8:10 pm, and the sun was beginning to set. Mark spat his chew into a styrofoam cup and looked concerned at his old friend.

"So, what do we know so far?" Mark asked.

"I think Mr. Thatch is our top suspect," Tanaka responded.

"So you think this guy is telling the truth and is some crazy cannibal serial killer, or is he just batshit crazy? What are we going to do with him? We have enough to hold him for tampering with evidence and basically confessing to the murders of four people, but we have no evidence that he did anything. Any shit lawyer will see that and just go for insanity," Mark said.

Tanaka frowned as he responded. "Yes, and no. I think he saw what happened or knows what happened, but I honestly don't think a man of his physical size and shape could do the things that we found today. Nor do I think he could have done what was done to the six other victims. Did Thatch look like the kinda man who could rip the shed door off at

John and Kelly's place? I do not, but I think he might know what did."

Mark shifted in his seat uncomfortably and spat in his cup again. "So do you have any theories on what is doing this? I mean, what in tarnation made those animal tracks we saw? They were not like anything I've ever seen."

Tanaka took a minute and glanced at the photo of his daughter.

"Well, other than some crazy old stories my grandfather used to tell me when I was growing up about old Navajo folklore… no. There are old stories about the Yee Naaldlooshii, or skin-walker, that we would hear as children to keep us in line as we were growing up. Like if you were bad, the Yee Naaldlooshii would come on the night of a full moon and eat your face off and shit like that. It was a man who would turn into a giant wolf and stalk people and kill them in horrible hateful ways. I know it's all crazy bullshit made up through generations of storytelling with my people. I mean, it's 1985 and if something like that did exist with today's technology, we would have found out by now," Tanaka said.

Deputy McFerrin politely knocked on the sheriff's door frame. She was holding a piece of fax paper.

"I'm sorry to interrupt you two lovebirds, but the results of the DNA testing from NAU came back for those hair samples and were just faxed over." She walked over and handed Tanaka the piece of paper. Tanaka looked at it and looked up at both of his officers.

"The results have two matches," said the sheriff. "Canis Lupus and Homosapien,"

Mark gagged, almost choking on his chewing tobacco.

"Jennifer, can you do me a favor and check the coroner's reports for the time of death of the other six victims and tell me if they occurred on nights of last month's full moon?" the sheriff asked his deputy.

Just as she was about to leave Tanka's office, they heard gunshots, and then the fire alarm went off.

Norman Thatch sat on the cot in his drab gray jail cell and stared at the wall, having not uttered a word since the interrogation room. Norman had not resisted, nor had he been impolite. He seemed to welcome his solitude and seemed to just patiently wait. Tonight was the last night of the full moon and Norman smiled at the thought of this as he felt the animalistic pull of the moon through the bars of his window.

A young officer in his early twenties came to the door of his jail cell with a plate of cold food. "Time to eat, Thatch," he said as he slid the tray of food through the slit in the cell door. "Whoops," the officer said as he let the tray fall to the floor. The metal tray clanked to the ground and what looked like some kind of brown meat and what passed for peas and carrots splattered all over the floor.

"Good luck with that," the officer said.

Just as the officer looked up from the tray on the floor, he noticed that Norman was now standing right in front of him. The officer was startled and jumped back in response.

"Excuse me, officer," Norman politely said.

Norman could sense the officer's fear, and it pleased him. The young man slowly placed his hand on his hip. Nervously, he readied his sidearm.

"Jesus! It's not very wise to do that, Thatch," the officer spat. Now holding his gun so that Thatch could see it.

"Would you like to see something really scary?" Norman asked politely with a smile. "I mean reeeally scary?"

The officer looked at him with puzzlement. Norman smiled, and the officer noted that the man's eyes had turned an unholy shade of yellow rimmed with red veins and he was beginning to sweat profusely soaking his blue sweat suit into a darker hue.

"What the hell is wrong with you?" the officer questioned.

Norman now started to convulse as the audible sounds of bones breaking and reshaping could be heard. The officer looked on in horror as the man began to change in front of his eyes.

"When I first changed, the pain was unbearable, but now I've grown to enjoy the sensation. I welcome it, and now I find it invigorating," Thatch said in a deeper voice.

His jaw began to extend as his cheekbones broke and reshaped. He fell to his hands and knees and arched his back as he began to twist. Norman's fingers started to lengthen and grow black talon-like nails from each digit. He groaned as his legs and feet elongated, making crunching noises and reformed into large wolf-like pads that now bent the wrong way for a man. Gray and silver hair sprouted from all over his body. His teeth made a plinking noise as they fell to the floor and very large dagger-like ones grew in their place. There was a ripping sound as his clothes tore and his body mass tripled in size. The wolfish face was no longer human.

The young officer's revolver shook in his hand as he aimed at the beast. His hands were now perspiring so badly that the handle of his pistol felt slick. Norman Thatch was no more. What stood in his place was a hulking gray and silver beast that stood close to eight feet tall. Its canine jaws opened wide as drool began to seep over its teeth and gums as it locked its yellow eyes on its next victim.

The officer panicked and fired all six of his shots into the holding cell. Four of the shots hit the massive beast in its chest without phasing it. The officer quickly opened the cylinder on his Colt revolver and pressed the ejector rod to empty the spent shells onto the floor. With his hands trembling, he fumbled for a speed loader on his belt and dropped it on the floor.

The beast was now standing at the door of the cell, looking at it as if trying to figure out how it worked. The officer scrambled for his second-speed loader on his belt and was able to reload and slam the cylinder closed. As he raised it to fire again, the immense werewolf grabbed the cell door with both of its massive hands and began to rip it off the hinges. The twisting metal creaked and snapped.

The officer once more began to fire wildly. This time landing all six shots center mass on the behemoth. In about three jerks of its powerful arms, the cell door came off the frame and was tossed aside as the monster stepped out to its freedom. The officer turned to run down the hallway. With his last heroic effort, he was able to make it to the fire alarm on the wall as the beast pounced on his back. Warm crimson blood sprayed all over the floor and walls as the sirens of the fire alarms echoed through the Coconino County Sheriff's Department.

CHAPTER NINE

DETROIT

MAY, 1987

Daniel lay in his bed at Henry Ford Hospital flipping channels on the TV and trying to cure his boredom. Stanley sat in his chair in the far corner, keeping him company. The doctors' plans were for him to have his casts removed after six weeks, then he would require more X-rays and the possibility of a new cast to be put back on.

At the moment, Daniel was kind of enjoying the steady drip of morphine they were constantly feeding him to keep him comfortable. Even though he told the nurses he felt fine, they gave it to him anyway. This was causing him to drift in and out of sleep, but he didn't mind the consistent state of high, though he could do without the dry mouth and constipation. Stanley pointed out the irony of the fact that Daniel was watching the soap opera General Hospital while lying in a hospital.

"Did you stop by my apartment and water my flowers?" Daniel mumbled to Stanley.

"You don't have any plants," he replied with a raised eyebrow.

Daniel looked at Stanley with a disoriented look on his face. "I don't?"

Stanley looked back at him and shook his head no. Stanley was wearing the same wrinkled gray business suit that he had on when Daniel had seen him last at Mac's bar. "So you wanna talk about what happened? The other day?" Stanley asked. Daniel looked at him with a glazed-over look in his eyes. "We've been over this before, Daniel. You have to do it right to end this."

Daniel seemed clueless about what his friend was saying. Just as he was about to respond to Stanley, Nurse Evans came into the room carrying a tray of hospital food and medication. She was in one of her usual overly joyful moods.

"Lunch time! How are we feeling today, Mr. Methric?"

Daniel looked up at her with a smile and with slurred words complimented her on her beauty. "Has anyone ever told you that you look like Whitney Houston?" The nurse blushed and set down his food on the hospital tray in front of him.

"I bet you say that to all the nurses, Mr. Methric. Today's your favorite. Meatloaf, and I brought you extra jello," she said.

Nurse Evans walked around to the foot of his bed to retrieve his chart and glanced at it.

"How long have I been here?" Daniel asked the nurse.

"It's been a week and a half so far since you came in," she said.

Daniel could see the sunlight coming through the old dusty curtains. When he began to shovel forkfuls of meatloaf into his mouth, he noticed a musky animal smell fill the room as he chewed. He sniffed at his next bite of meatloaf and shrugged because it smelled normal, so he shoved it into his mouth.

A low growl emanated from the corner of the room from behind the nurse. Daniel stopped chewing and his face lost all color while he let the food fall from his mouth as it hung open. Nurse Evans kept rambling on about what the doctor had next in store for him and what tests were scheduled later that day. But what Daniel saw was a huge gray beast that rose behind her. The beast's ears touched the ceiling tiles as its yellow eyes were fixated on Daniel's.

With his eyes as big as saucers, he pointed at the monster. Unable to form any words, his hand shook in terror. "Ma… ma… monster," he stuttered.

"So that's what Doctor Fraser would like to see…"

The nurse's sentence was cut short as the beast locked its jaws around her left shoulder and she started to scream. Blood pumped out all over Daniel's face. The beast shook and tore at Nurse Evans violently. Even after her screams stopped, the monster still tore pieces from her with its teeth and let the chunks fall. After it seemed like it was finished with her, it let the body fall limp to the floor. Daniel tried to scoot back in his bed but he was unable to due to the cast and machines. The beast stared directly at him and spoke.

"You can't stop me, Daniel," it said with a growl.

Daniel kept smashing away at the nurse's call button as he screamed at the top of his lungs for help. Its yellow eyes pierced into him.

"No one can save you, Daniel," the beast said as it slowly began to crawl up his bed towards him.

Daniel began to scream hysterically and frantically pressed the call button for help.

"I am coming Daniel. You're too weak to stop me." It bellowed as the massive thing inched its way towards him. A mixture of blood and drool dripped from its jaws.

"You are weak, Daniel," it said. Then it lunged for him.

Daniel shot up out of his nightmare and noticed the clock read 2:45 am. Disoriented, he told himself, it was just a dream. He turned on the reading light by his bed and pulled the wet covers off. This was when he noticed that the sheets were soaked with blood. His blood.

His spica cast had been torn off and was lying in chunks on the linoleum floor by his bed. He felt no pain or discomfort as he bent his knees and wiggled his toes. He felt all over his legs for any open wounds or lesions and he found nothing. Other than the blood.

To his surprise, he felt great. He did, however, find in his bed a collection of metal surgical screws, plates, and rods. Holding them up to the light with puzzlement, he examined them. They looked like surgical hardware.

"Those would be yours, Daniel," Stanley said as he looked at him from the corner of the room. "Like I said, Daniel, we've been over this a few times now."

Stanley stood up from his seat and brushed himself off as if it would help him unwrinkle his suit. He then began to walk towards the door. Daniel watched, still dazed by everything that had just occurred. Just before walking out the doorway, Stanley turned to Daniel with a very serious look on his face.

"Meet me at Mac's when you're ready to talk…again. For now, I'd get your skinny honky ass outta here before the nurses and doctors see you like this." Then he was gone as he crossed the threshold and exited the room.

Daniel swung his legs over the edge of the bed and stood up. Shocked at how he was able to do this after all that had happened. He recalled that his belongings were in the drawer of the nightstand next to the bed. He pulled open the drawer and grabbed his wallet and keys and made his way over to the window. Wearing nothing but his white hospital gown, he opened the window and began to crawl out. Realizing he was two stories up, he let out a gasp as his courage clawed its way out.

He clung to the windowsill with his fingers, his bare backside mooning the world below him. He just closed his eyes and let go. He landed in a squat and steadied himself with his hand on the ground in front of him. Once he looked up at the open window, he realized he had just dropped from a two-story fall and was unharmed. Standing up, he inhaled the night air in a deep breath and exhaled. He felt alive! He couldn't explain it, but he felt it.

Daniel decided to run as fast as he could, running through back alleys and passing bums that were warming themselves by barrel fires. He didn't seem to care as his white hospital gown flapped in the wind. He wasn't cold, winded, or tired. Daniel felt like he could run forever. Instead, he figured it was wise to get back to his apartment before some-one saw a crazy naked man in a hospital gown running down streets, and through alleyways of Detroit at three in the morning. As he ran, he couldn't stop thinking about his nightmare.

CHAPTER TEN

FLAGSTAFF

JULY, 1985

Tanaka looked at Jennifer and instructed her to grab as many officers as she could and help get the civilians to safety. There were about fifteen officers on duty at the station that night along with another thirty or so civilians who either worked in clerical positions or as dispatchers. The sheriff instructed her that the top priority was to get these people to safety. She nodded and exited the sheriff's office in a run.

Mark looked at Tanaka, "What's the plan, boss?"

The sheriff removed his .357 from its holster, opened the cylinder to double check it was loaded and quickly flicked it closed.

"Grab who you can and meet me down in the armory as quickly as possible. I have a feeling we are gonna need as much firepower as we can muster," Tanaka instructed.

Just as Mark started to move, they heard a howl echo through the halls of the sheriff's department.

"I think we are about to find out if your grandfather's stories were just bullshit or not," Mark said.

Tanaka shook his head in disbelief, "I'm afraid you might be right."

The sheriff stood in the armory handing out Remington 870 pump action shotguns and M-16 rifles chambered in 5.56mm. Mark had managed to gather up eight other deputies while Officer McFerrin had whoever was left to help get the civilians out of the station. Mark began handing out extra ammunition as Tanaka yelled over the blaring fire alarm.

"Ladies and Gentlemen, I want you all to know I have no idea what we are about to face, but I am pretty confident that the ten of us can handle this situation. Let's split off into two teams of five." He pointed to three male officers and one female officer. "You three go with Officer Winston. I want you to hold the floor in the main lobby in case whatever this is tries to get out through the front doors." He then pointed to the remaining four male officers. "The rest of you will come with me and we will go to the holding cells. There is only one way out of there and it will lead right to the lobby."

Another terrifying howl rang through the station.

"What the fuck is that?" the female officer said.

"It sounds even more pissed than before," Mark responded.

Tanaka wished them all luck and to stay safe and rely on each other and they would get through this. Then they all quickly left in their instructed directions. He had a very bad feeling about the situation, but he did not want to let his deputies know exactly how he felt.

"Beers are on me when this is over," Mark called out as he took his team to the lobby.

The werewolf that had once been Norman Thatch made its way down the hallways of the jail, slaughtering anything that moved. High-pitch sounds of the fire alarms sent it into a berserker rage as it tore open cell doors and mutilated other prisoners. The officers who had guard duty that night had already been pulled apart and eviscerated. It pulled one prisoner halfway through the bars before his arm tore off. It just left him hanging there limp, half in and half out of his cell.

After sensing nothing remained alive, it chuffed as if laughing at its handy work. The monster saw the steel door at the end of the holding cells and knew that was the exit. Once it got down on all fours, it began to run towards the exit, slipping in the pools of blood that slicked the linoleum floors as it tried to gain momentum. It threw itself into more of a rage when the door didn't give way after hitting it with its left shoulder. It reared back and tried again to shoulder-check the door open.

Tanaka and his officers were on the other side of the door as the beast threw itself at it. Dust fell from the ceiling tiles with each massive impact.

"I don't think that door's gonna hold!" one officer shouted over the fire alarm.

"Let's let this fucker tire itself out and once the door comes open, let's start blasting," another officer said.

Tanaka took a deep breath, raised his rifle and took aim at the door, "I want you all to hold your fire until whatever this is breaches that door and we have a full visual!"

The door began to buckle and the hinges began to creak giving them the sign that it would not be long before it was in the hallway with them. One of the officers started reciting the lord's prayer as his shotgun visibly began to shake.

"What the hell is this thing?" another officer asked.

With one final bash, the heavy steel swung open and smashed into the adjacent wall with a loud bang that made the officer's ears ring. The werewolf placed its hands on either side of the door frame as it pulled itself through the opening. There was about a five-second delay as the sheriff and his deputies looked at the creature in disbelief.

"Yee Naagloshii!" Tanaka said as he snapped out of his trance and raised his rifle to take aim. The hulking beast roared as it heard him say that word. Then they all opened fire on it at point-blank range. The beast roared again in rage at the nuisance and lunged for them with bloodthirst in its eyes.

First, it backhanded Sheriff Tanaka sending him flying into the wall and knocking him unconscious. Then, in a flash, it grabbed for the nearest officer firing a shotgun. It seized the officer by his face and, in one hard yank, pulled off his lower jaw. The officer dropped his shotgun and fell to the ground, trying to scream in pain as he went into shock.

The werewolf followed this move up with a quick stomp to the side of the man's head as he lay there, twitching in agony. The man's skull shattered, silencing him forever. Oozing brain matter and blood all over the floor beneath the werewolf's foot. The remaining officers simultaneously ran out of ammunition in their rifles and went for their sidearms. One officer didn't make it in time as the beast grabbed him by his head and, with incredible force, drove him into the opposite wall with a wet crunch as his skull fractured and he was killed instantly.

The last officer was able to fire off three rounds before the beast leaped over the other officers' bodies and snapped its jaws around his throat as it shook him like a dog would a toy. This horrific massacre was over in less than a minute. The beast was not here to feed; it was here out of pure hatred for man, and it was here to slaughter as many as it could.

Tanaka opened his eyes and there it was. It stood over him with one of its giant hands resting on his chest. He could feel its hot breath just inches away from his face. Rank odor of the beast's musk and carrion breath filled his nostrils. The werewolf just stared at him and emitted a low growl, as if warning him not to make a move. The creature's maw slowly opened as its saliva and blood began to slowly drip down onto the sheriff's face.

Tanaka lay there in silence and closed his eyes and accepted his fate. In his head, Tanaka could hear the sounds of his ancestors chanting in Navajo as he seemed to enter a state of serenity. Then the beast started to chuff, and he slowly opened his eyes. It lifted itself off him carefully so as not to crush him and turned its head towards the exit door. Tanaka realized this giant monster was laughing at him. Then, just like that, it turned and ran on all fours off down the hallway towards the lobby. Tanaka, still dazed, quickly grabbed for his radio to warn the others of the hell that was headed their way like a freight train.

Deputy Sheriff Winton's radio squawked as Tanaka's voice came over the small speaker in a panic.

"Mark! It's headed right for you. Everyone's dead! Our guns don't do shit! I repeat. Guns don't do shit!"

Mark hit the call button and screamed into the radio, "What do you want us to do?! Over!"

Just then, the beast came crashing through the door, taking the door frame and some drywall with it.

Tanaka screamed once more through his radio, "Run!"

PART II

"99 LUFTBALLONS..."

CHAPTER ELEVEN

STALINGRAD

NOVEMBER, 1942

The morning sun came through an opening in the treetops and its warming rays fell on Erich's face as he opened his eyes. He lay there blinking slowly, staring up at the treetops and blue sky, watching the steam from his breath fill the air around his face. A single snowflake floated through the air and landed on his cheek. Realizing he could feel the small drop of water run down his face, he raised his arms to look at his hands. His hands looked and felt as good as new. There were no more signs of hypothermia. His fingertips were no longer black with dead skin. When he opened his hands he could feel the warmth from the sun. He wiggled his toes in his boots and could sense the feeling was back in them as well. Slowly, he sat up and looked around, quickly realizing he was alone.

The fire pit in front of him was now just a pile of used coals, burnt logs, and ice. The frozen carcass of the elk still lay near the log Nikolia was sitting on, but the gypsy was nowhere to be found. The image of Nikolia's face lunging at him through the firelight was still etched into his memory. He wondered for a minute if Nikolia was really there or if it was all just a nightmare.

Erich stood up and brushed the light snow from his body and saw the ground was dark with frozen blood. He wondered whose blood it was. There was a dull ache in his shoulder and his jacket and uniform underneath were torn open, exposing his bare skin. His clothing was also stained a dark brown from dried, frozen blood.

He checked his shoulder through the tear and did not find any wound. Yet it was still stiff and ached. He looked up and could tell by where the sun was in the sky that it had to be late afternoon. Confused and disoriented, he searched the area for his rifle. He gathered up the German Mauser and slung it over his shoulder. He figured standing around wasn't doing him any good, so he decided to keep walking in what he thought was a western direction.

Erich walked for three days when he came to the edge of the forest. Not once did he feel that he had to stop to rest or try to get warm. The subzero weather no longer seemed to bother him. He had no aches and pains anymore from all the time he had spent cramped in the small space of his Panzer tank. When he exited the forest, the sun had already set and the full moon began to shine. The night sky was clear and full of stars and all the wonders of space.

He could see the lights from a small village off in the distance across a large empty field as the moonlight caused the undisturbed snow to almost shimmer like calm water. His stomach began to growl and cramp with hunger. He was famished like he had never been before. Even though he felt much better and more rejuvenated than he had in his entire life, he still knew he needed to eat. He could smell food being cooked off in the distance, which he thought was strange because he still had another 200 yards or so to go until he reached the village.

Erich longed for a hot meal and a warm bed. He smiled at the thought of a hot bath to clean off the remnants of war. He started to make his way towards the small village in hopes the inhabitants would be friendly and not see him as some Nazi monster.

Erich grew nervous as he walked across the wide open space. He did not want to be spotted by a Russian sniper and taken out after surviving all this way. Not knowing who occupied this little village made him grow weary of his decision the closer he got.

A loud humming noise rang in his ears, while a dull headache chiseled away at his temples. For some reason, he could tell it was coming from the full moon. It seemed like it was calling out to him. He realized he had only walked about forty yards across the wide open field when the strange hum in his head grew with intensity. The hunger pains in his stomach were becoming unbearable and his head started to throb. Sweat now soaked through his uniform. His shins and knees started to have pain shoot through them, causing him to drop to the ground. His body temperature began to rise drastically, so he removed his coat to cool off. This wasn't enough, for he felt like his skin was catching on fire. Erich removed his shirt and undershirt, which still gave him no relief as the perspiration increased.

"What is happening to me?" he said while he raised his arms in front of him.

Steam rose from the pores of his skin. It was like he had begun to boil. The hum in his ears was so intense it was all he could hear, and the pain in his legs started to spread throughout his entire body. He screamed in anguish as he watched both his hands contort and stretch in front of his eyes.

His fingers elongated and his fingernails began to bleed and fall out. Black, talon-like claws started to break through each of his fingertips while the back of his hands began to sprout hair. The pain was so unbearable, Erich blacked out.

On the outskirts of the little Russian village sat a small squabble of a cabin. Inside sat a Russian family, settling down for an evening meal. The day was your average day of chores and farming the winter wheat fields located to the north of town. Petrov had been married to his wife for nine years and the couple had an eight-year-old boy and a six-year-old daughter. They had spent the last few months in fear of a possible invasion by the German army. But today they seemed to feel more at ease. Word had traveled that the Soviets had begun to turn the tide against the Nazi army at Stalingrad.

The aroma of stew filled the small home. It was the first time in a long while they felt as if they could have a relaxing, family meal together. Tonight, they could not hear gunshots or explosions echoing off in the distance to the east. The night air seemed to be calm and peaceful.

Petrov bounced his daughter on his knee while she laughed as they sat at the head of their dining table. His son was setting the table as his wife was getting the stew ready to serve on their pot belly stove. The fire was roaring in the fireplace and candles were lit, giving the cabin a warm, comfortable glow. They all sat down at the table and began to enjoy this precious moment they had together.

At first, the noise started as a soft scratching at the front door. It was as if some small animal was asking to be let in from the cold. Petrov noticed it and stopped bouncing his daughter.

"Aw, papa, don't stop," she said.

"Hush, child," he replied.

The scratching began to grow much louder and turned into a scraping noise as if an animal was trying to claw its way through the door. Petrov's wife glanced at him with a startled look. His face had turned pale because they both realized he had yet to place the wooden bar across the door to lock it and keep them safe from what was outside. Petrov leaped from his chair, causing his daughter to fall and begin to cry. Her mother quickly scooped her up and then rocked her in her arms to comfort her. The father dashed across the room to reach the wooden bar that was leaning against the wall. As quickly as he could, he picked up the bar and placed it in the slots, locking the door from opening inward. After he slid the bar in place, the clawing noises stopped.

"What is it Papa?" his son asked.

Petrov did not respond. He just placed his forefinger over his lips to signal his family to stay quiet. With all four of their hearts racing, the doorknob slowly began to turn back and forth. Petrov motioned for his son to grab his rifle. Without hesitation, the young boy ran to the wall, reached up on his toes, pulled down the old Mosin-Nagant and rushed over to his father. His father took the rifle, checked the chamber, and placed the stock to his shoulder. After stepping back he aimed towards the home's entryway.

The doorknob stopped turning and the room was silent except for the crackle of the fireplace and the ticking of the clock above the mantle. Petrov could feel his heart hammering through his hands as he tightly gripped his rifle. There was a loud screeching noise as a set of claws dragged themselves across one of their windows on the opposite side of the cabin, startling them all. Then it stopped.

His daughter began to sob as she buried her face in her mother's bosom. The tension in the room grew and Petrov turned to look at his wife and daughter. There, he saw the beast's face through the window over his wife's shoulder. Its yellow eyes blazed with a murderous hunger, which chilled Petrov as if his blood froze solid. The beast bared its teeth as if to smile at him then it withdrew back into the darkness and was gone. With that image burned into his brain, Petrov ordered his family to stay away from the windows. The muffled cries of his daughter caused his hands to shake. His wife held the child close to her chest and quietly hummed her favorite Russian lullaby to comfort her.

There was now a low growl coming from the front door behind them. With a loud thud, the heavy wood began to shake violently. Dust fell from the rafters with every pound and shutter. He could tell the beast wanted inside. Quickly, he spun and fired a shot from his rifle through the front door. The shot was deafening in the small space and caused his wife to scream and his daughter began to wail.

"Papa?" his son asked, with tears streaking down his face.

"Stay with your mother and sister," he responded as he walked towards the door.

"Be careful Petrov," she said while trying to comfort their daughter.

He slowly crept towards the door. Every time a floorboard creaked, he closed his eyes and quietly took a breath. His heart pounded even harder against his chest cavity. He turned his head to his left so he could listen to what was beyond the door. There was no sound. All Petrov could hear were his daughter's quiet whimpers, the crackle of the fire dancing, and the ticking of their clock.

"Is it…" His wife's whisper was cut short.

Petrov held up a hand to silence his wife. He tried to listen as he slowly crept closer to the door. All was still. He walked over to the window next to their entrance and cautiously peered through the curtains. Big, soft snowflakes began to fall from the night sky as the wind began to whistle. Everything else was quiet. Petrov lowered his rifle and turned to his family with a sigh of relief.

"I think it's…"

With an explosion of broken glass, the beast cut him short. It reached in through the window and pulled Petrov through the small frame into the darkness. Petrov didn't have time to scream as he dropped his rifle. Large snowflakes and wind swirled into the room as his family stood speechless in terror.

The screams could be heard echoing through the frozen landscape as the full moon blazed above in the night sky.

Erich came to the next morning in the center of what was left of the small Russian village. He was naked and no longer emaciated. His skin was smeared with dried blood and he frantically stood up with no memory of what had taken place since he stepped out of the forest the night before. He slowly spun in a circle and took in the horror that surrounded him. Bodies of men, women, and even children lay torn apart and scattered as far as he could see. The wet snow was stained with their blood. Smoke billowed from some of the houses as they smoldered in ash and small fires still danced in their place. It was a massacre like nothing he had ever seen in all his time in the war. It brought tears to his eyes as he tried to process what he was seeing.

He heard someone clap, causing Erich to turn around. There stood Nikolia, clapping his hands together with a wondrous smile on his face.

"That was magnificent, comrade. I honestly only expected you to kill one or two of them, but instead, you killed this entire village. Such determination and tenacity like nothing I have ever seen. Such anger and rage, yet so graceful like ballerina. It truly was breathtaking to watch the slaughter unfold," Nikolia said, as he stopped clapping.

Erich fell to his knees and looked down at his palms. They were crusted with dried blood, and that was all he could take. His vomit began to paint the white snow with more blood and chunks of meat as he bent over and retched. He could see a small human finger lying in the contents of his stomach in front of him.

"Come now, don't be upset. Rarely, someone like you comes along that embraces the gift so quickly on their first night," Nikolia said.

The German looked up while the tears on his face mixed with the dried blood, causing it to run like mascara.

"What did you do to me!" Erich screamed.

Nikolia tilted his head to one side and looked down at him with empathy. "Do not be sad, little one. I gave you gift that will stay with you forever. You now are perfect like me. You will never have to worry about the diseases or plagues of man, nor will you ever grow old. I have never seen someone in my centuries of life take to this gift as well as you have. It will not take long for you to be strong like me."

Erich lashed out in a fit of rage as he lunged at Nikolia. "You made me a killer!" he roared. As he reached for the gypsy's throat, Nikolia effortlessly smacked him aside with the back of his hand like an annoying child.

"Please, you are still just a pup. One day you will embrace the gift and you will thank me." He turned around and began to walk off.

Erich lay there on his side as he watched the man walk back towards the forest.

Nikolia stopped and turned to him once more, "Oh, beware of silver, for it is one of the few things that can end your life if used correctly. Good luck, little one."

As the cold wind whistled, he watched a snow devil twirl and dance through the dense air. The whirling vortex began petering off into nothing as Nikolia disappeared into the forest.

CHAPTER TWELVE

AMARILLO

FEBRUARY, 1986

Tanaka Chee sat on the bed in Room 16 at a small motor court motel off I-40 just outside of Amarillo, Texas. In the center of the light brown motel carpeting was a large bloodstain. A trail led from the center of the room to the bathroom. Three naked bodies lay strewn on the floor just outside an open closet door to his right. These were the bodies of three teenage girls who had gone missing a few days earlier from the campus of Amarillo Community College.

Tanaka was slouched over with his elbows on his thighs, deep in thought. He looked down at the suppressed Glock 17 dangling in his right hand. It was loaded with 9mm subsonic silver bullets that he had custom-made. The full moon peeked in through dusty red and brown curtains and cast the room with a muted red glow. This just enhanced his already bleak mood. He bowed his head while his long braids slightly swayed back and forth as the memories of the massacre back at the Coconino Sheriff's Department filled his head. Everything that led him to his current situation.

Most of his deputies and one of his closest friends, Mark Winston, had been torn apart. The monster named Norman Thatch was responsible for all of this. His daughter, Barbara, was still missing and presumed dead. Though her body was never found, he hoped to at least discover what had happened and gain closure.

Thatch was a lycanthrope. Or more commonly known among his native people as the Yee Naaldlooshii. A man or woman who would turn into a wolf beast by the light of the full moon. Folklore had many names, but the most common was "werewolf". Something that Tanaka had never believed to be true until now.

Once it tore through the officers standing guard in the lobby like they were helpless jackrabbits, the Yee Naaldlooshii made its way up to the roof of the building and disappeared into the darkness. Ever since that horrendous night, the murders in Coconino County had stopped. Tanaka believed that the beast had moved on. Away from northern Arizona and was still out there somewhere.

After burying their friends and loved ones, Tanaka handed in his badge and walked away from a total of twenty years of work in law enforcement. Now he devoted his life to tracking down and killing Norman Thatch, no matter the cost.

He took the time to sit down with the tribal elders of the Navajo Nation, who once knew his grandfather, and learned what he could about the legends of the Yee Naaldlooshii. Then he studied as much as he could about its strengths and weaknesses. He discovered that their greatest advantage was convincing the world it did not exist. To remain in the shadows, away from the knowledge of man. The creatures seemed to have learned over the years that if man became aware of their presence, they would once again organize and hunt them down.

With the help of the then-rookie deputy Jennifer McFerrin, he was able to cross-check other departments' databases, looking for similar cases across the United States. Of course, just about every major city had missing person cases. What they were looking for involved large animal attacks that were similar in depth to the ones that happened in Coconino County. Since they knew what to look for, they found more cases than he expected.

It appears that around the late 1940s, similar cases popped up in New York City, New Jersey, Richmond, Savannah, Jacksonville, and down to Miami. At first, it was just a couple here and there and nothing on the magnitude of what happened in Flagstaff. These were all major cities with far more resources than most rural American towns. They both cringed at the thought of how many similar cases were in the rural areas where people were more private and kept to themselves.

There was a break in the killings that matched his MO for about ten years. Tanaka had a theory that Norman possibly set up shop around the Florida Everglades. That would have been a perfect place for a Yee Naaldlooshii to hide and lie low for a while. People disappeared in the Everglades constantly and were never heard from again.

It wasn't until the late 1960s that similar murders started up again in New Orleans, but something had changed. Not all the cases fell on nights of the full moon. Tanaka thought this was odd at first, but after checking with more of the tribal elders of the Navajo Nation, he learned why. The person cursed by the Yee Naaldlooshii would no longer be solely tied to the nights of the full moon after time went by. The curse would grow and slowly take over the host, pushing what was left of the person's humanity out leaving only evil behind.

After New Orleans, it moved on to Albuquerque by the early 1970s, then up to Salt Lake City, and eventually up to Portland where there was a major string of homeless murders that were swept under the carpet. From Portland, he believed it went up to Seattle in the early 1980s and finally made its way to Coconino County in 1985. If Tanaka had to guess, he would say there were over 100 cases here if he included the missing persons' reports in each city around the time of the killings. But these were just the major cities. It made him shudder again at the thought of what happened in the remote areas in between. Places like the reservations and poorer communities had to have been hit hard throughout the years.

One thing that worried Tanaka the most was the random murders that began to pop up in those same major cities after it appeared that Thatch had moved on. They did not last very long, and they were small, but there was no doubt that they were there. Tanaka knew that Norman could not be in two places at the same time, so this meant only one thing: there were more out there.

He knew the bite from the Yee Naaldlooshii was the only way to spread the curse, though it was very rare for someone to survive an attack. Seeing firsthand what the beast could do, he knew a person's chance of survival was slim. This made him wonder if Norman did this on purpose. Was he turning people? Was he trying to grow his numbers? Was he creating a pack or was he just so twisted that he was trying to leave something behind to continue killing after he was gone? There were so many questions Tanaka wanted answers to.

After Northern Arizona, he found reports of missing campers and animal attacks up in Denver, then down to Colorado Springs. By the start of the new year, Tanaka was ready to start up his manhunt hoping he could learn about the fate of his daughter and stop the Yee Naaldlooshii from spreading its curse and murdering more innocent people.

Tanaka first called up an old friend by the name of George Seff, who lived out near Indian Head Mountain in Seligman, Arizona. George was a trapper and gunsmith by trade who lived off the grid and knew Tanaka's wife and daughter. He felt for the man's grief and wanted to help his friend in any way he could. Tanaka had placed an order for George to make him various calibers of silver ammunition. Seeing how the one thing that all the folklore and stories about the Yee Naaldlooshii and lycanthropes had in common was a weakness of silver. So Tanaka thought this was a good place to start.

The Navajo Nation had donated most of their silver bullion to him. They knew what his plans were and supported him where the proper authorities would have locked him away. He brought enough silver for George to make 900 rounds of ammunition.

Since silver did not perform like lead when it was being molded into a bullet, George had to make all custom molds for each bullet caliber so the bullet size would be accurate. Silver is less dense than lead, so it didn't make the greatest, most accurate bullets. George, however, was a wizard when it came to ballistics. If there was anyone who could make a silver bullet work, it would be him.

Out of the 900 rounds, each caliber was made into batches of 300. He had rounds made for his .357 revolver, subsonic 9mm rounds for his Glock 17, and lastly 12 gauge slugs for the up close stopping power of his Remington 870. George even refitted the barrel of his Glock to take a screw-on suppressor, which he also supplied him with. Tanaka liked the idea of having his automatic suppressed. This would allow him to get into situations that require more stealth than brute force. Tanaka was not a brute force-oriented person and preferred to use that to his advantage.

The work was top-notch and took George about two weeks to complete. In the meantime, Tanaka stayed at his cabin and they reminisced and told stories about his wife and daughter. Shortly after George completed his order, Tanaka loaded up his late-model Chevrolet K5 Blazer. He placed a phone call back to Flagstaff to speak with Deputy McFerrin.

She informed him that there had been three murders and a few missing persons reports that all centered around the full moon in Midland, Texas, in December 1985. Everything seemed to match Norman's MO. So Tanaka figured this was a good place to start, and he headed out to the oil fields of West Texas to see what he could find.

CHAPTER THIRTEEN

MIDLAND

JANUARY, 1986

By the time Tanaka got to Midland, Texas, the trail seemed to have gone cold. However, he did find out some interesting information regarding the case. Four oil workers had gotten drunk and decided to wander around in the fields during the night of a full moon in mid-December of that previous year. Three of the men were torn to pieces and left for dead, but the fourth man survived.

The authorities reported that the men were attacked by a large pack of rabid coyotes. Tanaka thought this was one of the most dim-witted theories he had ever heard. He knew firsthand what those bodies would have looked like and no pack of coyotes were capable of doing that to grown men.

What caught his attention was this man by the name of Jonathan Murphy. He survived the attack with only minor scrapes and bruises. After the incident, he was taken to the nearest hospital, where he was found to be in good health and discharged the next day.

Midland was not a particularly large city so Tanaka decided to stick around and start asking the locals about what had happened the previous December. It didn't take long for him to find something. All he had to do was visit a small bar that was located off Interstate Twenty. It was a frequent stop for oil field workers and other blue-collar locals.

Everyone there seemed to know Jonathan Murphy and told stories about how he was not the same after the attack. After Jonathan was discharged from the hospital, he told insane stories about a giant beast that attacked him and his friends. He went into great detail about how they were gruesomely torn to pieces. Jonathan told a few colleagues that the great beast had bitten him and left him for dead. Being the small town that Midland was, everyone knew that he was found wandering the oil fields before being taken to the hospital. Once the doctors looked him over, they found he did not have wounds or marks to support his stories.

One of the waitresses told Tanaka that Jonathan had become increasingly aggressive and easily agitated, which was very unlike him. Everyone seemed to agree that before the incident, Jonathan was a soft-spoken sweet man. Tanaka was able to find out that he had become a recluse in his single-wide trailer. Murphy lived just south of town, out on State Road 349. With less than a week till the next full moon, Tanaka got a room at the Armadillo Inn down the road and figured he would take a look around.

Periodically he would check back in with Deputy McFerrin in Flagstaff. She would share any new findings related to possible attacks by Thatch. Per Tanaka's requests, she would also run background checks. McFerrin was not able to pull up any history on Jonathan Murphy. It came back squeaky clean. The man didn't even have any parking tickets. She was also able to find Jonathan's address for him, so Tanaka headed out to pay him a visit. He just wanted to ask a few basic questions regarding what had happened.

Tanaka pulled his Blazer into the dirt driveway of Jonathan's trailer. Right away, he noticed that the place was extremely isolated from any other surrounding houses, trailers, or businesses. The man's yard was mostly dirt, like most places in West Texas. A single Honey Mesquite tree large enough to cast shade over the man's dilapidated single-wide was the only vegetation in the yard.

Tanaka put his truck in park, stepped out and walked towards the man's home. He had his revolver tucked into his belt and concealed by his plaid button-up shirt. Jonathan's 1982 Ford Pickup sat with about an inch of Texas red dirt that covered the hood and windshield. This told Tanaka that it had not been driven in some time.

As he approached the front stoop, he noticed a rank smell coming from a garbage can just to the right of the storm door. Jonathan had set his garbage out some time ago and it was filled to the top with empty raw meat packages. Every package was covered in flies and maggots as they baked in the Texas heat. The smell was rancid, and Tanaka had to focus to keep his gag reflexes at bay. He removed his cowboy hat and knocked on the man's trailer.

"Who the fuck is it?!" a man yelled from inside.

"Are you Jonathan Murphy?" he responded.

"What the fuck do you want?! Leave me alone!" the man screamed through the door.

Tanaka could hear rustling from inside the single-wide and could hear the sound of some glass bottles breaking. He took a cautious step back from the door and held his hands up to show he was unarmed.

"My name is Tanaka Chee. I used to be the sheriff in Coconino County up in Flagstaff, Arizona. I just want a moment of your time to talk about what happened last December out in the oil fields," he said.

There was a long pause from inside and he could see the man was peeking through a set of blinds in the front picture window to his left.

"I told the police everything that happened and they didn't believe me. Nobody believed me. Why should I talk to another pig?" the man said from behind the window glass.

"Jonathan, I said I was the sheriff of Coconino County. I am no longer a police officer. Also, I believe your story is true because I've seen it too," Tanaka said.

There was another long pause and Tanaka debated on just putting his boot through the door and pulling the man out by his hair because he did not have time for this.

"Seen what?" the man shouted back.

"The Yee Naaldlooshii, or what you white people call a werewolf," Tanaka said.

Again there was a pause and just before Tanaka had had enough of the heat and the rank smell of the man's garbage, he heard a series of deadbolts unlock and the door slowly pulled inward. He carefully readied himself in case he needed to reach for his gun. Standing in the door frame behind the storm door was a man of average height who looked nothing at all like the man in the pictures that was supposed to be Jonathan Murphy. Tanaka could tell in the man's eyes it was him, but the rest of him had changed drastically.

The man standing before him was gaunt, filthy, and had heavy bags under his eyes. He resembled a cancer patient who was going through chemotherapy and hadn't slept for a month.

"I suppose I should let you in, eh Tonto?" Jonathan said nervously as he scratched at his left bicep, then scratched the back of his neck.

Tanaka ignored the racial stereotype and allowed the man to open the door for him. Tanaka placed his cowboy hat back on his head and was very careful not to touch any part of the storm door or frame so as not to get his fingerprints on anything as he stepped inside.

To his surprise, the inside of Jonathan's trailer stunk worse than the overfilled garbage can baking in the sun outside. Tanaka instantly felt unclean. He doubted if a shower could fix that feeling. The man's home was in shambles, filled with garbage and empty whiskey bottles that clinked against his boots.

Inside was foul and he could sense a mixture in the air of human excrement and stale cigarettes. The living room was dark and musty while the Texas sun was muted by brown dingy curtains with dust-covered blinds. Jonathan plopped down on a stained white couch that was piled with debris and more empty bottles. The man lit up a cigarette and motioned for Tanaka to take a seat. The overstuffed La-Z-Boy chair to his left had a giant wet spot on the seat cushion. Tanaka graciously declined the offer and remained standing, still cautiously aware of his surroundings without being obvious.

"Sorry for the mess Tonto, but I haven't been feeling myself lately. Whiskey makes the voices in my head stop," said the shell of what was once a healthy man. "Hell, I used to be a lightweight. One Bartles and Jaymes and I would be three sheets to the wind. Now I'm drinking at least a fifth of whiskey a day. A fucking day, Tonto. If ma could only see me now."

Tanaka noticed that the man had a nervous twitch when he spoke and his right hand trembled as he raised his cigarette to his mouth and inhaled. He took a minute to watch Jonathan's next few actions. He tried to determine if this man was a threat in his current state.

"Can you tell me what happened that night out in the oil fields when you were attacked?" Tanaka asked.

The man nervously crushed out his cigarette butt and reached for another pack of Pall Malls.

"Well, the boys and I had a couple soda pops on the tailgate of our trucks after working in the fields all day. It was a common thing we would do on a Friday. The boys liked to shoot the shit. Get their buzz on. Just basic redneck Friday night bullshit. Being a lightweight and all, I only had two beers, and I was all set." The man paused to take a swig out of a random bottle that was lying on his couch next to him. "Honestly… don't remember much of what happened. What I do remember though… I will never forget."

"What happened next?" Tanaka asked.

"One minute we are laughing and telling jokes and the next minute we hear this howl that was off in the dark across the fields. I'll tell you what Tonto… I about pissed myself after hearing that." He said and stared down at his feet for a minute before looking back up at Tanaka. "I ain't never heard anything like that before. Sure, I know what coyotes sound like, but whatever this was sounded pissed off and big."

Tanaka shuddered at the memory of that sound. Even the thought of that horrible night back in Flagstaff sent a chill down his spine. It would haunt him too for the rest of his life.

"Then we saw these yellow eyes glowing from behind an oil rig about thirty meters out from where we were standing." Jonathan continued. "Like something from hell's asscrack was sizing us up for dinner."

The man paused for another drag of his cigarette and a pull from his bottle. It was like he was trying to swim his way to the bottom.

Tanaka noted that Jonathan's ticks and twitches began to get worse as he continued his story.

"We figured someone was fuckin' with us or the fumes and heat had played tricks on our minds. Regardless, we figured it was time to get the fuck out of there fast," he said. "Next thing I know, this giant gray beast that looked part man and part wolf leaped out of nowhere and onto Bubba Ray's back."

He stopped and looked up at Tanaka. Then Tanaka motioned to him that it was okay and to keep going. With a shaking hand, he raised the cigarette to his mouth once more before continuing.

"He screamed like mad as the thing took a chunk out of his left shoulder. That was all I needed to see, so I turned tail and bolted in the opposite direction. I think we all did that. Well, except for Bubba, cuz he was being eaten at that moment. I just ran and ran, no clue where I was headed. All I knew was I had to get away from whatever that thing was." Jonathan looked at him with an ashen face.

Tanaka once again gestured to him to continue.

"I just kept runnin'," Jonathan said. "I could hear it as it galloped after me. Its snarls and breaths were right behind me. It was so close I could smell it. Next thing I know the damn thing claps its jaws around my shoulder then throws me about ten yards."

Tanaka frowned as he watched the man tick and nervously scratch at his neck. He began to wonder if this was a sign of the curse that ran through his veins.

"So it did bite you?" Tanaka inquired.

"Sure as shit! Thought I was dead. Next thing I know, I'm waking up in the hospital. No bite wound, no scar. My shoulder just ached, and the hospital discharged me the next day with a clean bill of health. Clean bill my ass! Look at me! Something's wrong with me now and I ain't right in the head no more…" He noticed Tanaka was just staring at him.

"You still listening, Red?" he asked.

"I am. Please continue." Tanaka said.

"The voices started about a week ago. Telling me to do all sorts of horrible things. Not to mention I'm always starving. I just can't seem to satisfy my appetite," Jonathan said.

Tanaka nodded to the man and wanted to wrap this conversation up because just being in the man's home alone was giving him a pit in his stomach.

"I believe you, Mr. Murphy. Thank you for taking the time to speak with me," Tanaka said.

Just as he turned to leave, the man called out to him. "Wait, you said you saw the beast too?"

Tanaka nodded without turning around. "Yes. It killed a bunch of people I cared about. I'm going to find it… and kill it."

Tanaka opened the storm door with his elbow, once again careful to not get his fingerprints on anything inside the trailer. He already knew what he had to do, and it was not going to be pretty. He crossed the man's front yard got in his truck and drove off.

Jonathan Murphy stood inside his storm door and watched the Blazer leave as he took another swig from his bottle of whiskey.

When Tanaka returned to his motel room, he quickly stripped down, got in a hot shower, and went over his thoughts on what Murphy just told him. When the hot water hit his back and the steam filled his nostrils, he breathed deeply and pondered whether or not to burn his clothes. There wasn't enough soap in the shower for him to get clean.

He just couldn't seem to get all the filth from Murphy's off his skin.

After his shower, he picked up the phone and checked in with Deputy McFerrin back in Flagstaff. The deputy informed him that there was another series of murders with the same MO up in Amarillo however, they did not fall on the night of the full moon. Both Deputy McFerrin and Tanaka knew that it had to be Thatch. Before he hung up the phone, he told her that he had a few loose ends to tie up here in Midland. Then he would be on his way up to Amarillo in about two or three days.

Tanaka was going to pay Jonathan one more visit before he left. If he was bitten by Thatch, then he was more than likely going to turn during the next full moon, which was in two nights. He figured this would be a good way to test out the new ammo that George made for him. Tanaka lay on his bed in his motel room reading from Guy Endores' *The Werewolf of Paris* until slumber finally took hold of him.

The next day Tanaka stopped by the local hardware store before he met with Jonathan later that night. He needed to grab a few supplies. The young man behind the cash register just looked at him oddly as he rang up a shovel, hacksaw, two rolls of duct tape, contractor bags, latex gloves, work gloves, and a pack of Dentyne chewing gum.

"Looks like someone's having a party tonight," the younger man said.

Tanaka just paid the man in cash and winked without saying a word. Then turned and left the store with his items.

He drove his Blazer out to State Route 349 and pulled off on the shoulder about a half mile from Jonathan's mobile home. Tanaka turned off his truck and patiently waited for the sun to go down and the full moon to rise. Finally, when the sun dipped below the horizon, he started up his truck and made his move.

With his driver's window down and his headlights off, he slowly crept into Jonathan's driveway. The lights were on inside the single-wide and Tanaka could see the flicker of the television as he imagined Murphy was sitting on his couch watching TV and drinking whiskey.

Tanaka opened his box of latex gloves, pulled out a pair and put them on. He reached into the large duffle bag that was on the passenger seat of his truck and removed his Glock. Pulled out the suppressor that George had supplied him with and screwed the cylinder to the end of his pistol. Tanaka knew that this trailer was so isolated that no one would hear a gunshot. It was Texas, after all. If you stood still long enough, you would eventually hear a gunshot coming from somewhere. He was still not going to take any chances, which is exactly why he had George make him the subsonic rounds for his 9mm. Subsonic rounds greatly diminish the sound of a gun being discharged, especially when paired with a suppressor. They were not completely silent like the movies, but from a distance, the untrained ear would have a harder time picking up what it was. Tanaka retrieved a magazine filled with silver rounds from the duffle bag and slammed it into the handle of the pistol. He pulled the slide back and checked the chamber to make sure everything was working accordingly and chambered a round.

His theory with the 9mm was that if the silver had to remain in place, he didn't want to shoot someone in human form and have the bullet exit the body as it could with a larger caliber weapon like his .357 revolver. Tonight, he figured it was a good night to test that theory.

Just as he looked up to see the full moon glowing in the clear Texas sky, there was a loud crash and a scream from inside Jonathan's trailer. The lights in the window went out, leaving only the flicker of the television set glowing through the blinds.

Tanaka stepped out of his truck, careful not to slam the door, and walked towards the man's home with his pistol at the ready.

As he approached, he heard Jonathan screech from inside the mobile home and Tanaka quickly made his way to the front entrance. After he opened the storm door quietly, he blasted open the front door with a hard kick of his boot. He was shocked at what he saw.

There inside on the floor was Jonathan Murphy. The man was on his hands and knees, bellowing in agony as his bones broke and reshaped. The only source of light in the trailer was that of the television. It showed a monster truck rally as Bigfoot crushed a row of cars. The man's eyes were yellow and rimmed with red veins and his jaws extended and began to fill with elongated canine teeth. His hands began to stretch and cover with hair as he looked up at Tanaka with a painful and terrified look in his eyes.

Tanaka slowly walked over to Jonathan and aimed his pistol down at the man's forehead and noticed a single tear falling from his right eye.

"I'm sorry," Tanaka said as he quickly fired three rounds of silver into the man's head, causing him to fall limp to the floor.

Tanaka returned to his Blazer and opened the tailgate, pulled out a garbage bag, a roll of duct tape, and the hacksaw. With a heavy sigh, he returned to the man's home to finish what he started. Eventually, he returned to his truck with the garbage bag. Its contents were wound up tight and sealed with duct tape and placed in the back of his Blazer.

After he got in the driver's seat and closed the door, he consulted his road map of Texas to find the most discreet way to get to Amarillo. Luckily, it was all pretty much discreet because there wasn't much in between Midland and Amarillo. It was about a four to five-hour drive. He was going to avoid going through Lubbock just in case he got stopped for any reason. He felt his odds were better on back roads and smaller state route highways so he started up his truck and drove off leaving the man's disheveled single-wide behind.

He prayed to the creator that he would not have to do this to his daughter Barbara someday. After about two hours of driving, Tanaka found a remote area where he buried Murphy's head in a dirt field about fifty yards from the road.

CHAPTER FOURTEEN

DETROIT

MAY, 1987

IT had been two days since Daniel returned to his apartment after he exited the hospital. He lay in his twin-sized bed and stared at the ceiling fan as it slowly spun over him. He was still trying to process what had happened to him and how he was able to heal so quickly, let alone survive. Did it all actually happen, or was most of it a nightmare?

It had to be the morphine that made those dreams so vivid and surreal, he thought.

What was it that Stanley wanted to talk to him about? And was he really there at all? The plastic hospital bracelet on his left wrist assured him that he was, in fact, at Henry Ford Hospital. He reached over and tore the bracelet from his wrist and flung it across the bedroom. Now he worried the authorities would try to find him. He didn't know how they could because his expired driver's license was from New Mexico and they did not have his current address. There was no phone in his tiny apartment and he paid his rent on time every month in cash. Daniel did not have a bank account or credit cards and kept all his money stuffed under his twin mattress, which totaled around $5000.

His job down at Puzo's Market paid him in cash, and Mr. Puzo never asked him any questions. Which reminded him that he had to go down to the market today and make sure he still had a job after being gone so long with his recent trip to the hospital.

His bedroom was small, with just a bed that butted up against the western wall. This was so the window that faced east let the sunlight into the room every morning. There was a nightstand next to the bed where a lamp and a wind-up alarm clock sat. A stack of old paperbacks lay on the floor next to him. Adjacent to where he lay was a dresser, and next to that was his closet. The walls were bare throughout the entire apartment and were a dingy color of white. Daniel had not even been there a year and honestly didn't know if he was going to stay once the remainder of his lease ran out.

Daniel suffered from selective amnesia throughout most of his life. The majority of his memories were spotty at best. He could not remember his parents or even where or when he was born. His New Mexico driver's license stated his birthday was December 10th, 1946. Though he had no recollection of this, he still went by that as his birthdate. Daniel figured something happened in his life years ago that was so traumatic it caused him to either forget or block out large chunks, if not most, of his past. He had no memories of childhood, his teens, or his twenties or thirties. No memories of school or college or any family whatsoever. To him, it felt like he was always in his early forties, with small blotches of living in different places around the United States. He thought he remembered living in New York City, which might have been the late 1950s and sometime after that, he was down in Miami, Florida. He then remembered traveling out west to Albuquerque, New Mexico, which is when he believed he got his driver's license because it expired in 1973.

He remembered bits and pieces of living in the North West around Seattle and Portland, but for the life of him could not remember when that was. Before coming to Detroit, just under a year ago, he was living in Columbus, Ohio, where he worked in a butcher shop in an older part of town.

Sometimes Daniel heard a voice in his head that made him question his sanity. None of his memories made any sense to him and to cope with this Daniel self-medicated with booze and pills. He often drank until he blacked out and woke up in unappealing locations, sometimes without clothes and with no memory of the previous three days. Daniel would keep telling himself that he was going to seek help soon, but like every addict, he kept putting it off.

He shuffled his way out of the bedroom and down the hallway to the bathroom to brush his teeth. Then continued down the hallway and paused just inside his living room. A lone green leather recliner sat in the center facing a small twelve-inch black-and-white TV that sat on a milk crate. There was a tall floor lamp next to the recliner and a TV tray on the opposite side. Daniel kept his apartment very tidy, which wasn't a stretch because there really wasn't anything in it.

This is pathetic, the voice inside him said.

Daniel sighed to himself as the voice badgered away at him.

Why do you keep me in this hellhole? it continued.

Daniel tried to ignore it as he pulled down a bottle of Old Crow stashed in a cabinet above his refrigerator.

This is what insanity is like, he thought to himself.

The whiskey burned his esophagus as it went down and left a small ball of warmth in his stomach. Wincing, he took another swig and then placed the bottle back up into the cupboard.

You cannot ignore me, Daniel. You cannot stop me. The voice said.

He made himself a sandwich and shuffled back towards the hallway, taking bites as he returned to his bedroom.

You are nothing. You are a waste. I am coming, Daniel.

"Go away," he muttered to himself.

He opened up his closet door and suddenly, the beast was in front of him. It lashed out from inside the closet with lightning speed and grabbed Daniel by his throat. With a grip like iron, it lifted him off the ground, causing his feet to dangle a foot from the floor. Its eyes were now filled with resentment and impatience. Gums curled up over massive teeth as it snarled. Daniel could feel the creature's hot breath against his cheeks. He tried to scream, but the monster's grip was too tight. So he did the next best thing he could do. He wet himself.

The beast sniffed the air and began to chuff. It was laughing at him.

Pathetic whelp, the beast said in a deep baritone voice.

Daniel frantically fought the monster's grip. He clawed and tried to strike the beast, but his attempts to free himself failed. It lowered its head and stepped into the bedroom, carrying Daniel by his throat. There was nothing he could do.

The great beast tilted and turned his head as it watched Daniel squirm in his grip. It was like watching a sadistic child hold a fish out of water. With one claw, it reached down and slowly eviscerated Daniel just below his abdomen. He could feel his warm insides pour down the front of his legs as they left his body.

Weak... the beast spat.

When Daniel came to, he was still standing in front of his empty closet. There was no giant beast. It had not sliced his stomach open and as far as he could tell, all his organs were still on the inside. He stood there for a minute trying to ignore the wet spot in his shorts. These hallucinations were becoming more frequent. With a heavy sigh, he bowed his head in shame and returned to the bathroom to clean himself up.

After a quick shower, he pulled out a pair of old blue jeans and an Aerosmith t-shirt then realized he recently lost his favorite pair of Adidas high-tops. Bummed, he settled for the only other pair of shoes he owned, which was a pair of grass-stained white no-name high-tops. Daniel got dressed, finished his bologna sandwich, and left his apartment, locking the door behind him.

Hopefully, Mr. Puzo would understand why he was gone for so long and missed the past few days of work. Daniel stepped outside his apartment complex and inhaled the summer air which contained the odors of car exhaust and marijuana smoke.

"Morning, Sam," he said to the homeless man who sat next to his stoop.

"Morning, Ralph," the bum replied.

Daniel laughed to himself at the bum's response. They did this every time they saw each other, referring to a Looney Tunes Cartoon.

He paused there for a minute, trying to recollect what day it was. "It's Sunday!"

He dug in his front pocket for some loose change and darted straight over to the red news rack that was a few steps from his building and had the words Detroit News written on the side of it. He deposited twenty-five cents into the slot, opened the graffiti-covered door and pulled out the Sunday edition of the local periodical.

This brightened his day because the Sunday edition had the colored funny papers which he loved to read. The funny papers were an entire section of colorized versions of his favorite comic strips, instead of the weekly black and white ones you found at the end of the Sports section. He was excited to see what Bill the Cat was up to this week in his favorite comic by Berkeley Breathed titled "Bloom County".

Daniel figured he'd head over to Marge's diner a few blocks away, enjoy a cup of coffee, and read his newspaper before heading over to Puzo's to explain what happened and why he was gone. Daniel stuffed the folded newspaper under his left arm and strutted down the block.

Marge's Diner was your ordinary choke and puke, located three blocks west of Daniel's apartment building. Marge was a heavy-set Polish woman in her early sixties with short gray curly hair and a surly attitude. She always summed herself up in one description; fat and sassy. Inside was your standard diner motif of subway tile, a few booths, and yellowed nicotine-stained walls. Marge stood behind the counter taking orders and her cook, Ken, was in the kitchen slinging food on his flattop stove. The entire place smelled like burnt grease, fresh coffee, and stale cigarettes. The diner had a healthy amount of customers, as she did every Sunday morning. Daniel sat perched at the bar by himself, sipping on his cup of coffee while intensely reading the Sunday paper.

A waitress by the name of Cassy plopped down on the empty stool for her break next to Daniel and lit up a cigarette. Cassy was in her mid-thirties with long brown hair tied back into a ponytail and had appeared there ever since Daniel started coming to Marge's. Her olive skin, high cheekbones, and model-like physique made her the most gorgeous woman Daniel had ever seen.

He had a massive crush on Cassy from the first moment he saw her and would blush a little every time she came around him. Cassy was the kind of person who would touch him when she spoke. She would either rest her hand on his forearm or squeeze his bicep. He liked this innocent form of physical connection, and it gave him butterflies when she did it. Cassy would always make time for him. They would talk about her day and her dogs. For the life of him, he could never remember the names of her two dogs.

"Morning, Daniel," she said as she put her hand on his forearm.

"Hi Cassy, how are you doing?" Daniel said as he looked up from his paper.

"I'm okay. I miss my puppies. How are today's Sunday comics?" she inquired.

"The Lockhorns were great today and so was Crankshaft," Daniel said as he sipped from his cup.

She pointed out the headline on the front page of the newspaper that read "Four People Dead And The Detroit Police Still Have No Leads."

"Pretty scary stuff, isn't it? I mean, is there a crazy person running around killing people?" she asked as she took a drag from her smoke. Daniel peered up from his comics, looked over at the grim headline and frowned.

"Yeah, that is pretty bad. It is Detroit though. Doesn't that stuff happen all the time these days?" Daniel asked.

"Well, I read somewhere that the victims were dismembered," she said, taking another drag.

"Okay, well, I guess that doesn't happen all the time," he replied. A perplexed look came over Daniel's face as he looked at Cassy. His palms began to sweat as his heart began to speed up.

"What is it, Daniel?" she asked curiously.

"Cassy, would you like to have dinner with me sometime?" he asked as his gut instantly turned upside down.

Cassy blushed. "I would like that very much, Daniel."

"Awesome! How does tomorrow night sound?" he asked anxiously.

She nodded to him like an excited little schoolgirl. He took a deep breath and wiped his palms on his thighs. He hadn't asked a girl out on a date in a very long time. Wrangling up the opposite sex was not always one of Daniel's strong suits. He was much more of a book-reading introverted type and didn't get out much.

"I kinda don't have any wheels at the moment, so how about we meet up at Vince's over on Springwells Ave. for some old-school Italian? How does 7 pm sound?" he asked.

"I can totally meet you there. That sounds outstanding, and 7 pm is perfect," she replied excitedly.

"Okay great! I have to get going now and get down to Puzo's to see if I still have a job. It's a long story. I'll tell you tomorrow," Daniel said.

Laying a dollar on the counter to pay for his coffee, he stood up and headed for the door. She smiled and nodded and continued to finish her cigarette. Just before Daniel opened the diner door to leave, Marge called out to him while cashing out another customer.

"Hey, Daniel. You want your Sunday paper?" she asked.

"Nah. I left it for Cassy to read. See ya soon, Marge," he said as he turned and darted out the door.

"Cassy?" Marge questioned as the door closed behind him.

Daniel walked into Puzo's market around one in the afternoon. The old Italian was restocking a bin of cantaloupe melons as he looked up and saw Daniel walk through the door. Mario was a short, full-blooded Italian immigrant who relocated to Detroit from Chicago in the early 1970s. The story goes that he was an informant for the FBI and helped take down one of the largest Chicago crime families, then entered witness protection and was moved to Detroit. These stories were neither denied nor confirmed and he never really spoke of his life before living in Detroit. He and his wife Sharon lived in a studio loft above the small corner market and were always working. Daniel was their only other employee who worked part-time because the old Italian couple could not afford to pay any full-time workers.

"Hello, Daniel. Glad you finally decided to show up," the old man said as he wiped his hands off on his red apron and placed them on his hips. Daniel could sense the disappointment and annoyance in his tone.

"I'm so sorry, Mr. Puzo. I wanted to come in and apologize for leaving you high and dry like that," Daniel said. "That was very uncool of me and I promise it won't happen again."

The old man just blinked at him and sighed heavily. Daniel then explained to him what happened with his run-in with the Detroit Sanitation department and his stay over at Henry Ford. Daniel was careful to leave out certain parts but assured him he was okay. The old paisano was not stupid by any means and knew Daniel had problems mentally and with alcohol. He was always a little extra lenient with him. Not to mention his wife had a major soft spot for Daniel and he would never hear the end of it if he let him go.

"Okay, Daniel. I believe you and I'm glad you're okay. Besides, Sharon would murder me if I fired you. I don't know why she likes you so much," he said. Daniel blushed and looked down in shame. "How about you get to work and help me move this crate of cantaloupes back to the stockroom?"

Daniel quickly hopped to it and picked up the crate of melons. He couldn't afford to lose this job. Not for financial reasons, but more for his sanity. Working at Puzo's helped keep Daniel grounded. This was his pulse to reality. He would miss the interaction with Mario and would miss talking with the customers who came in. Some of these customers he had gotten to know by name. His mind never wandered while he was at work. To the best of his knowledge, he never had any hallucinations while at work, either. There had been no "episodes" per se. He was a hard worker and Mario gave him a sense of purpose. In a life that he seemed to flounder through, Puzo's market was his anchor.

CHAPTER FIFTEEN

AMARILLO

FEBRUARY, 1986

A month after the incident in Midland, Texas, Tanaka found himself sitting on the bed in Room 16 of the small motel on the night of the next full moon. The room was under the name Sebastian Crosswell, who was also the man lying in the bathtub with two silver bullets in his chest and one in his head.

Crosswell was a twenty-three-year-old bartender at one of Amarillo's downtown nightclubs. He was the only survivor of three college kids who were attacked the previous month out at the Cadillac Ranch off I-40.

This case was much different from Murphy's. He didn't speak of any rabid beasts or being bitten. Sebastian told the authorities that he was knocked out cold during the attack and woke up to find his friends dead. The other two students shared the same savage animalistic attacks as the others, but the survivor appeared to have gotten away unharmed. After all this, he just went home and continued his life as normal.

Way too normal, Tanaka thought.

The man didn't seem to grieve for his friends who had just died. For the first two weeks, he went to work on time and did regular things.

Just like an average person would. One that hadn't been attacked by a werewolf.

How could this man who just survived a run-in with Thatch plug back into society so easily? Tanaka thought.

Tanaka had stopped by the man's work to see if they could talk. Crosswell just ignored him and asked for his drink order. This interaction led Tanaka to think he was a self-absorbed little prick. After that, he decided to follow him every day to and from work. He never let the man out of his sight. Nothing was out of the ordinary until about two weeks before his first full moon.

Crosswell stopped going to work and instead checked into Room 16. The only time he would leave was when he went out to eat or stopped by one of the local bars near Amarillo Community College. He would also frequently bring young college girls back to his room.

On the day of the full moon, Tanaka paid a pizza delivery kid $100 to let him deliver the pizza to Room 16. The delivery boy could have cared less. He made some extra money and didn't have to do anything but leave. When Sebastian came to the door, he was introduced to the business end of Tanaka's silencer.

Tanaka calmly forced himself inside and right away noticed the aroma. When he questioned the man about the smell, he just pointed to the closest.

"Why, it's the girls. I gave them a time-out. Would you like to see them?" Crosswell asked with a smile.

"I want you to open that door, Sebastian... slowly," Tanaka replied while pressing the barrel of his pistol to the man's forehead.

"Okay. Okay," he said with his arms up in the air. "Geez, you are no fun. No fun at all."

The man turned and walked over to the closet door. He slowly turned the handle and gave the ex-sheriff a playful smile. Just like a child about to show his father a surprise. Tanaka grew tense.

When the door slowly creaked open, the rancid odor got worse. Crosswell let the weight of the bodies push the door open the rest of the way and they flopped out onto the floor. Before the two men lay three teenage girls. They were all naked, with bruises and contusions all over their bodies.

Tanaka could tell these were the bodies of three girls who had been recently reported missing. They reminded him of his daughter. The thought of her suffering a similar fate made his mind spiral down a dark path. He just stood there looking at them for a moment, then glanced up at Sebastian, who just politely smiled at him and shrugged.

"See. Just like I tol…"

Crosswell was not able to finish his sentence before Tanaka raised his pistol and put a bullet in his head and then two more in his chest. Blood splattered on the walls and ceiling before his body dropped to the floor. He took a minute to erase the memory of his daughter from his mind. He didn't have time to be sad. He had a job to do.

Tanaka dragged the bartender's body into the bathroom and placed him in the bathtub. The way he saw it was if he was wrong, and the man wasn't bitten by Thatch, he just solved Amarillo's missing college girl's case. He wasn't worried at all about this getting back to him and knew that the local police department would learn that the bodies in the closet were put there by Sebastian. They would more than likely theorize that one of the girls' fathers had found out about Crosswell and come to his room for some "Cowboy" justice. It was Texas, after all.

What Tanaka was worried about was what they would think when they found his head was missing.

Once he cleaned up the mess he had made in Room 16, Tanaka knew it was time to leave Texas. He checked back in with Deputy McFerrin in Flagstaff from a payphone at a rest area just east of Amarillo. The trail had gone cold. There were no more leads and there had not been any murders that the deputy could find that led them in a direction.

"So what do you think, boss?" Jennifer asked.

Tanaka held the phone receiver to his ear and paused for a minute. He was looking for a pattern. There wasn't one.

"Thatch is playing a game," he said. "I think he knows I am following him. I can just feel it in my gut."

Jennifer let out a heavy sigh. "Do you think he's been sticking around and staying hidden?"

"Yes," he replied.

"So where does that leave us?" she asked.

"Whelp… I first started to think he was doing this to slow me down and keep me busy. This way, he could stay a few steps ahead of me. Thatch knows I would stick around and clean up his mess before moving on." Tanaka went on, "I don't think that's the case anymore, Jen. I think he's been doing this and watching me all along. I mean, I could be wrong, but I don't think that I am."

"Okay, I think you might be on to something," she responded.

"See… Norman is not only a psychopath, but he's a sociopath, too. I think he thinks he is the top dog here. His ego is too big, and he has to watch and relish in his work." He theorized further. "I think his arrogance will be what leads us right to him. Or right to me."

"Are you thinking about setting a trap? Do you remember what he did here at the station? He's a one-man wrecking crew. I don't think you will have much luck going head-to-head with him," the deputy pointed out.

"I have to be smarter," he said with confidence. "I am going to have to find a way to catch him with his guard down."

"How the hell are you going to do that? I mean, the guy is like the Terminator. I honestly don't think he ever has his guard down," the deputy said with both sarcasm and sincerity.

"Believe me, I know. I also need to take him alive," he said.

"Umm, you can't be serious, boss. That's utterly insane," she said concerned.

"I have to. I need to know what happened to Barbara. I have to know if she is, in fact, dead." She could tell by the sound of his voice that he was exhausted. "I have to know Jennifer."

"Okay… I get it. So what's the plan from here?" she asked.

"I'm gonna head up to Oklahoma City. I could use a break to collect my thoughts. I'll check in as soon as I get a room and give you a number to reach me at," he explained. "I need some time to think and figure out our next move. Maybe try to get some actual sleep."

"Okay, sounds good. I'll keep my eyes peeled on my end and you touch base with me when you can," she instructed.

"Sounds good. Bye," Tanaka said as he hung up the pay phone.

Tanaka had rented a room at the Knights Inn when he got to Oklahoma City. He tried to clear his head, but the horrors from Room 16 were still fresh in his mind. Had that been Barbara's fate? Had Thatch killed his daughter? Did the man toy with her like Crosswell did to those college girls, or did the beast tear her apart? He could not get these thoughts to stop running through his head on constant replay.

He needed some fresh air, so he decided to go for a walk and find some food for a change of scenery. Hopefully, some hot Chinese food would help him stop ruminating on the events of the past year.

He found a small quiet restaurant and ordered the sweet and sour chicken and sipped some warm tea. The hot beverage had a sort of soothing effect on him as he drank it. For the first time in a while, he was able to slow down and think more clearly.

Tanaka sat with his food, reviewing his notes and studying a map of the United States.

Where the hell are you Norman, and where are you headed? he thought to himself.

He remembered when he discovered Emily's body back in the Coconino National Forest. Thatch had been watching him and even called out to him from a distance. This further supported his theory that Norman was sticking around. The fact that he allowed himself to be taken in by Mark and placed in the interrogation room just proved his arrogance.

Why? Tanaka thought to himself in between bites. His right leg jiggled up and down as he sat at the table, deep in thought.

Why the hell would he do that? Why bring attention to the fact that he even existed? I mean the Yee Naaldlooshii 'can' be killed. Why bring yourself out into the open? Allowing people to learn more about what he was, he thought.

Tanaka summarized that Thatch had not come across a challenge like this. It would have to eventually get boring being at the top of the food chain. Being more or less immortal and having no real natural enemies would probably get old after a while. The nature of how the beast killed was so brutal and full of malevolence that it reminded him of an angsty teenager rebelling against his parents. He followed no laws of nature whatsoever.

Tanaka knew predators hunted for food. They hunted for survival. Thatch hunted to kill and inflict as much pain as possible. The level of his rage was evident in the way he slaughtered his way across northern Arizona.

Why did he leave me alive back at the station? he thought. Tapping his chopsticks on the side of his plate to a steady rhythm as his brain turned.

"Because he's fucking bored," he said out loud. "The fucker is bored."

At that moment, he realized that leaving Barbara's fate unknown would be the greatest damage Norman could have inflicted on him. What kind of evil would do such a thing? To leave him alive and drag him along in this little game of hide and seek. Norman was in complete control of the situation. Tanaka knew that he needed to come up with a plan to change that.

He found he did his best thinking while walking through the Oklahoma City Zoo. There was something about watching the animals in their daily routines that he found soothing. He knew it was cruel for the white man to keep them in cages, but there was nothing he could do about that. Nonetheless, it was a peaceful place to be.

A growing sense of paranoia, however, began to creep its way into Tanaka's head. He now couldn't go anywhere without feeling that he was being watched.

Was Norman there in OKC? Was he lurking around every corner, just far enough out of sight to pull his strings like a puppeteer?

Tanaka sat on a bench one afternoon in front of the primate exhibit with a notebook. He was watching the monkeys play and jump from tree to tree as he jotted notes down as if he were brainstorming ideas for a plan.

Storage Space. Concrete Room. Drugs? Zip Ties. Poison? Wolfsbane? Flame Thrower? Landmines? Fire? Surface-to-Air Missile? These were all things he jotted down on his paper. Going back and scratching out the ideas that seemed a little too far-fetched.

After about an hour, he noticed that the monkeys in the cage started to become increasingly nervous. Shortly after that, they began to get aggressive with each other. They began to scream and cry out. Tanaka paused and thought this was odd. He had been coming here every day for about two weeks and had never seen them exhibit this behavior. After a few minutes of this, they all just stopped. He noticed they were quiet now. Just like that, they went from howling mad to silent. Tanaka noticed that all the animal exhibits seemed to be quiet.

The people in the zoo walked around, not noticing anything was out of the ordinary. Parents with their kids still pointed and laughed at the chimpanzees and any other animals they found silly. Families walked past him as they would any other normal day. Tanaka, however, knew something was wrong. Something made all these animals quiet down. Something or someone was here.

"Norman," he whispered to himself.

Tanaka stood up from his bench, gathered his things, and looked around. He scanned the area, trying to keep a watchful eye on what was going on.

He saw nothing. Norman wasn't anywhere at all. All he saw were people enjoying their day at the Zoo. Kids were laughing and playing while their parents were annoyed. Nothing was out of the ordinary, yet he couldn't shake this feeling. The feeling that he was being watched.

I must be getting paranoid, he thought to himself.

After waiting a few more minutes, he figured it was time to go. He needed to get back to his motel room and check in with Deputy McFerrin back in Flagstaff. He needed to see if there were any more leads or any new information. So he made sure he wasn't followed and made his way back to his truck and headed back to the Knights Inn.

Norman stood under a tree about fifty meters from the primate exhibit at the Oklahoma Zoo. He watched Sheriff Tanaka sit on a bench, watching the monkeys doing monkey stuff or whatever it was those vile creatures did. He was wondering what exactly was going through the sheriff's head.

Is he thinking about me? I so hope he's thinking about me, he thought to himself.

He stayed just out of sight while eating a bucket of fried chicken. With a grease-covered hand, he reached in and pulled out a chicken thigh and began to crunch away, bones and all.

While sucking and licking the grease and chicken skin from his thumb, a ball bounced in front of him. It stopped just within reach. He ceased what he was doing and peered down at it with puzzlement.

"Hey mister… you gonna throw that back or what?" A little girl called out.

He looked at her and smiled. Setting his bucket of chicken down, he reached over picked up the ball, and studied it.

It seemed to have some kind of Japanese cartoon character on it.

"Well?" the girl called out with annoyance.

"I'm sorry, little one. This just reminded me of something," he said to the child, then tossed it back to her.

"Tabatha! Stop bothering that man," her mother called out from behind her.

"You're weird, mister," the little girl said.

"Tabatha!" her father snapped.

"Is she dressed for rain?" Norman asked.

"It's her favorite outfit, and she seems to want to wear it all the time," the child's mother said.

"I'm sorry, sir. Our child doesn't seem to have a filter," the man said as he walked over to him.

The child's mother gave her a scolding look.

"What?" Tabatha said back to her mother.

"The name's Norman," he said. Then he wiped his hands off on his pants and shook the man's hand.

"Bill, that's my wife Kim. I see you have met our daughter, Tabatha." The man said while shaking Norman's hand.

"You folks live here?" he asked.

"Sure do. Born and raised," the man said with pride. "How about you, Norman?"

"Nah. Just passing through. I've never been to Oklahoma." He replied while he smiled at the little girl.

Over the man's shoulder, he noticed Tanaka gather up his things and hurry off. Tabatha noticed this as well. She began to think something was very different with this man named Norman.

"How do you like it so far?" Kim asked.

"It's great. I've only been here two days and I really don't know my way around. Wouldn't mind if someone showed me around or gave me some suggestions," Norman said politely.

"Sure, we were just headed over to see the wolves. Tabatha hasn't seen them before," the man said.

Tabatha clenched her mother's hand tightly at the thought of having to see this stranger any longer.

"Oh, I love wolves. Mind if I tag along?" Norman asked nicely.

"Yeah, for sure. Let's go," Tabatha's father responded.

As he let the young family lead the way, Tabatha turned to look at Norman. Norman just smiled at her and his eyes flashed to yellow.

The next day Tanaka returned to the zoo like he always did, only to find it was closed due to some kind of accident. He was only able to get as far as the main gate where he was refused entry. He knew there had to be a death for them to shut down the entire zoo for further investigation.

"Hey, what happened in there?" Tanaka asked the young officer stationed at the gate.

"Sorry buddy. Can't say much, but there was an accident involving the wolf pen and some young family." the officer said. "Awful, if you ask me."

"Thanks. Do they have an idea when it will reopen?" Tanaka asked.

"Nope. They need to rule out whether it was just an accident or if homicide needs to take a look," the younger man answered.

Tanaka turned around and went back to his Blazer. He sat in the driver's seat, thinking over what had happened there the day before.

Thatch... he thought. *It has to be Thatch.*

He called Deputy McFerrin on a pay phone from the parking lot of a Waffle House.

"Hey, it's me again," he said.

"Anything new?" she asked.

"There was an incident here at the zoo yesterday. Remember how I thought I was being paranoid?" he asked.

"Yeah. You think he's there, don't you?" she questioned.

"Yes. I'm going to stay here another week. I want to wait and see what the news reports have to say about what happened yesterday. It can't be just a coincidence that I was just there and then there's an accident at the wolf pen," he explained.

"Okay. That makes sense. I'll see what I can dig up. Be careful boss." She insisted before they both hung up.

When the news finally broke of the incident at the zoo, they deemed it an accident. A young couple and their young daughter seemed to have fallen into the wolf pen and got attacked. A zoo keeper found some of the wolves feeding on the remains of the family. The authorities figured that the child must have fallen into the pen and her parents tried to save her.

Tanaka knew this was not just an accident. He knew it was way too much of a coincidence for this to happen the same day he had been there. This had to be Thatch. There was no doubt in his mind that this was all connected.

A few days after the incident, he received a note from the office at the Knights Inn informing him that he had mail. Tanaka walked down to the office and the man behind the counter handed him a postcard that was addressed to him. The postcard had a picture of Graceland, the house that Elvis Presley lived in when he died in Memphis, Tennessee.

The card was addressed to Tanaka Chee and read, *Hugs and Kisses. Wish you were here!* It was signed with the initials NT.

He instantly knew exactly who this was from. It was postmarked three days before he received it. He did not doubt that Norman was goading him on. Tanaka returned to his room and placed a call back to Flagstaff. Deputy McFerrin didn't have any new information for Tanaka. There had not been any recent reported attacks or missing persons reports that matched Norman's MO.

He told her about the postcard he received and that it was postmarked from Memphis, Tennessee. This meant that Norman had been in Oklahoma City. She agreed that Memphis would be his next move. Knowing it more than likely was a trap, Tanaka agreed and hung up the phone.

"I've always wanted to go to Memphis," he said to himself.

CHAPTER SIXTEEN

RUSSIA

NOVEMBER, 1942

Erich had gathered up a set of clean clothes and a pair of dry boots. He took a hot bath in one of the small homes that was now unoccupied. He had taken the time to collect all the bodies he could and stack them in the center of the village. The casualties totaled forty-seven, which included men, women, and about fifteen children. Once he respectfully collected them all into a massive pile, he located some kerosene and lamp oil and dosed them with it. Erich then found some matches and set them ablaze. As the flames danced in the air and the smell of burning flesh scorched his nostrils, he wept.

He wept for the lives that were lost by his hands and whatever curse Nikolia bestowed upon him. He gathered up a few supplies for his trek and placed them in a leather backpack. Lastly, he picked up Petrov's old rifle and started his walk across the frozen prairie to the west towards occupied German territory.

It took him nineteen days to cross the harsh Russian landscape before reaching the first German outpost. He had to stay clear of a few Soviet patrols and dodge being spotted by the occasional aircraft.

The frequent snow squalls covered his tracks, but he still backtracked a few times to be sure and throw off anyone who might be tracking him.

Still, he couldn't help but ruminate about Nikolia Sergeev and what he had done. Nikolia's eyes and teeth were still burned into his memory. Was the mad gypsy centuries old? What exactly was Nikolia and what had Erich become for that matter? Had he slaughtered an entire village even though he had no memory of it? These were all things that ran through his mind constantly as he trudged along, unable to put it all behind him.

He managed to shoot an elk cow at one point. Though he was never a hunter, he was able to strip what he thought was the meat from the animal and make a campfire. The meat was stringy and undercooked, but he didn't mind. For some reason, he seemed to like it that way now.

Some days he walked all day and night and some days he rested. He didn't need to rest as much as he thought, but it was good for him to sit still to make sure he was not being followed. He crossed frozen streams and raging rivers, which made his clothing freeze solid at one point, causing him to stop and set up another campfire to thaw them out.

While cleaning the carcass of a rabbit he shot, the knife he was using slipped and sliced the inside of his palm wide open. Erich quickly tore up some rags and wrapped up his hand. Two days later, he removed the bandage to check his wound and nothing was there, not even a scar.

"What have I become?" he asked himself as he sat all alone in the solitude of the Russian wilderness.

When he got to the German outpost, he asked the officer at the gate to see General Hans-Valentin Hube right away. Erich had to retell his story over and over again until he was finally in the General's presence. They did not believe him at first. There was no way a man could have walked back from Stalingrad through the Russian climate and arrived unharmed. The German army had lost so many troops that winter to the harsh cold, and it was not humanly possible for any man to accomplish this task.

Instead of believing him, the general and his commanding officers decided they should lock him up for wasting their time and concocting such a ludicrous story. In one last-ditch effort to prove his story true, he pulled the knife he was carrying from his belt and rolled up his left sleeve. He slowly dragged the blade up his forearm, cutting a twelve-centimeter gash as blood followed gravity and began to pool in his palm.

"See this? Lock me up if you have to, but come check on this wound and I guarantee it will be healed in two days or less," Erich said. The commanding officers didn't care. The guards were ordered to take him away and tossed him into a cell.

Out of curiosity, the general did check back on Erich a day later and, after having his bandage removed, saw that the wound was completely healed. General Hube was now convinced the German soldier was telling the truth. Whatever was inside Erich, the general thought could be something that the Führer could use in Germany's favor. General Hube was going to personally escort Erich back to Zossen, Germany, and to the headquarters of the Nazi High Command. In his debriefing, Erich purposely left out the part about Nikolia and the small Russian village he visited nineteen days earlier. Instead, he told them he passed out from hypothermia shortly after he made his escape from the Battle of Stalingrad, and when he woke up his body had changed or adapted to survival.

Over the next four and a half days, they shuffled him from outpost to outpost with the utmost urgency until they reached Ukraine. There they traveled to Kyiv, where they boarded an armored SS train that would take them to Berlin, Germany. From Berlin, he was then to be sent south to Zossen, Germany, to meet with Hitler's Oberkommando des Heeres, or "High Command" of the Nazi army. The train ride to Berlin would take three days, so Erich got comfortable and settled in for a long commute aboard the locomotive. They would only make a few stops for them to relieve themselves and eat. After they embarked from their last stop, the armored train would have to run all through the night to arrive in Berlin by morning. They all had no idea what was in store for them when the sun fell behind the horizon and the full moon rose.

The colossal armored behemoth barreled down the tracks, its arms and pistons pumping away, turning its drive wheels. Her headlamp cut through the falling snow as the Nazi Swastika on the front plate of the enormous engine warned all those around to stay clear. She was covered in large armor plates that held scars and stories of previous battles. The powerful engine carried a single armor-covered car that housed General Hube, two high-ranking commanders, and fifteen elite Waffen-SS soldiers. Transporting Erich back to Berlin was of the utmost priority because the general thought he might hold the key to unlocking a new breed of super soldier. General Hube smiled at the thought of an unstoppable army that could lead Germany to victory on the eastern front, crushing the Allied armies. Heinrich Himmler had personally instructed the general that he would be waiting for the train to arrive and it was his responsibility to protect the asset at all costs.

Erich sat in his seat and gently swayed from side to side as the train clicked and clacked down the tracks toward their destination. The presence of the Waffen-SS always made him nervous. These were the kind of men who pulled women and children from their homes and committed horrible crimes in the name of the Führer and enjoyed it. They were not the kind of men you could reason with let alone have a simple conversation. These soldiers' minds had been brainwashed and reprogrammed to follow the Third Reich's narrative, no matter the cost or loss of life. Their black uniforms with red swastika armbands were truly an imposing sight and could unnerve the strongest of wills. A few of them peered through the slits in the armor plating, scanning the landscape with their MP-40s at the ready.

The German MP-40 was more commonly called "The Grease Gun," by Allied forces. This submachine fired a 9x19 mm Parabellum round out of a thirty-two-round magazine at 500 rounds per minute. They were nasty little things in the right hands. Each Waffen-SS soldier aboard the train was armed with one.

Across from Erich sat the General who was watching him intensely as the vibrations of the train caused them to sway in unison. Erich had no idea what to talk about with this man and wondered how many people had died under his orders. German soldiers were one thing, but the true Nazis were terrifying. Evil to their core.

"The great Himmler himself wants to meet you and will be waiting for us on the platform in Berlin when we arrive," the general said.

Erich tried not to squirm in his seat as the man spoke of Hitler's number two in command, Heinrich Himmler who was the leader of the Nazi SS. He was just as feared and more ruthless than the Führer himself. If he was going to be meeting Himmler, Erich knew this was not going to lead to something good.

"You should feel proud that you are about to help strengthen the Fuhrer's cause and hopefully turn the balance in our favor," General Hube said with great pride.

Erich quietly nodded and noticed it was starting to get increasingly warm in the passenger car.

"Is it warm in here to you, General?" Erich asked while unbuttoning the first few buttons of his uniform.

"No, not at all. I find it quite pleasant at the moment," the general replied.

Erich began to perspire heavily as a humming noise began to throb in his ears. The General reached into the breast pocket of his uniform and pulled out a metal cigarette case that had an iron cross on one side and a swastika on the other. Opening it like a billfold, he removed a cigarette and closed it with one hand. While tapping the tobacco-filled tube on the metal case, he looked directly at Erich, sensing the change in his demeanor.

"Is something wrong, Erich?" The general asked as he placed the cigarette into his mouth and allowed the nearest SS soldier to lean over with his lighter and light it for him.

Erich's sense of smell was all of a suddenly incredibly sensitive. The smell of the smoke from the general filled his nostrils with an over-powering scent. Erich's hearing suddenly seemed superhuman and he could hear the general's heart beating as well as the heartbeats of every other person in the car. As the hum grew louder in his ears, his skin began to feel like it was boiling. He closed his eyes and tried to control his breathing as the train rocked him from side to side. The general just watched in intrigue while he slowly smoked his cigarette.

The pain began to start in Erich's joints and spread throughout his body as he could no longer contain himself. He let out a horrible scream as his bones began to break and reshape. The general and his troops watched in fright as Erich's body contorted and his eyes became yellow with red veins around the edges. He tore his uniform open as his ribs began to pop and crack and hair began to cover his body. His face and jaw broke and elongated as his skin stretched and his mouth began to fill with sharp teeth in place of where his human ones once were. Erich fell to his hands and knees between the seats as the General stood up and backed away to the other side of the train car.

The SS soldiers surrounded the General whose back was now against the wall. The Nazi soldiers raised their grease guns towards Erich, who was still screaming out of sight behind the cover of the train's seats. His vocabulary quickly dwindled and had now turned into snarls.

"Do not fire until I say so!" General Hube ordered.

The beast that was Erich Kaiser slowly stood up. Its massive head almost touched the ceiling of the passenger car. It looked directly at the general with eyes filled with malice as its chest heaved.

Werwölf," the general said out loud as the beast tilted its head back and howled. It was so loud in the small space that it caused the Germans to cover their ears to keep from blowing out their eardrums. General Hube could not believe what he was seeing in front of him as he tried to regain his senses. The werewolf was a thing from old legends and made-up stories of fiction, yet here it was standing right in front of them sizing them up with murderous intent. The beast crouched with its arms cocked back and its claws spread wide as it roared at them.

"FIRE!" the general screamed to his men.

All fifteen of the Waffen-SS troops unleashed a barrage of bullets from their submachine guns into the monster standing in front of them. In under ten seconds, they had each emptied their thirty-two-round magazines into the beast, simultaneously reloading another magazine and systematically began firing again. The sound of empty brass hitting the armored walls and floors of the train car sounded like metallic rain under the deafening sounds of the full auto sub-gun fire.

The werewolf held its ground not ten meters in front of them and roared as it recoiled in pain, instinctively using its forearms to block its face from the onslaught of lead the soldiers were providing. The Waffen-SS were trained to handle their MP-40s with precise accuracy. Especially at such a close range, so the majority of their shots were hitting the beast in its center mass.

In under two minutes, the Germans had exhausted all of their ammo having each emptied four, thirty-two-round magazines totaling close to 2,000 rounds into and around the beast. Any rounds that did not hit the monster ricocheted off the armor plating and bounced around the passenger car causing some minor injuries to the men firing their weapons. As the moment seemed to move at a snail's pace, the smoke began to settle revealing the werewolf was down in front of them.

The beast hunkered down on all fours, bowing its head and supporting itself on its knuckles with clenched fists. Pools of blood were collecting on the floor beneath it as it pushed itself into an upright stance, towering over the men. The beast's gray fur was spattered and soaked with blood that still dripped to the floor. It looked directly at General Hube, who stood in both terror and awe at what was before them.

One SS Soldier broke the silence by screaming, "Heil Hitler!" and drew his Luger in one hand and his knife in his other and charged the werewolf. He fired as he closed the distance between man and beast. It just calmly swatted away the man's pistol and snatched the man by his throat. The soldier managed to drive his knife into the beast's forearm before it placed a hand on his collarbone and yanked off his head. His spine came along with his head in a spray of blood and gore. The entire time, the beast never took his eyes off the general as he tossed the man's head in front of his antagonists. It seemed to curl its lips up over its teeth in a sort of Cheshire Cat smile. The remaining fourteen soldiers all turned to look at each other, knowing they only had two choices left. They were going to die fighting or die not fighting.

"HEIL HITLER!", they all belted in unison as they drew their knives and pistols and charged as one to their deaths.

Like a pack of hyenas attacking an injured lion, they leaped and piled on top of the eight-foot monster, stabbing and shooting it wherever they could find an opening. In an almost methodical manner, the beast peeled the men off him one by one, biting, crushing, and pulling off arms and legs and tossing them aside like rag dolls. Hitler's elite special forces were disposed of in just a few minutes, leaving the two commanders and General Hube at the far end of the train watching in disbelief.

In a fit of rage, like a child throwing a tantrum, the werewolf stomped on any remaining soldiers that still moved or breathed. After it made sure none of the men had survived, it turned its gaze back to the remaining men at the other end of the passenger car. One commander drew his Luger pistol, put the gun to his temple, and pulled the trigger, spraying brain matter all over the wall as he fell to the floor. The werewolf slowly began to step towards them, its musky odor mixed with the coppery scent of blood.

General Hube grabbed the last remaining man next to him and shoved him in the path of the beast as he turned towards the door to the train engine and began to fumble the lock with shaking hands. The commander slipped and fell in a pool of warm blood and intestines, then looked up at the beast that was glaring down at him.

Panicking, the General was still struggling to operate the lock when the beast reached down and lifted the screaming man by his face. With a wet splat, his head was driven into the wall to the right of the general's, crushing it like an overripe melon. The man's screams stopped as the monster just held his corpse against the wall. General Hube slowly turned to find the beast lowering its head to look at him eye to eye as its lips curled over its gums, revealing rows of blood-soaked teeth. The man's sphincter let loose filling his pants with feces as the beast quickly lashed out, closing his maw around the general's cheekbones and muffling his cries to God.

As the werewolf let both bodies fall to the ground, he saw the door to the train engine slowly unlatch and crack open. The beast chuffed as it realized it was not finished with tonight's slaughter.

CHAPTER SEVENTEEN

MEMPHIS

APRIL, 1986

Tanaka walked up and down Beale Street in downtown Memphis on a Saturday night in late April. It was hot for this time of year. The temperature had to be in the upper 80s and the humidity was around 75%. The smells of BBQ ribs and the sound of blues music bounced off the buildings in the historical district. He had never been here and if the situation were different, he might have enjoyed himself. Since Beale Street was a heavily trafficked tourist area, he figured this would be a good place to keep an eye out.

Tanaka had been in Memphis since the end of March and hadn't turned up any leads on Thatch yet. With another full moon done and gone, he didn't have anything to go off besides a postcard and his gut. His gut told him Norman was still here somewhere.

He had spent most of his days out in the open walking around Beale Street, Midtown, and South Main Street in hopes of drawing Thatch out into the open. So far, he had not had any luck. There had been no signs that Norman was still there.

Deputy McFerrin did inform him that in the last month there had been a spike in missing persons reports, but other than that, they had nothing. There were no related homicides or animal attacks. Even during the full moon. Tanaka began to fear that something bad was going to happen soon. That was Thatch's sadistic nature. He didn't know when but could feel it in his gut that soon a sign would be coming.

Tanaka heard some music he liked, so he decided to walk into Rum Boogie, have a beer, and get off his feet for a bit. He pulled up a stool at the bar and ordered a cold domestic. After he took a swig, he sat in thought and slowly peeled the label off the bottle. The band launched into an Elmore James song.

Where the hell are you? he thought to himself.

Hidden by the crowd across the street, Norman watched Tanaka walk into Rum Boogie. He was enjoying the game they were playing. Not to mention how very impressed with the man's resilience and attention to detail. He smiled at the thought of that night in Flagstaff. The look on that big oaf, Mark Winston's face before he eviscerated him, was priceless. He figured it was about time he might wanna give Tanaka some kind of "bone".

Norman had shaved his beard completely off. His hair was now about shoulder length and he tied it back into a ponytail. He wore a black Adidas tracksuit which included a black zip-up jacket and matching running pants with the signature three white stripes down the sleeves and pant legs. Norman had on yellow-tinted aviator glasses and dangled a toothpick in his mouth as he greeted strangers with a smile as they walked past.

His eyes combed the crowds on Beale Street looking for just the right opportunity when he noticed a young drunk couple stagger into Handy Park on the eastern end of Beale. He sat on a park bench, watching them stumble and giggle from the night's libations.

"Evening folks," Norman said politely to the couple as they tried their hardest to navigate the sidewalk.

"Oh hello there," the woman said in a thick Minnesota accent as the man just seemed to giggle and exhale deeply.

"Are you folks okay? You both look like you could use a hand. Beale Street at night isn't the safest of places," he said with concern. The couple swayed back and forth to keep their balance looked at each other and began to laugh.

"Please, please. I do not mean to sound creepy. It's just that I've lived here all my life and I've seen a thing or two happen down here at night. I would hate to see a young couple such as yourselves have anything happen to them on their vacation," Norman said with a warm smile.

"How did you know we were tourists? It was our accent, wasn't it?" the woman asked.

Norman politely shrugged, acknowledging the woman's question.

"I sense you have an accent as well. Is it Dutch?" the woman asked.

"You know what? I get that a lot. A guy out west just recently asked me that same question. It's German actually. Vu know vat zey zay, vu can take zee German out of Germany, but vu can not take zee Germany out of zee German," he said with a chuckle.

"I thought you said you lived here all of your life?" the man questioned.

Norman just smiled and waved his hands around vivaciously. "Well, most of my life. My family fled wartime Germany in the early 1940s, getting away from all that insanity to raise a family. They were fascinated with American southern culture and food, so we ended up here. Names Norman, by the way. Norman Thatch." He held out his hand to greet him with a shake.

His face was so alluring that she couldn't resist his invitation.

"I'm sorry for my husband's rudeness, Norman. My name is Judy and this is Timothy." She greeted Norman's handshake as her husband stumbled and giggled.

"I truly apologize if I've come across as a weirdo, but I was sincere about at least making sure you two get to your car safely. You look like you've both enjoyed your evening and could use an extra set of eyes over to the parking structure," Norman explained in a soft, charming tone.

"Sure, why not? As you can see, my husband's a handful right now." She declared as she pointed to the buffoon next to her.

"How long are you folks in town for?" Norman politely inquired.

"Oh, we are here till the end of April. We wanted to stay an entire month and maybe look at real estate along with taking in all the tourist bullshit," Judy said.

Norman smiled as he helped navigate them back to the parking garage that was about five blocks north of Beale Street's hustle and bustle nightlife.

He purposely avoided any dimly lit portions of the walk and made sure they stayed out in the open to calm the woman's nerves.

"So what brings you two to Memphis?" Norman asked.

"The music. My husband here is a big Elvis Presley fan and has been for years. So we figured we would head down here and see Graceland as well as experience Beale Street," Judy said.

Norman nodded in approval as they turned a corner. "Well, those are good reasons. Have you discovered some of the food here? Some of the best BBQ ribs you can get," Norman said. "If you're ever able to come down here in May, the Memphis in May festival is to die for. It's nothing but great blues music and BBQ pork for as far as you can see for three days."

Judy's face lit up at Norman's description.

"Is that the one that's over in Tom Lee Park?" she asked.

"Yeah! That's the one. I saw BB King perform there once. John Lee Hooker too," Norman said excitedly. They started to enter the parking structure where the couple's car was parked.

"What floor are you guys on?" Norman asked as he looked at the markings on the wall, indicating which way they should go.

"Oh, we are on level C. Help me get Drunks McGee here up the stairs," Judy said as she struggled to steady her husband.

Norman carefully took Timothy by his arm and helped him climb up the steps to level C, keeping him from face-planting at any moment.

"We are this way," she said as they left the stairway and crossed into the garage. Judy and Timothy's 1972 banana yellow Monte Carlo was the only car parked on the entire level.

Norman could sense this made Judy tense up and begin to perspire.

"God, is he getting heavier?" Norman said with a chuckle.

"Ha, ha, yeah, I think he is," Judy said, lightening the mood as they crossed the wide open space of the empty garage.

"Hey. Are you guys into horror?" Norman asked playfully.

"Like what? Books and movies and stuff? Yeah, sure, I'm a big Stephen King fan and we loved the movie American Werewolf in London," she said.

Norman seemed to stick up his nose at the mention of the movie.

"Bah! That movie was just bad comedy. They got it all wrong. To suggest we just run around on all fours like a dog subservient to man is insulting," Norman blurted out.

"Excuse me? Did you just refer to yourself as we?" Judy said in perplexity as she began to nervously look around as they reached the car.

All she had to do was unlock the car door and stuff Timothy in the passenger side, then run around the back of the car to get into the driver's seat. She would just fire up the Monte Carlo and head back to their hotel room down on South Main, which was on the other side of town. Judy didn't want to show it, but she was getting increasingly nervous about their decision to let this strange man walk them back to their car. Norman could hear the woman's heartbeat increase as he could tell she was trying to figure out if this was a smart decision or not.

"Hey you guys, wanna see something really scary?" Norman asked, pulling down his yellow-lensed glasses.

Judy's face went into pure terror as she looked into his yellow eyes. Norman just smiled, showing off a mouthful of razor-like teeth.

Judy shot awake early the next morning to find themselves inside the front seat of their car. Timothy just moaned as the smell of booze made her wince. She noticed her right forearm was stiff and there was some dried blood on her light blouse.

"Timothy! What the fuck is this blood from? What the hell happened to us? Who or what was Norman?" she said as she checked for her purse and his wallet.

Timothy just farted and rolled over to his side in response to her hysterical questioning.

"God Damn it Tim!" she yelled as she rolled down the driver's side window for fresh air.

She didn't notice that anything was missing from their possessions. There wasn't even a dollar gone from Timothy's wallet and all their credit cards and IDs were in place. She noticed the keys were in the ignition, so she turned it over and started the Monte Carlo. She put the vehicle in reverse but sat and wondered what had happened the night before.

Did one of them fall right before getting into the car? Did Norman just put us in our car safely and then leave? She sat, trying to remember what had happened the night before.

Judy vaguely remembered something was wrong with Norman's face before she blacked out. She couldn't help but think of his yellow eyes and whether or not he had sharp teeth. Finally, she just shrugged it off to the fact that they were talking about horror movies before she blacked out for some reason. She drove off and exited the parking structure. Then headed back to their hotel room, where she would nurse her husband's hangover away.

As she drove, Judy tried to put together the events of her evening. Meanwhile, Norman was driving a stolen station wagon north on I-75. The Chevy wagon was white with fake wood paneling and a rear seat that faced backward. The family of three that owned the vehicle was in the first stages of rigor in the back of the car amongst their luggage. Norman playfully tapped his fingers along to the music that was blaring on the radio. He inspected his face in the rear-view mirror, wondering if he should shave again today.

"99 Luftballons. Auf ihrem Weg zum Horizont. Hielt man fuer UFOs aus dem all," Norman sang along to the radio, tapping the steering wheel in a syncopated rhythm. He grinned a bit at the thought of leaving Tanaka with some presents back in Memphis.

That should keep the man busy for a very long time, he thought.

Judy was not the first or only person Norman had bitten during his brief time in the city. He had infected five other people who in the next few days would change for the first time in the light of April's full moon. Who knows, they might even infect a few more poor souls in the process. Norman knew that Tanaka wouldn't move on until he made sure there were no more like him in Memphis. He grinned a shark-toothed smile as he drove across the river and under a sign that said: "Welcome to Ohio".

CHAPTER EIGHTEEN

For some time Tanaka didn't find any evidence of Norman even being in Memphis. Other than the postcard he was sent, there seemed to be no leads. The sign he was waiting for happened soon enough when numerous attacks started popping up all over the city that month. No reported deaths, just people stating they were attacked by a large animal. The majority of them had no memory of exactly what happened, nor did any of them show any signs of any harm. The police just ruled it out as prank calls and paranoid delusion.

Tanaka knew these were not prank calls. He also had no real way of telling how many people Thatch attacked. Seeing how no one was murdered and that no one sought medical attention. If the reports were true, he was very worried. This would mean that Norman had infected a handful of people and that was going to be very bad.

Tanaka would have to wait until the next full moon to see what kind of mess he had in store for him. He felt it was his responsibility to stick around as long as it took. He didn't want any more blood on his hands.

Just before May's full moon, Tanaka received another postcard to his hotel room. This one was from Columbus, Ohio. The back of the card just read *Hugs!!!* Tanaka knew that Norman sent this right before the full moon on purpose. Forcing him to choose to either stay in Memphis or pack up and head to Ohio in search of him.

He had to purchase a police scanner to help keep an ear on what was happening around the city during the nights of the full moon. When the attack reports started coming in, he was able to get to the crime scenes very quickly. Being a civilian now made it so his hands were tied as far as involvement. So he kept his distance but was still able to get a few glimpses of the murder victims. He needed to make sure they matched the MOs he was looking for. He also wanted to know about survivors. The last thing he wanted was for this curse to spread even more.

He double-checked his information to make sure, but it seemed to happen in the same areas as the people who had reported being attacked by an animal. Seven attacks in total. Seven murders in total. That was a lot of ground for him to cover in a short amount of time. The last thing he wanted was to have someone taken back to the police station for questioning. He didn't want someone else to make that mistake.

Luckily five of the seven murders were isolated incidents. The police found mangled bodies in different locations all over the city. Everywhere from alleyways downtown to city parks. Three of the victims were homeless people and two of the victims were tourists who happened to be in the wrong place at the wrong time.

The police had no leads, and they took nobody into custody regarding the killings. Tanaka really couldn't tell yet if they were all done by just one of Norman's offspring or if it was multiple. He knew from firsthand experience how much ground just one of these monsters was able to cover. So all he could do was wait and see.

The remaining two attacks, however, were in a place of residence. From what he could gather, Thatch bit someone and they came home and ended up killing their significant other. The Memphis PD did not know what they were looking at or what to search for, but Tanaka did.

Since the murders were so animalistic, they wrote off the spouse as a suspect. There was no way that a human being committed these murders. That was one thing the Memphis PD got correct.

Tanaka had Deputy McFerrin call in some favors and speak with the Memphis Police. She explained to them it would help out an ongoing investigation she was heading if she knew how many supposed animal attacks had been reported in April. The deputy spun some story about a Satanic Cult that had been poisoning people's minds into thinking animals attacked them. She wanted to cross-check the names of the people who called in to see if there was a relation to her case in Arizona.

McFerrin gave Tanaka four names. She was also able to run background checks, and they all came back clean. All four were residents of the city of Memphis. Two of the names matched the two residential attacks.

To Tanaka's luck, they were both located over in Midtown and not far from one another. He patiently waited for the police to leave the residence of the first name on his list. They did not take the man in for questioning. They just took the body away and left him with the mess to clean up. He had about three hours before the night of the full moon began, so he did not have any time to waste.

Tanaka went to the man's neighbors and asked a few questions. Informing them he was an investigative reporter and was looking into a string of animal attacks that an escaped zoo animal might be linked to.

"Yeah, I heard all sorts of racket coming from that house last night. I heard his wife scream, and I swore I heard a howl." One of the neighbors explained.

"Did you hear or see anything else?" Tanaka inquired.

"Nah… My wife and I hid in our basement the entire time," the man responded.

"Smart man. Thank you for your time, sir. I hope you have a good day." Tanaka said and shook the man's hand and left.

He got a similar response from other neighbors. All of them seemed to hear the same thing, but no one saw anything. Or if they did, they were keeping their mouths shut.

Who was gonna believe anyone who claimed they saw a giant werewolf strolling down the streets of Midtown? he thought to himself as he walked up to the stoop of the first name on his list.

Tanaka knocked on the door and looked around to make sure no one noticed him. He did make note that the Memphis PD did not station an officer outside this man's house. He thought that was odd but took into consideration that with what happened the night prior, they were probably overwhelmed and shorthanded.

"WHAT?!" a man screamed from inside the house.

"Hello? I was wondering if you could answer a few questions regarding the death of your wife. I know it's a horrible time, but it will only take a moment," Tanaka probed.

"You the cops? The press?" the voice yelled back. "I am done answering questions!"

"I'm neither sir. Just a guy who lost his wife in a similar situation last month and I'm trying to put the pieces together. I don't mean any harm, and anything you tell me stays with me. You have my word." Tanaka said through the door.

There was a long pause. Tanaka wore his duffle bag over his shoulder and kept his hand on the grip of the silenced pistol inside. He tried to not bring attention to the fact he was wearing latex gloves or give off any threatening body language. Which was very hard to do when talking to a stranger while holding your hand in a duffle bag.

The door cracked open a bit, and the man peeked through the crack at Tanaka. His eyes were bloodshot and his face was covered in stubble. The man looked like he hadn't slept in a month. Tanaka just gave him a warm smile.

"May I come in?" he asked. "I won't take long."

He seemed to stand there and think it over for a moment, then opened the door all the way and let Tanaka in.

"Yeah, come on in… and you better make this quick." The man said and turned around to walk into his living room.

Tanaka stepped inside the house and closed the door behind him. With the man's back still turned to him, he retrieved his pistol and shot the man in the right arm. The result was exactly what he had expected.

"It burns! Why did you shoot me?! Why does it burn?!" the man spat as he gripped at his arm.

Tanaka saw his skin start to bubble around the bullet wound. Then, without giving it a second thought, he put two bullets in the man's head and he dropped to the floor.

Now's the fun part, he thought and let out a sigh as he set the duffle bag on the ground.

Tanaka felt it was a smart move to wait till after dark to finish up. This meant he would not have time to get to the next residence before the full moon rose in the sky. He hated the fact that he wasn't able to do anything, but he couldn't be seen in broad daylight removing a man's head from his house. Especially after he had spoken to a few of the neighbors.

He left the man's headless body on the floor of the living room next to his wife's blood stains. Carefully, he searched the house for some sort of case or luggage to place the man's head into, so he was able to carry it back to his truck without giving off suspicion. Tanaka was able to locate a small carry-on suitcase with wheels.

Well, that is kinda morbid, he thought to himself, but he knew it would have to do.

Tanaka placed the head into one of his contractor bags, zipped it up inside the carry-on and went out the back door and down the alley that was behind the house. He had parked his truck a few blocks over so he would have better luck without someone writing down his Arizona plates.

Before he got to his Blazer, he heard a howl in the distance. This caused his heart to sink because he knew he was not able to get there in time before it would kill. It would have been suicide for him to try and take any of these beasts on at night when they were fully transformed. So he had to block the thought out of his mind and complete the task at hand.

The next morning, between his police scanner and the television news stations, he learned there were four more murders. Once again, no survivors were reported. Tanaka called back to Flagstaff first thing in the morning.

"Hellooo," a groggy McFerrin answered.

"Shit. I forgot the two-hour time difference," he apologized.

"It's okay, boss. What do you have for me?" she yawned.

"We had four more murders here last night. All matching the same MO." Tanaka got to the point. "That means either one got lucky and was able to knock out two in one night or we have more of these than we thought."

"Well, that's quite possible. Look at how much damage Norman was able to do," she noted.

"Yeah, but that was in Northern Arizona and wide open spaces with not a lot of people around," he then pointed out. "This is Memphis, and there are people everywhere. Call it a hunch, but I need to prepare for the latter."

"Okay. Let me see what I can find out and get back to you around noon Arizona time," she replied while still half asleep.

"I am going to pay a visit to the next name on my list. Talk to you soon." He hung up the phone and went back to watching the news.

Tanaka had to move quickly but also had to be extremely careful not to bring unwanted attention to himself while he was there. If four more monsters were running around the city, that meant there would be four more headless bodies shot with silver bullets for the police to find. He had to make sure he calculated every move. If he were arrested and taken out of the picture, God knows what would happen to the city and how many lives would be lost.

Like the day before, he parked his Blazer a few blocks away from the next name on his list. He carried his duffle bag over one shoulder and tucked his hair under a Memphis Birds baseball hat the best he could. The woman he was looking for was named Ida Rose.

From what Deputy McFerrin told him, she would be an African American woman about the age of seventy-two.

When he got to her address, he found Ida sitting on a swing on her front porch. She was wearing a flowered robe and drinking from a glass filled with iced tea.

"Afternoon, ma'am," he said with a polite smile. "Mind if I ask you some questions about what's been going on around town?"

She took a moment to study him. He could tell she knew something. This woman was not like the others he had been in contact with. She was much more lucid and together.

"I suppose so, Red. Come on up and have a seat." She gestured to Tanaka to sit.

"Thank you very much ma'am, I'll try not to take up too much of your time," he said as he climbed the steps of her stoop and took a seat.

"Stop calling me ma'am. The name's Ida… but something tells me you already know that." She said while glaring his way as she rocked back and forth. "I'd offer you some sweet tea, but I don't think you want any of this batch."

"Okay, Ida it is," Tanaka said with a smile. "I would like to offer my condolences for the loss of your husband."

"Oh, would you now?" she asked. "What would you know about that?"

Her response took Tanaka by surprise. This woman had a fire in her. He respected that. It also saddened him to know what her fate would be.

"I pretty much expected someone like you to come along eventually. You see, Red, I know what I am. So did my husband. We tried to take care of it ourselves, but as you can see, that didn't work out. Figured it was only a matter of time before someone came to end this. Honestly,

I'm glad you came." Her words struck him like a bullet.

"So you know what I am here to do?" he asked.

"Yes… Tried to do it myself last night." She paused, then took a sip of tea. "See my late husband, Arnold, used to be a doctor. He ran a private practice out of our home for years. Over that time, he collected a lot of prescription drugs of all types. Liquid morphine would be one of them."

Ida paused and took a long sip from her iced tea again and Tanaka put two and two together. He also filed that bit of information away as it gave him an idea.

"So what I did last night was mix up a giant batch of this here sweet tea and pour in enough morphine to cause a mad elephant to drop dead. Tastes horrible too. I gulped the entire pitcher down, then tried not to piss my pants. That's something you will understand when you're older," she said with a small chuckle.

"What did you do after that?" Tanaka asked, eager to hear the rest of her story.

"Whelp, I locked myself in the basement and peacefully laid down and went to sleep. Hoping that would take care of things. As you can see by the fact that we are talking to each other right now, that did not work," Ida said.

"Did you get out of the house last night?" Tanaka asked with concern.

"Don't think I did. When I came to this morning, I was still in the basement. Tore the shit out of the place, but didn't look like I had enough strength to get through the door," she said, exacerbated. "I'm tired, Red. So tired. I loved my husband very much, and he meant the world to me. Now he's gone."

"I want you to know I'm after the thing that did this to you. I believe he killed my daughter, and I watched him slaughter a lot of my friends back home. I promise you that I will put an end to this nightmare," he assured the woman.

"I'm very sorry to hear that. Mind if we just sit for a while longer? It's a nice day and I would just like a few more moments of peace," she said as she rocked in her swing and looked out towards the street.

"My grandfather would always say 'The Great Spirit is everywhere. He hears whatever is in our minds and hearts, and it is not necessary to speak to him in a loud voice'," Tanaka responded.

"I like that," she replied with a tired smile.

They both sat quietly and watched the neighborhood children play and go about their unblemished lives.

Tanaka took Deputy McFerrin's call at the time she requested. He ran down the events of the day and what had happened. It made them both sad but also relieved that it didn't lead to more bloodshed.

"I've been keeping an ear to the ground in Columbus, Ohio, by the way. It's been pretty quiet. Just an armed robbery and a couple of stolen cars were reported. Seems like Thatch must be keeping a low profile. I wonder what's going through his head," the deputy said.

"Me," Tanaka responded.

"You think so?" she inquired.

"Yes. I think for some reason this is a game. I think he is waiting for my next move and when I will arrive in Columbus," he said bluntly.

"As far as the new killings around Memphis were concerned, it looks like it was tourists and homeless people. I couldn't find anything that tracked back to any of the addresses on your list," she said.

"I'm gonna go check out these last three remaining addresses today and see if I can clean up this mess as quickly as I can," Tanaka explained.

"Keep me posted," Deputy McFerrin said as they both hung up the phone.

Since last night was the third night of May's full moon, he worried the trail might go cold soon. Tanaka was hoping to find these names before June's moon. The pressure was excruciating. The stress alone had started to eat at him.

He came up empty-handed with all three residences he visited. He could not visit all of them at the same time. So after he found that none of them were home, he picked one and watched it from his truck.

Come on... Where are you? he thought as his leg jiggled up and down with impatience.

He waited outside till morning. No one came in or out of the house. Tanaka even walked over when the sun came up and beat on the door to double-check. Nobody appeared to be home. There wasn't a sound coming from inside.

"Shit!" Tanaka spat.

He walked back across the street, got into his truck and drove back to his hotel room to try to get some sleep. He figured he would just have to wait for the news reports and see what the police scanner had to say. Exhaustion began to set in and he wondered how much longer he could keep this up.

CHAPTER NINETEEN

DETROIT

MAY, 1987

Daniel had on his best blue jeans, his favorite Thin Lizzy concert t-shirt, and a blue sports coat when he stepped out of the cab in front of Vince's Italian restaurant. He handed the cab driver a ten-dollar bill and thanked him. "Hey man, make sure you get it right this time," the cab driver told Daniel, who just blinked at him with a confused look. The cab sped off and Daniel turned to find Cassy waiting for him outside the restaurant. She was still in her waitress outfit and must have come straight from the diner. He didn't care what she had on because, to him, she was beautiful regardless.

"Hey, Cassy. You weren't waiting too long, were you?" he asked.

"No. Not at all. I just arrived when you did, actually," she responded.

They both hugged and entered the restaurant, where Daniel asked the hostess for a table for two. The hostess guided him to a table in the far corner of the restaurant and placed two menus on the table. Daniel pulled out the chair for Cassy to sit down, then walked around the table and took his seat. Daniel thanked the hostess, who just gave him a very odd look and walked back to her station at the front of the restaurant.

The atmosphere was perfect, Daniel thought. The Italian restaurant was softly lit and there were small votive candles on every table. This gave Cassy's face a wonderful, angelic glow. A man played old Italian love songs on a piano in the opposite corner, which added to the romanticism of the room.

"What's good here?" she asked Daniel.

"Oh man, everything. The pasta is made fresh, and it's all amazing," he said as he perused the menu. "Everyone from Frank Sinatra to Muhammad Ali has dined here. So this place is real old school."

"Okay, why don't you order for me," she said.

Eventually, the waiter came over to take their order and Daniel ordered the Veal Scallopini and ordered the Pasta Alla Carbonara for Cassy. The waiter cocked an eyebrow, then scribbled the orders down on his notepad, nodded, and turned around back towards the kitchen. Daniel's heart was pounding, and he took a sip from his water glass.

"So, Cassy, tell me more about yourself. How long have you worked as a waitress? Do you like the job? Do you have any aspirations in life? What's your favorite color? Mine's red. What do you do for fun? Do you like to read? I like tacos. Do you like tacos?" Daniel rattled off as his brain yelled at him to slow down, to no avail.

Cassy grinned and stared at Daniel with amusement.

"It's okay I guess. I only started doing it to help pay for night school. I was trying to go for my master's in psychotherapy, but that's been put on hold for now. I like red too. What about you Daniel? What do you do for a living?" she asked.

Daniel took another sip of his ice water and wiped the sweat from his hands on his jeans. He couldn't remember the last time he was on a date with a woman, let alone talking with a woman as pretty as Cassy.

He hoped his nervousness wasn't showing. He paused for a minute to collect himself and not to sound like a teenage boy.

"Well, I work part-time over at Puzo's Market and other than that, I enjoy reading horror novels and comic books. I have an apartment over on Grand River and Joy Road not far from the expressway. It's not much, but it's cheap and it's home for now," he said.

She lit up a cigarette and flicked the ash into the ashtray as she blew smoke upwards towards the ceiling.

"For now?" she questioned.

"Yeah, my entire life I haven't stayed in one place too long and I guess I got gypsy in my blood. Probably not the best thing to say on a first date, eh?" he said while nervously taking another sip of water.

Cassy smiled timidly and blushed a little. The waiter returned to check on Daniel and he ordered whatever beer they had on tap and gestured towards Cassy, who nodded in return. So he changed his order to two beers. The waiter cocked an eyebrow at him, then went to go fetch his drink order. When he returned, he placed the two glasses of beer in front of him and walked off. Daniel handed one of them over to Cassy, who took it from him with a smile.

"Should we cheer to something?" he asked her.

"Sure. Let's cheers to our health and hope for a long, happy life," she said in return.

"Prost!" he said, then they clinked their glasses together, took a drink, and smiled at each other. The waiter came to the table with two steaming plates of hot food and set them both down in front of Daniel.

"Oh, this one is for her," he said as he passed the Pasta Alla Carbonara over to Cassy. The waiter shook his head and shrugged, then turned and walked off to check on his other customers.

"This smells amazing and looks so elegant," Cassy said as she looked at the plate full of angel hair pasta with small bits of fatback pork.

Daniel leaned over his plate, took in a huge whiff and inhaled the wonderful smells of the thinly sliced veal, garlic and wine sauce. "Let's eat, shall we?" he said as she nodded in excitement.

There was a moment of silence as they enjoyed their food, savoring every bite. Daniel couldn't remember the last time he ate something this succulent. It was a real culinary masterpiece. The waiter returned and Daniel ordered another round of beers and asked him if he could get two shots of Four Roses bourbon. The waiter nodded and shortly returned with his drinks. Cassy and Daniel talked for another hour after finishing their meals, laughing and smiling at each other. Daniel was feeling a connection with Cassy and, at the rate this date was going, he could see himself settling down for a while here in Detroit. The thought of things progressing with her made him smile. He was completely at ease in her company and felt they had some sort of bond.

"You know what? For the life of me, I cannot remember the names of your two dogs. I know you would always tell me about them every time I came into Marge's," Daniel said.

"Oh, you mean Princess and Pepper?" she responded.

"Yeah, that's them! What kind of breed are they again?" he asked.

"Yorkshire Terrier. God, I miss them," she said as her demeanor changed from happy to sad. She then quickly excused herself, got up from the table and walked off to the ladies' room. Daniel took a minute to wonder if he had offended her in any way because her mood instantly changed at the mention of her dogs.

The waiter returned and handed Daniel his check. "I'm sorry your friend could not make it, sir. Would you like me to box up the Carbonara for you?" he asked.

"What? Oh, she's in the restroom right now and no thank you, we won't be needing a box," Daniel responded.

"Very well, sir," the waiter once again gave him an odd look and walked away.

As Daniel was counting out his money and calculating a tip, Stanley pulled out the chair across from him and sat down in the same seat that Cassy was sitting in. He just glared at Daniel with a huge smile.

"What the hell are you doing here, Stanley? Get out of here. I'm on an actual date," Daniel demanded.

Stanley just clicked his tongue and shook his head. "Man shhiiit, what am I doin' here? What the hell are you doin' here?! I told you to come see me at Mac's because we have to talk and time is of the essence. As in within the next week because after that, it will start all over again."

"Yeah, I remember what you said. How about I come by tomorrow afternoon? Until then, scram and let me enjoy the rest of my date with Cassy. She could be back at any moment and I don't want to explain why you're sitting in her seat," Daniel said.

Frustration began to build in Stanley's face.

"I could strangle you right now, Daniel. For fuck's sake man, how many times do I have to go over this with you? She's not fucking real. She's all in your head. The girl is dead. Has been for a fuckin' while now. You have been sitting by yourself the entire time. I don't know how else to say it."

Daniel's eyes squinted in disbelief. "You are making no sense whatsoever Stanley. She was just here a minute ago and left to use the bathroom. Now get the hell out of here before she comes back. I will see you tomorrow afternoon. Now take your heebie jeebie mumbo jumbo and leave. Now, please."

Stanley stood up, brushed off his wrinkled suit and sighed in further growing exasperation.

"If I could smack the shit out of you, I would, Daniel. Haven't you noticed the odd looks everyone has been giving you as you sat here all night talking to yourself? Can't you see this entire plate of cold food sitting here? The very fabric of your mind is being torn apart. Not everything is what you think it is."

"Halt die Klappe!" Daniel spat in German as he slammed his fist down hard on the table.

The entire restaurant halted as if a record skipped, and they all looked directly at Daniel, embarrassed and confused by his outburst. He tried to compose himself. He also had no idea how he knew how to speak German.

"Nice, Daniel," Stanley responded.

Daniel squinted his eyes again at him.

"Leave Stanley," Daniel said firmly.

"Hey, don't shoot the messenger man. I am seriously only here to help. Or at least try to help," he said. Then he turned and left.

Daniel fidgeted in his seat as he watched Stanley leave. After he made sure his bill and tip were correct, he tried to forget the conversation he just had as he waited for Cassy to return from the restroom. She never returned.

PART III

"THERE IS NOTHING SO ELOQUENT AS A RATTLESNAKES TAIL..."

CHAPTER TWENTY

BERLIN

NOVEMBER, 1942

The train never made it to Berlin when it was expected. It took three days for the German army to locate the colossus 100 miles west of Berlin. It went as far as it could without an operator and eventually ran out of steam and momentum. Then it came to a halt and sat motionless collecting snow. The horrors within sealed away from the outside world. Himmler gave very strict orders not to open any of the doors. He wanted it undisturbed when it arrived. Himmler was to be the first one to see what was inside.

A crew of engineers was tasked with pulling the train into the station with another steam engine. This arduous task took them almost the entire day. Growing increasingly impatient, Himmler, surrounded by Waffen-SS and his Gestapo, waited for the train to come to a halt in front of the boarding platform. Steam bellowed out from around the engine that towed in the armored juggernaut that just sat silent on the tracks before them. The Reichsführer took off his small circular glasses and wiped the condensation off them with a handkerchief before placing them back on his face. Then he ordered one of his stormtroopers to open the door to the passenger car. When the seal to the door was broken, it caused the soldier to turn his head and gag. Himmler placed his handkerchief over his nose and mouth and stepped across the threshold and into the train car.

Dried gore and bullet holes covered the walls inside the car while the bodies of the eighteen men lay strewn all over in various forms of dismemberment. The sounds of empty brass clanked under Himmler's boots as he stepped. He paused and looked around in awe at the destruction that was once an impenetrable mobile command station. Erich Kaiser lay in a fetal position in the center of the car. He was naked, unconscious, and covered in blood.

"What do we have here?" Heinrich said.

He knelt and checked for a pulse and confirmed that Erich was alive and seemed to be uninjured. The Reichsführer called for his men to carefully gather him up. Then instructed that he was to be taken to Wewelsburg immediately.

"I want him sedated as much as possible and do not speak of this to anyone," Himmler barked at the SS soldiers.

He then turned to his Gestapo. "I want you to destroy this train and burn all the remains." Then the Reichsführer pivoted and quickly left.

They took Erich to Wewelsburg Castle, located about five hours southwest of Berlin. The triangular-shaped castle had three large cylindrical towers at the end of each point of its triangle, which were connected by massive walls. Wewelsburg belonged to Heinrich Himmler, who purchased the castle back in 1933 and it served as the headquarters for his Waffen-SS. It eventually became commonly known as the Nazi Temple of Doom.

In the bowels of the castle hidden beneath the north tower is where Himmler had his secret laboratory. Here he had his scientists conduct horrible experiments on prisoners from the nearby concentration camp. Doing unspeakable things in the name of science.

Niederhagen was the smallest of the Nazi Death Camps and sat just off-site to Wewelsburg and a good portion of its prisoners were Soviet POWS, Jehovah's Witnesses, and Jews. The Commandant of the camp would instruct his guards to randomly select five or six prisoners at a time and send them up to the castle. There they would be taken down to Himmler's laboratories and experimented on to better help the fatherland. The Reichsführer fully believed he was doing good and these inhuman experiments were to help Germany gain an edge in the war against the Allies. Erich was now Himmler's top priority and pet project. He did not know what Erich was, but he believed that through him he would unlock secrets the world had never seen.

The Reichsführer kept Erich quiet from the Nazi High Command as well as the Führer himself. Himmler wanted all the secrets he was hoping to unlock for himself in hopes of someday usurping Adolf Hitler. Taking his Waffen-SS west across the Atlantic Ocean to bring the fight to the capitalist pigs, conquer the United States, and reform it under his reign and his vision.

When Erich finally came to, he had been placed in a small cell beneath the castle where he had been cleaned up and dressed in a pair of trousers and a button-down shirt made out of coarse gray-blue striped material. It was very similar to what they wore in the concentration camps. His little dingy cell had only a small cot for him to sleep on, with a pillow and a blanket. There was a toilet off to the side against the stone wall, and the room smelled like earth and mold.

Himmler was seated on the other side of his cell door just beyond the reach of the bars. He was sitting in a chair with his legs crossed in front of him, smoking a cigarette and calmly watching Erich inside his cell. Erich sat on the cot and through the dim light looked at Himmler. He was starting to wish he stayed in his Panzer tank. What now felt like a decade ago had only been just a little over a month.

"Erich Kaiser, is it?" Himmler finally broke the silence.

"That is correct," Erich replied.

His interrogator took a long drag from his cigarette and slowly blew the smoke out the side of his mouth. Erich could hear droplets of water in the distance adding to the tension of the situation.

"So, would you like to tell me what happened on my train? Please tell me what exactly happened to my men," Himmler stated calmly.

Erich rubbed the bridge of his nose with his forefinger and thumb as his eyes grew dark and filled with hopelessness. *Of all the possible people he would be answering questions to, it had to be this madman,* he thought.

"I honestly don't remember, sir. One minute General Hube was talking to me and the next I know I'm sitting in this cell talking to you," Erich said.

"I find that interesting," Himmler said as he took another drag off his cigarette, looking at the man in the cell with ice-cold eyes. "They were torn apart, Erich. You don't mind if I call you Erich, do you?" Himmler asked.

Erich nodded in agreement but did not speak.

"Fifteen of my highly trained Waffen-SS, two commanders, and one General were torn to pieces and fed on by what looked like a wild animal. Something that was able to withstand a hellstorm of gunfire and still be able to cause so much damage. I believe that something was you, Erich," Himmler coldly stated.

Erich's hands started to tremble as he looked away from the man's gaze.

"I'm sorry about your men. I honestly have no recollection of what occurred the last few nights aboard that train," Erich said.

"General Hans-Valentin Hube was a coward and an imbecile. You did me a service. The rest are replaceable. Besides, I believe you could be the key," Himmler said.

Erich continued to sit on his cot and listen.

"There are quite a few tests I would like to have my men perform on you. I believe the key to victory lies inside you. You are possibly the answer to years of research," the Reichsführer stated.

"What kind of tests?" Erich asked nervously.

Heinrich Himmler nonchalantly removed the Luger from his side holster and shot Erich in the center of his forehead.

CHAPTER TWENTY ONE

MEMPHIS

MAY, 1986

The third night of the next full moon brought four more dead bodies to the city of Memphis. This time, however, there was a survivor. A group of FedEx workers who had gotten off work late were attacked before they reached their vehicles. One man managed to get away when the beast struck them.

While in the hospital, a man named Ned Steiner babbled about some giant beast that sank its teeth into him, and then let go. While it began to tear through his coworkers, he ran. The man ran back into the building and hid in the bathroom. He remained there until the authorities found him the next morning.

Ned Steiner was delusional and was forced to take a medical leave from work for a month. After that, the man seemed not to leave his house again. He just holed up with his wife at their farmhouse.

Tanaka had watched the three remaining addresses on his list for the rest of May and into early June. Still, he found nothing. He even had flowers delivered from an anonymous person and they just wilted and died on their respected front porches. So he thought it was best to switch gears and keep an eye on this survivor named Steiner.

The Steiners lived in a farmhouse that was about twenty minutes outside the city. Tanaka welcomed the change of scenery, but it also made it hard for him to keep an eye on the previous three addresses he had been watching. This made him a little uneasy because it gave him anxiety. He didn't want to run the risk of someone else being killed or infected because he was spread too thin.

When he spotted Mr. Steiner's wife leaving the house one day, Tanaka noticed that she had a black eye. That let him know he was making the right decision. Now he had the face of someone who was surely going to die by the end of this lunar cycle. He made this couple his top priority. He could not let this woman die at the hands of her husband's curse.

Tanaka kept an eye on the house from afar. He also tailed the wife on her daily errands and tried to get a glimpse of the husband. Ned Steiner never left his house. As far as Tanaka could see, the man didn't go out for anything. He seemed to make his wife do everything that involved going outside. She went to the grocery store every afternoon and seemed to bring back a lot of food for two people to consume daily.

One day, he decided to go in for a closer look around the back of the farmhouse. Doing his best to stay out of sight, he peeked in one of the windows. The house seemed a mess. Ned stood in the kitchen barking orders at his wife. Tanaka quickly noticed he had a lot of telltale signs that he had been bitten. He experienced the ticks and twitches as well as the constant intake of food.

Tanaka kept a watchful eye over Mrs. Steiner. He felt like he was backed up against a wall. On one hand, he needed to wait and be sure and take care of Ned on the first night of his change like he had done with the others. On the other hand, if he didn't do something fast, this man was going to do something dark as Crosswell did back in Amarillo. So he figured it was time to get in closer.

Samantha Steiner pushed her cart down the aisle of the Piggly Wiggly and paused to read a box of Rice-a-Roni. She had to pull her sunglasses down to read the box better. The sunglasses covered up the black eye that her husband had recently given her. Ever since he had gotten attacked after work and returned home from the hospital, he was different. Much different.

Ned Steiner was always somewhat of an asshole to everyone around, but he was never physical with her. That was something that started after the attack. He had grown extremely aggressive and seemed to be overly paranoid about everything. She understood some level of PTSD, but this was a bit extreme. It was like he had become a different person from the man she married last year.

She was stuck with him. Samantha was originally from Belfast, Ireland and had applied for citizenship right after they got married. So if she left him now, she would have to leave everything she worked for here in Memphis and go back to Ireland. That was something that kept her up most nights. She didn't want to leave her friends or her house. It wasn't much, but it was her home. All she could do for now was wait and see if whatever he was going through passed.

He was, however, eating them out of house and home. She had read stories about PTSD affecting people differently. Binge eating was a coping mechanism some people used to get through the stress that was affecting them.

"Doorknob?" asked the Native American standing next to her in the aisle.

"Huh? I beg your pardon?" she retorted.

"Sorry, couldn't help but notice your eye. I've walked into a couple of door knobs myself," Tanaka responded.

She looked at the Navajo with intrigue as she readjusted her sunglasses. Something was calming about this man. Plus, you didn't see many Native Americans in Memphis, Tennessee.

"Oh, yeah. Door knob," she responded and turned her cart, and continued down the aisle.

"I didn't mean to offend you in any way," Tanaka tailed after her.

"You didn't. I'm a big girl and can take care of myself," she said coldly.

"I can see that," he said before he was able to stop the words from flying out of his mouth.

Samantha halted and spun around. Blasting Tanaka with a stern look. She paused briefly just before she opened her mouth to speak.

Tanaka stepped back a bit as if to give her room to explode so he wouldn't get sucked up into collateral damage.

"That came out horribly," he said as he rubbed at the back of his neck. "It's just my late wife was always the kind of person who tried to help people and at least listen to their stories in hopes of helping them."

Samantha just continued to glare at him, but was starting to warm up to the man.

"You just look like someone who could use someone to talk to right now. That's all. I don't mean to be rude or imply anything," Tanaka said. He held his hands up in hopes of keeping the peace between them. "Name's Tanaka Chee."

She held her ground and continued her glare. Samantha was good at holding things close to her chest. She was raised to believe that showing emotion was a sign of weakness. That hadn't gotten her far in life nor did it work in her favor. Ned had put her through hell over the past few weeks at home and she could use someone to talk to. Even if they talked about something or nothing at all, she could use the company.

"Also I don't know anyone with an accent like yours. Is it Irish?" Tanaka asked politely.

"I'm sorry to hear about your wife. My name's Samantha. Yes, I'm from Belfast. Do you usually try to pick up married women down at the Piggly Wiggly?" she asked in a snarky tone.

Tanaka could tell she was letting her guard down and was slowly starting to open up.

"Nope, first time," he chuckled. "Besides, it's not like that. I just figured you could use an ear to lean on. Maybe over a cup of coffee next door?"

"Hmm. So do you think I'm just gonna walk next door and meet up with a stranger for coffee and a therapy session?" Her glare was still cold as ice.

"I get it. How about this? If I see you, I see you. If I don't, I don't," Tanaka said with a shrug. "I'm ready to cash out and hopefully I'll see you over there."

"Okay, have a nice day if I don't see you," Samantha said.

A few minutes had passed, and she was checking out at the cash register. As the bag boy placed her groceries into her cart, she couldn't stop thinking about Tanaka. It wasn't a physical attraction. Even though he was very handsome for his age, it was the fact that she believed he was being sincere. She loaded her groceries into her International Scout and against her better judgment proceeded to walk across the parking lot to Anthony's Steak and Eggs to meet a complete stranger for coffee.

Judy Auerbach sat in the living room of a house that was not hers. The family photos on the walls and the memories they created there were also not hers. She had killed them all on the first night of her change, erasing these memories from existence. This was her house now. She came and went as she pleased and even introduced herself to the neighbors as a relative who was house-sitting while they were out of town. Everything was so much clearer to her now. Her late husband was a weak buffoon who would have amounted to nothing. Her life as a whole would have gone nowhere. Was she supposed to just be a housewife in Minnesota for the rest of her life? Was she to just be complacent and accept her fate? What was the point of life anyway? The beautiful man named Norman had changed all this for her, and she was grateful.

She felt so alive now. Felt in control of her life for once and in charge of her own destiny. She could feel the power running through her veins as she sat on the couch. Naked and covered in dried blood, she watched her right hand open and close. Relishing in the way she felt now. Eventually, the television caught her attention.

"The Memphis Police Department discovered two bodies related to last month's animal attacks," the anchorman said.

Is that so? Judy thought to herself, as she looked on with curiosity.

"A woman by the name of Ida Rose and a man by the name of Brad Smith were both found in their homes earlier this week. Both victims had recently lost their spouses to what the authorities believe to be a random animal attack. These attacks occurred in Midtown," the anchorman continued. "Both bodies were decapitated and the heads are yet to be found. The Police have no leads at this time."

"Well, well. What do we have here?" Judy said with a wolfish smirk.

CHAPTER TWENTY TWO

Tanaka sat in his hotel room. The heat and humidity were starting to get to him as beads of sweat dripped down his forehead. Being from northern Arizona, humidity was not something he was used to. He looked long and hard into his own eyes, hoping this was all a dream of some kind and he was going to wake up back home in Flagstaff with his daughter and her friends.

After realizing he had been sitting there for a good ten minutes, he decided to check with Deputy McFerrin. He ran down the recent events and how he had made contact with Samantha Steiner. They had a nice conversation over coffee and he got her to open up and finally let her guard down. She had invited him over to the house to meet her husband and have dinner with them. She thought it would do their relationship good if they both had someone to talk to who could relate to what they were going through. It also just so happened to be on the night of the next full moon, which was in two days.

"So, do you think the husband is going to go along with this?" she asked.

"Nope. All I need to do is get into the house and I can take it from there," Tanaka responded.

"So once inside the house, are you just gonna start slinging hot silver?" McFerrin pressed.

"No. I plan to get him to let his guard down until the change starts to take effect. She has to see this. Otherwise, I am just going to waltz in and murder her husband. I think she is smart enough and strong enough not to let anything happen to her over the next two days," Tanaka replied.

"Do you still think there's possibly a fourth we don't know about?" the deputy asked.

"Yes," Tanaka said bluntly.

"Okay, well, be careful," she said. "I've still been keeping an eye on Columbus, and it's still quiet there. Nothing has been reported. Not even on the night of the last full moon. Maybe Norman has moved on?" she asked.

"No, he's still there. He's just lying low, seeing how I handle Memphis and waiting for me," he said while he slowly flipped the channels on the television.

"Any luck with the other three addresses?" she asked.

"No, but as soon as I hang up with you, I am headed over to scope them out and see what I can find," he said.

"Alright, keep me posted. I'll check in soon." They both hung up the phone at the same time.

Tanaka clicked off the TV and grabbed his duffel bag. He double-checked the contents to make sure he had everything and slung it over his shoulder. Once he was in his truck, he headed out to check on the remaining three addresses in hopes of turning up something before the next full moon.

It wasn't until his third stop that his curiosity was sparked. He could see that lights were now on in the home as twilight began to approach.

"Bingo," he said out loud.

He circled the block a few times until he saw movement inside the house. That was his cue.

What Tanaka didn't notice was sitting across the street. Judy Auerbach casually perched on a bench leaning back with disdain. Her eyes followed Tanaka down the sidewalk and up the steps of the old house.

"I seeeeee you," she whispered with excitement.

Tanaka arrived at the Steiner's farmhouse about an hour before sunset. He hoped that this was enough time to let their guard down, but not enough time for things to escalate with her husband if he became violent before the change. He tucked his revolver in the small of his back and brushed himself off.

When Samantha came to the door, he noticed she had a fresh black eye. This was going to make taking care of her husband much easier.

"Doorknob?" he asked when she opened the door.

"Yeah," she said as she blushed.

She welcomed him into their farmhouse, which was decorated in hunter greens and dark browns. He was about to take off his boots when she told him that wasn't necessary.

Ned Steiner was sitting in his recliner in the living room watching a football game. Tanaka couldn't tell who was playing because he wasn't a sports fan in the least bit.

"Ned, this is Tanaka. Tanaka, this is my husband Ned." She said while she motioned back and forth with her hands.

Ned just turned and gave a stern look. Tanaka could tell right away this man was infected.

The man's facial features had already changed from when he first saw him through the kitchen window.

"Tanaka, eh?" he replied as he scratched at the back of his neck. "What kinda name is that? You don't look oriental."

Samantha just sighed and watched how Tanaka was going to respond to her husband's bigotry.

"It's Navajo. I'm originally from the Navajo Nation in northern Arizona," he politely replied and smiled at Samantha.

This man has the patience of a saint, she thought.

"Never been," Ned replied and turned back to watching his sports ball.

Why does lycanthropy make white people even more dickish? Tanaka thought and laughed to himself.

Samantha looked at Ned with disapproval before offering their guest something to drink.

"I have iced tea and cold beer. Would you like either of those?" she asked graciously.

"Tea would be nice," he replied.

As she showed him into the kitchen, he noticed out of the corner of his eye that Ned was still glaring at him. By now, he knew he was in for a very awkward night.

Samantha walked over to the refrigerator, pulled out a pitcher of iced tea and poured some into a glass. He noticed that there was a cast-iron skillet on the stove that had some hamburgers cooking.

"What smells so good?" he asked.

Samantha walked over to the table and set the glass of tea in front of him. She sat down and smiled at him.

"Oh, I made hamburgers, corn on the cob, and I have some sweet potatoes in the oven," she said. "Everything's ready if you would like to eat now."

"Sure, that sounds good," Tanaka said with a smile and took a sip from his glass.

He watched her retrieve a plate and start serving out food. He couldn't believe how much this woman reminded him of Barbara. Even though she was probably seven or eight years older, the resemblance and body language were uncanny.

"They got hamburgers out on the reservation, Navajo Joe?" Ned said as he stomped into the kitchen.

He pulled out his chair causing a shrill squeal. Then sat down while grinning at Tanaka. His face was gaunt and the bags under his eyes were heavy.

Can I just shoot this prick now? Tanaka thought to himself while just smiling at the man in return.

"Stop it, Ned. He is our guest and is here to help," she said exasperated while setting a plate down in front of both of them.

"Tanaka used to be a sheriff in Flagstaff, Arizona until his daughter was killed in a vicious animal attack. He's here to help us. He knows what you are going through," she said as she sat down at the dinner table.

Ned just glared at them both while he shoveled food into his face like a slob. Tanaka tried not to squirm in his chair as the man smacked his lips and chewed with his mouth open.

"She's right. I am the retired sheriff of Coconino County," he replied as he took a bite of his meal.

"Is that so? I thought she said Flagstaff, not Kokomo or whatever county you just named," he replied.

"Flagstaff is in Coconino County," Tanaka quickly responded without hesitation.

This man was getting on his last nerve. It would only be a matter of time before he was taking a hacksaw to his neck.

"Well excuse the fuck out of me, Geronimo," Ned spat, causing food to fly out of his mouth.

"Ned!" Samantha cut in.

"Was he always like this, or did he just recently turn into a prick after the incident?" Tanaka said to Samantha.

Her mouth dropped open at his comment. Ned slammed his fork down at the insult.

"Listen here, you red-skinned fuck! You're in my house eating my food! Show some respect!" Ned belted out.

Tanaka looked at the clock on the stove and saw there were another fifteen minutes or so before the moon began to rise. He also noticed that Ned was starting to perspire profusely.

"My apologies. I do not mean any disrespect," Tanaka responded while holding up both his palms.

"Let me ask you something there, Navajo Joe. Did you come here to steal my wife from me?" he said coldly. "You are practically old enough to be her father.

"Ned!" Samantha spat again.

"It's okay. I get it. No, it's nothing like that at all, Ned," Tanaka said with empathy.

"Let me ask you this, then. What are you planning to do with that pistol tucked away in your back?" Ned said while he wiped the sweat from his brow with a napkin.

"What?!" Samantha quickly questioned.

"I'm guessing it's a .357 or .44 by the looks of it. Pretty bulky to conceal under your shirt," Ned said with increasing anger.

"Well, this has gotten awkward," Tanaka said.

He reached behind, retrieved the revolver and placed it on the table in front of him. His right hand still rested on the handle.

"What the fuck, Tanaka!" Samantha said as she shot up from the table.

"Told ya," Ned said as he continued to eat.

"Please sit down, Samantha. I am not here to hurt you," Tanaka said calmly and motioned for her to sit.

"Why do you have a gun?!" She demanded as her Irish temper started to flare.

"Well… about that," Tanaka responded.

Before Tanaka could say anything else, Ned began to scream in pain. He knocked his plate on the floor, spilling food everywhere. His bones began to make an audible crack as they began to reshape into something hideous.

"NED!" Samantha screamed.

"I'm gonna tear you both apart!" he growled in response. "It hurts so bad, but I am going to make it hurt more for you both."

As her husband contorted and began to change, Tanaka slowly raised his revolver and cocked the hammer. Samantha began to back away from the table as she looked on in horror and disbelief.

"I'm sorry, Samantha, but you had to see this." Tanaka then fired a round into Ned's chest.

The velocity of the .357 pushed Ned off balance and he dropped to the floor out of sight under the table.

"Holy shit! Holy shit! What the hell just happened?!" Samantha screamed as she looked at Tanaka in shock.

"It wasn't a random animal attack. A werewolf bit your husband," he responded in a calm demeanor.

Before Samantha could respond, they heard a growl coming from underneath the table. A clawed hand reached up and grabbed the table. Still not fully transformed, the thing that was Samantha's husband heaved itself up from the floor.

His eyes were bloodshot and his mouth was misshapen, filled with sharp teeth. Tanaka noticed that his shot was not a killing blow. The bullet passed through the rib cage, missing its heart and puncturing a lung. It took small shallow breaths as it seemed to gasp for air.

"Well, that's not good," Tanaka muttered as he backed away from the table.

Before he could get another shot off. Samantha shot past him in a flash. She brought the cast-iron skillet down across the thing's face. The blow knocked it back and showered it with hot grease.

"You son of a bitch!" she cried out as she struck it again with the skillet.

Samantha swung the pan again, causing the creature to fall to the ground. The thing roared in pain as she continued to bash its skull in over and over.

"I hate you! I hate you! I hate you!" she repeated with every blow.

Tanaka had to pull her off to get her to stop. As she stood there with tears streaming down her cheeks, he felt sorry for her. Ned was probably a decent man a month ago and not the misshapen abomination lying on the floor.

"It's okay… you can put the pan down now," Tanaka said as he tried to calm her.

She refused to let go of the cast-iron skillet as she tried to regain her composure. Neither of them could take their eyes off the thing that lay on the floor in a bloody pulp.

One of its eyes was still intact and glared at them both with hatred. Its chest slowly moved up and down as it gasped for air. Gurgling and whistling as it breathed shallow breaths.

"It's going to start healing soon," Tanaka said.

"Do it," Samantha said with no remorse.

Tanaka walked over to Ned Steiner and shot him in the chest and once more in what was left of his head.

Tanaka sat Samantha down and was very empathetic to her. The woman not only just lost her husband, but she also bashed in his head with a cast-iron skillet as he turned into a werewolf. He couldn't imagine how she was going to process this.

"I am very sorry you had to go through all of this, Samantha," Tanaka apologized.

She still held onto her frying pan and stared blankly at the remains of her late husband on the floor. There were no more tears or sobs, just silence. She seemed to be in a catatonic state of denial of what had transpired in the last fifteen minutes.

Samantha finally broke the silence. "You used me, didn't you?"

Tanaka paused for a minute, trying to be careful what to say next. He didn't want this to escalate any further than it already had. So he knelt in front of her and placed his hand on her thigh.

"Yes," he said coldly.

Yadila, he thought. Smooth Tanaka.

"You used me to get to him, didn't you?" she asked without taking her eyes off Ned's body.

Tanaka waited to make sure she didn't have anything else to say before he went on. When she finally looked at him, he began to explain.

"Listen. This was going to go down one of two ways. You would have died tonight, or if you were lucky, he would have just bitten you," he said in a calm voice. "If he would have bitten you… Well, then I would have come after you, eventually. Both ways would have ended in your death. I am truly sorry you had to go through this, but you would not have believed me if I told you that your husband was a werewolf."

"That's cool," she said emotionlessly. "It's cool. I'm fine. Everything's cool. Seriously it's cool."

Tanaka was able to get her to release the cast-iron skillet and he placed it on the table. He took a napkin from the table and wiped the tears away from her cheeks. No matter how unbelievable this situation was, she could tell this man cared about her.

"So, werewolves are real, huh?" she asked while staring blankly at the body of her husband on the floor.

"Yes, they are. I've been chasing the one that I believe killed my daughter and a lot of my friends back in Flagstaff. I believe he's been around for quite some time and has killed a lot of people. I tracked him here to Memphis a few months ago. Before he got away, he managed to bite and infect a few people here in the city," Tanaka explained.

"Did he bite Ned?" she asked.

"No. I have only been able to kill three of the ones he turned so far. I believe there are three more here in Memphis. I'm afraid we will see more news reports tomorrow regarding other murders that probably occur tonight." Tanaka replied.

"Why?" she asked.

"This thing is pure ch'įįdii, and it pleases it to cause carnage and chaos. It has been playing a game of cat and mouse with me ever since last year. It is doing this for fun," he said, still holding his hand on her thigh.

"Ned used to be a good man. I mean, he was always an asshole, but he wasn't a fucking asshole," Samantha said. "He didn't change until after he was attacked."

She stood up to compose herself and began to pace the kitchen. Tanaka just gave her time to process.

"So, what do we do next?" she finally asked.

"Cut off his head and dispose of the body," Tanaka said with a shrug.

"Say what now?" she replied.

CHAPTER TWENTY THREE

Tanaka and Samantha had buried Ned's headless body about forty yards from the back of her farmhouse. Then they dug a hole for his head another forty yards from that. Her house was twenty minutes from the city limits and she had no neighbors nearby. So they didn't have to worry about anybody seeing what they were up to.

Tanaka helped clean up the kitchen and remove any evidence that led to foul play involving the disappearance of her husband. She would contact the authorities first thing in the morning and explain to them that they had a fight and he stormed off and never came home. She had the black eye to prove it.

Tanaka didn't think the police would look too much more into it with everything else that was going on. He just hoped that this wouldn't come back at some point and bite him in the ass.

"Maybe I should sleep on the couch tonight?" Tanaka said. "You have been through a lot."

"Yes, please. I don't think I am going to be able to sleep for the rest of my life knowing these things exist," she replied. "Let me get you some blankets and a pillow."

After he got situated and she went back to her bedroom, he lay there on the couch, staring up at the ceiling. It was very hard for him to clear his head. The thought that more werewolves roamed the streets of Memphis and the fact that Norman was still out there smoldered like hot coal inside him. He was starting to feel the exhaustion and fatigue of all this and began to wonder how much longer this journey would take. Sleep finally took hold and he drifted off.

The next morning, Tanaka and Samantha went over the plan before he left. She was going to wait an hour and then call the police and report her husband missing. Tanaka had to check in with Flagstaff and work on tracking down the last two names on his list. He had told her that he would be back later in the day to check on her.

After he left, Samantha made a pot of coffee for herself and turned on the news. The first thing she saw was a news story about two murders that had occurred on Mud Island back in downtown Memphis. Two people had been attacked by what the authorities believed to be the same wild animal that had been plaguing the city. The Police still seemed to be at a loss and did not have any leads at this time.

The next story was about a possible suicide. A man had walked in front of a moving train, causing his body to be tossed out in pieces over a quarter mile. She wondered if this had anything to do with what was going on. Was this one of the people Tanaka said had been bitten? Because that is what she would have done if it were the case.

Back at the hotel, Tanaka had called up Deputy McFerrin and explained to her everything that had happened the night before. He also told her that one of the names on their list had committed suicide by stepping in front of a speeding train.

"You think that would do the job?" she asked.

"Yes. There wasn't much of the body left to come back from," he pointed out.

"So that leaves two more?" she asked.

"Yes, for now," Tanaka said. "I have one more name on my list and I believe there is an unknown floating out there somewhere."

"How are you holding up?" she asked.

"Exhausted and pretty beat up, but I'm hanging in there," he replied. "This Samantha Steiner reminds me of Barbara in so many ways. I am grateful that I was able to be here."

"Just be careful. I still have nothing coming in from Ohio. It's like Norman has just up and disappeared," Deputy McFerrin said.

"He's there. Hell, he could be here for all I know. I doubt it, though. I don't think he could be that close to me without some kind of sign," he said. "I also have something I want you to do, deputy. I'm going to give you a phone number for a man out on the reservation I want you to contact. If you can't get through to him, I'll give you his address as well. His name is Mato Coldfeather. I need him to make something for me. I have a theory to try out."

After he provided her with the information on Mato, they said their goodbyes. Tanaka turned on the television and his police scanner to get up to date on last night's events before he headed out in search of the last name on his list.

Judy Auerbach stood out of sight across the street from the Knights Inn and watched Tanaka leave in his truck. She was starting to relish this new life of hers. She enjoyed the hunt as much as the killing. From time to time she wished that Norman were here so she could thank him properly for this gift he had passed down to her. After she took care of this little Indian fellow, she planned on searching for her alpha. They could be together, hunt together and most importantly, kill together.

Judy tailed Tanaka all over the city in her late husband's Monte Carlo. She followed him to a restaurant where he sat for an hour and ate breakfast. After that, he drove to Mud Island to look at the crime scene from the night before. This made her smile, knowing that someone was appreciating her work. It made her excited to know that this unsuspecting man would end up another mangled corpse for the police to find.

Tanaka picked up on the Monte Carlo behind him since he left the diner earlier that morning. He noticed a middle-aged woman was driving and she was doing her best to not be seen. He laughed at how horrible a job she was doing.

"Who do we have here?" he asked himself. In the rear-view mirror, the yellow sedan slinked in and out of the traffic behind him.

Too sloppy to be a cop or a fed. Besides, who tails someone in a bright yellow car? he thought as he turned down a street.

He came to the last address he had written down for a man named Arthur McAllister. As he drove past the house, he could tell no one had been home for some time. The mail was still piling up on the porch and the flowers he had delivered were still wilted and dead by the front door.

Deputy McFerrin's background check said that McAllister worked in road construction. His foreman had informed Tanaka that he had not been to work in about a month. The man just seemed to have disappeared. He didn't have any family or many friends in the area. His neighbors had not seen him in or out of his house over the past month. Tanaka was starting to wonder about this one.

Judy watched Tanaka slow down and park at McAllister's house. A man she had been somehow drawn to. She sensed as if the gift was trying to bring the two of them together for some reason. When she did meet Arthur McAllister, she was extremely disappointed at how much of a sniveling wimp he was. He was not willing to embrace what Norman had bestowed upon them. Once she realized he was useless and a complete waste, she removed his head from his body with her bare hands in disgust. Now here she was again, circling his house, following a man who seemed to know something about what they were.

Tanaka just kept circling the block over and over again. He wanted to send a clear signal to whoever was following him that he knew she was back there. He began to wonder if this was the fifth victim Norman had infected. After about six laps around the block, his tail got the message and eventually broke off and drove away.

After Tanaka was sure the mystery woman was gone, he returned to the Knights Inn. He picked up the phone and checked in with Deputy McFerrin.

"I picked up a tail today," he said

"Who do you think it was?" she asked.

"I don't know, but if I had to guess, I think it's our fifth werewolf," he responded. "She tailed me for the majority of the day and to McAllister's."

"She?" the deputy inquired.

"Yeah, middle-aged woman with blonde hair. She was horrible at tailing me," he chuckled.

"Any luck with Arthur McAllister?" she asked.

"No. I would like you to call the Memphis PD and ask them to do a wellness check at his residence. Tell them you are a concerned neighbor," he instructed.

"Yeah, I can do that. Ohio is still quiet and there have not been any other related reports or news stories outside of what's going on there in Memphis," she said.

Tanaka paused for a minute, wondering what Thatch was up to. He had been quiet for a long time now and that did not fit his pattern.

"I went out and saw Mato for you and he said he would get right on whatever it was you wanted him to do," she said.

"Good. I need something that can give me an edge. I don't think I can get close enough to Norman or a mature werewolf without being detected," Tanaka explained.

"Care to tell me what he's making for you?" she asked.

"No. I don't want to jinx myself and have it not work," he responded.

"Well, is it possible that you will be torn apart if it doesn't work?" she questioned.

Tanaka could tell she was concerned about him. They had both been through a lot together. She was his lifeline to a past life that Norman had destroyed. He also realized that he could not be doing this without her.

"Correct. If I die, you will know it didn't work," he laughed dryly.

Deputy McFerrin let out a heavy sigh and hung up the phone. Tanaka gathered a few things and left to check on Samantha to see how she was doing.

Samantha welcomed him with a hug and invited him in for some coffee and some dinner. They ate quietly and both seemed to enjoy each other's company without having to say a word.

"How are you doing?" Tanaka asked and finally broke the silence.

"Well, considering I was bashing my husband's head in with a cast-iron skillet less than twenty-four hours ago as he turned into a werewolf, I'd say pretty good," she replied.

Tanaka empathized with her. Part of him felt that a lot of this was his fault. If he hadn't gone after Thatch, then it might not have led him to Memphis.

"Look. I think I would feel a lot safer if you stayed here," Samantha said. "Out back above my garage is a loft. It's not much, but it has a bathroom, running water, a telephone and a TV. You are welcome to use it for the remainder of your stay here in Memphis. You can go ahead and check out of that shithole Knights Inn you have been staying at."

Tanaka thought about it for a minute. He figured this would be a smart move. His motel room had been compromised by whoever this woman in the Monte Carlo was. It was probably time for him to find a new base camp until he wrapped up here in Memphis and headed to Columbus.

Tanaka was careful to make sure he wasn't followed after he checked out of the Knights Inn. Once he brought all his belongings up into Samantha's loft, he contacted Flagstaff to inform McFerrin that he had relocated. He provided her with his address and phone number and she informed him that she would give Mato his new address and to expect a package soon.

That night was another full moon and for now, Tanaka thought it was best for him to sit tight. He and Samantha sat in her living room and watched the evening news.

A report came on about a man named Arthur McAllister who had been found in his house decapitated. The police had gone over for a wellness check. His body appeared to have been there for a few weeks. The police had no leads and didn't feel it was related to any of the other murders that had been happening around the city that summer.

"Wasn't that one of the names on your list?" Samantha asked.

"Yeah, it appears to have worked itself out," he responded.

Unbeknownst to both of them, the beast was watching them carefully through one of the windows of Samantha's farmhouse. She was much more careful this time not to be seen. She would return when it was right. Judy's beast wasn't quite ready to end her little game.

CHAPTER TWENTY FOUR

Another month had passed since Tanaka relocated above Samantha's garage. Memphis had been quiet ever since he saw the woman in the Monte Carlo tailing him. His police scanner didn't speak of anything related to the previous attacks. The local news stations had even quieted down.

Even though Tanaka welcomed the downtime, it worried him. It made him uneasy that this was the calm before the storm. Soon this beast would come for him and possibly Samantha. He was kicking himself daily for not getting the license plate off the Monte Carlo.

He stayed in contact with Flagstaff daily. Deputy McFerrin had told him that Thatch had also remained quiet. This worried him even more. Just because it wasn't being caught by the police or reported by the news didn't mean it wasn't happening. He was afraid Norman had just become more careful to cover his tracks. He felt that as soon as he moved on from Memphis, he would start right back up again.

Tanaka sat at a desk in Samantha's loft and studied a map of the United States. Trying to see if he could see a pattern in where Thatch had been and possibly where he was going.

There was a knock on the door.

"Looks like you have a package here," Samantha said with a smile.

Tanaka took the package from her, walked over to the desk and opened it with his lock blade. Samantha peered over his shoulder in curiosity.

"I had a theory about using wolfsbane. Seems to be a very common legend among different cultures that lycanthropes don't like it," Tanaka said while he pulled out the contents of the package. "So I had an old childhood friend back home make something for me to try out my theory."

He retrieved two leather cuff bracelets and set them on the desk. They were well-tanned and dark. They had a second layer with what looked like hemp twine attached to them. Just a few simple strands of hemp braided together like a rope. Next, he removed a large eye dropper bottle that contained a tincture made of natural oils and wolfsbane.

The tincture was to be used generously to soak the braided twine. The leather was used as a barrier for his skin. This way, his skin wouldn't absorb any of the wolfsbane. Wolfsbane was poisonous and could make a person very ill or lead to respiratory problems.

In theory, once absorbed, the brackets should be able to mask his scent from the Yee Naaldlooshii. Allowing him to go undetected. They hoped that each application would last for at least a week before needing more applied.

"You think it will work?" Samantha asked.

"The elders have been correct on just about everything," he responded.

He planned to start up a search for the woman in the yellow Monte Carlo. They had two more nights before the next full moon and he wanted to try to get a head start on finding her.

It didn't take long for Tanaka to find the yellow Monte Carlo. It was parked at a residence in Midtown. He had McFerrin run the plate. It had belonged to Timothy Auerbach. He was one of the tourists who was found dead a couple of months ago. That would have been the first night of murders committed by Norman's creations.

Timothy had a wife by the name of Judy, and her family had reported her missing after the death of her husband. From the description McFerrin gave him, this was the woman who was tailing him. The home where the Auerbach's car was parked was registered to a family that Tanaka knew was probably dead and the authorities just had not found them yet.

Tanaka rented a car this time and parked it down the street from the house. He wore the wolfsbane bracelets that Mato made for him in hopes of remaining undetected. Judy would make a move sooner or later and he would be there waiting. He left Samantha with some silver slugs for Ned's old 12-gauge shotgun, just in case something happened while he was gone.

With a copy of George Carlin's latest book in her hand, Samantha stood in her kitchen waiting for the teakettle to whistle. She looked up at the wallpaper and winced. Samantha despised the hunter-green paper, which also contained small prints of numerous types of waterfowl. The decor was something Ned had insisted on.

"God, I hate this house," she said as she turned off the burner.

Once the squealing kettle began to calm down, Samantha poured the hot water into her brown coffee mug. She dunked her tea bag up and down in the hot water. She was comfortable in her sweats and reading to avoid thinking about the full moon and Tanaka's absence. She just wished what he had to do was over soon.

A startling crashing noise caught her attention outside causing her new motion lights to turn on. She peered through the vertical blinds on her glass door wall. Then she scanned the back patio and backyard for anything out of the ordinary. The lights were off in the apartment above the garage, so she knew that Tanaka was still gone. Something had knocked over the garbage. Samantha just figured it was a couple of raccoons on the prowl.

"Tanaka will pick that up in the morning," she said to herself.

Then she heard a soft knock at the front door which caused her heart to skip as she looked at the clock on the kitchen wall. It read 10:45 pm.

Maybe it was Tanaka, and he forgot something, she thought hopefully.

Setting her mug and paperback book down on the kitchen counter, she cautiously entered the living room. Her eyes were locked on her front door and she stood very still and tried to listen.

"Who the hell would stop by at this hour, if it's not Tanaka?" she muttered.

After the longest thirty seconds of her life passed by, her heart raced. The doorknob started to turn. It moved back and forth ever so slowly.

"Shit!" she whispered and hurried back into the kitchen and grabbed the phone receiver from the wall.

The phone was dead. She pressed down the switch hook a few times to see if she got a dial tone and it was still dead.

"Fuck!" she said. "Okay… Samantha, you can do this. It's probably nothing, but just to be safe, let's go grab the shotgun from the bedroom."

Tanaka had left a box of silver slugs for her husband's old Winchester double barrel. However, she hadn't loaded it yet. This made her begin to panic. Whoever or whatever was at the door began to pound rapidly with heavy booms. Samantha didn't hesitate and she darted for the hallway.

The giant beast smashed its way through the front door, causing wood splinters to fly throughout the room. She cleared the hallway and made it down to her bedroom. A flash of charcoal fur flashed in her peripheral vision.

With a burst of speed, the beast covered the distance to the hallway, knocking over lamps and chairs out of its way. Samantha dove into her bedroom and slammed the door and locked it triumphantly. Not sure exactly what she was going to do next but she took the small victory.

Trying to catch her breath, she opened the nightstand drawer and pulled out the box of silver slugs. She could hear the beast as it sniffed at the crack at the bottom of the door like a dog. Samantha cracked open the breach on the old Winchester Model 21 and dropped two shells in. Quickly, she slammed the shotgun closed as she heard the beast growl outside the door. Making sure the safety was off, she aimed from the hip and blasted a hole through the bedroom door. The slug hit just above the halfway point, causing a pumpkin-sized hole that sent splinters everywhere.

She hit whatever it was on the other side because it yelped out in pain. Samantha didn't waste any time and fired another round through the lower half, hoping to put another slug into the beast as it lay on the ground. She cracked open the shotgun over her knee, ejected the two spent shells, dropped in two more and slammed it closed. She grabbed four extra slugs and put them in the pockets of her sweatpants as she carefully listened for any rustling on the other side. There wasn't a sound.

Samantha slowly opened what was left of the bedroom door and peeked around the frame. The hallway was empty and there was wet blood splattered on the wall in front of her.

"Well, you definitely hit the fucker, that's for sure," she quietly told herself as she inched her way down the hallway.

Tucking the butt of the shotgun to her right shoulder, she carefully waved it side to side, scanning for any movement. As soon as she made it to the end of the hallway and checked the living room to her right, the power went out.

"Of course. Of course it cut the power," she mumbled, still waving her shotgun in all directions.

Instinctively, she flipped the light switch on the wall as she entered the kitchen. Nothing happened.

"Shit! Damn it," she cursed to herself.

Her heart raced like a runaway train as she slowly crossed the kitchen floor toward the dining room table. She walked over to the door wall and reached for the chain that opened the vertical blinds. With a quick flick, the blinds opened about halfway. Pointing the shotgun towards the glass, she saw that there was nothing there.

She turned around to head back towards the kitchen when she heard a clicking noise at the glass. That was her first glimpse of what a fully transformed werewolf looked like.

On the other side of the glass stood the seven-foot beast. It was tapping on the glass with the claw of its forefinger as its yellow eyes pierced right through her. She was too terrified to scream.

The beast stood on two legs and she could see that its left shoulder hung limp. There was wet, congealed blood spattered all around the wound.

"Bet that hurt, didn't it?" she said.

It growled back at her.

She raised the shotgun and fired off one of the barrels. The door wall exploded in a shower of cascading shards. Between the noise of the blast and the explosion of glass, she turned her head and closed her eyes. This caused her to jerk and her aim to be off.

When she opened them, she noticed nothing was there. Just a large hole in her kitchen letting in the night air. She quickly opened the breach and pulled out the spent shell. Then she reached into her pocket retrieved another slug and dropped it in the empty tube. Slamming the old Winchester closed, she carefully looked around the kitchen.

With both the sliding glass and the front door destroyed, there was a heavy breeze coming through the house now. Trying to navigate her way across the disheveled living room, she kept her eyes on the front door and bay window. She slowly backed her way toward the corner of the room, keeping a watchful eye for anything that moved. There was now a musky odor in the house. Just before she inched to the corner, she felt its warm breath on the back of her neck.

Her lower lip began to quiver as the beast began to growl. It happened so quickly that Samantha didn't feel any pain.

When Tanaka returned home the next morning, Samantha's house was swarming with police cars and paramedics. He knew this was bad. Very bad. His hands were shaking and his palms began to sweat. He had to take a few minutes to compose himself before he approached the house. Finally, he parked his truck down the street. He knew the Memphis PD would have a lot of questions for him. Not to mention if they checked his truck, what they would find.

Tanaka wasn't hugely worried about being caught with firearms since he could prove he was a retired sheriff. He was worried about what they would say when they found the silver bullets; bullets that could be traced back to a few headless corpses that were recently found over the past few months. He couldn't just drive off either. He owed Samantha more than that.

As he remained seated in his truck, he ran down a few scenarios in his head. All of which led back to them searching the house and lifting his prints off everything. He would have to return soon and make a statement with the police. He had to think of something quick because the longer he waited to return to his loft, the more suspicious it would look. Tanaka quickly spun the truck around and sped off. He would find a place to stash the weapons and ammo. Then he would return home to Samantha's. This was going to be tricky because it was Memphis, which meant there were a lot of great places to stash things. The problem lay in whether it will be there when you return.

Tanaka had to come up with an alibi for where he was last night. Before returning to Samantha's house, he stopped by a drive-in theater that was nearby. He searched through the garbage and found a ticket stub from the double feature the night before and placed it in his jeans pocket.

When he arrived, he was greeted right away by the Memphis PD. He was quickly questioned by the homicide detectives working the crime scene.

"Morning officers. Can someone tell me what's going on here? Where is Samantha?" he asked the two detectives before they could question him.

"By Samantha, you mean Samantha Steiner?" the first detective asked. "I'm sorry to inform you that her body was found in her living room."

"A woman called in this morning that she heard noises at this house last night and that the police should get there right away," the second detective said.

The other officer looked at his partner like he was about to smack him upside the head for saying that. The second officer just shrugged back in response. Tanaka frowned at that information.

What woman? There isn't a neighbor around for miles, he thought to himself.

"What is your relation to Mrs. Steiner? Did you know her husband, Ned?" the second detective asked.

Tanaka paused for a few seconds to think and keep his cool. He knew right away this was the work of Judy Auerbach. She had to be the one who placed the call to the police.

"I've been renting the loft above her garage for the past couple of months. We met in town shortly after her husband ran off. We've become decent friends," he said. "So she let me rent her loft after Ned bailed."

"Is there someplace else you could stay tonight, mister.?" the first detective asked.

"I'm sorry. My name is Tanaka Chee and I'm the retired sheriff of Coconino County, Arizona."

The two detectives were both taken aback by his name and former place of employment.

"Are you the sheriff who survived that terrorist attack in Flagstaff last summer?" the first detective asked.

Tanaka didn't know how to answer that. He hadn't heard that it was labeled as a terrorist attack. This explains why they didn't see the similarities in murder cases. Tanaka just nodded at them.

"Holy shit!" the second detective said.

"Sir, it's an honor to meet you. If there's anything you need while you're in town, just let us know. Also, would you mind coming down to the station tomorrow to answer a few questions? I know there's a lot of people there that would love to meet you," the first detective said.

"Yeah, sure, that's fine. I can just get a room over at the Knights Inn. As long as I can get my stuff out of my loft as soon as you're done," Tanaka said.

Both detectives looked at each other and shrugged.

"Sure. I don't see why that would be a problem. We will let you know tomorrow when you come down when you can get your things," the first detective said.

Tanaka saw what they were doing, retired sheriff or not. He was their top suspect at the moment. He didn't want to make any waves or ruffle any feathers, so he agreed to come into the Department, answer a few questions and do a formal statement.

"One last thing before I go. Is there anything you can tell me about what happened here last night? I mean, between us cops?" Tanaka asked politely.

"Yeah, it looks like an animal attack. Similar to the others that happened over the last couple of months," the second detective said.

The first detective once again looked at his partner as if he was going to smack him.

"What?" he replied. "What's he gonna do with that information?"

"Thanks for your time, gentlemen. I will see you in the morning," Tanaka shook their hands and left.

That night Tanaka sat in his truck outside the house where Judy Auerbach parked her husband's Monte Carlo. He couldn't sleep after what had happened. The guilt was beginning to get to him. If his daughter had not been out in the woods, then this entire game would not be personal. Tanaka was hellbent on getting revenge on, not only Judy Auerbach, but Norman Thatch.

CHAPTER TWENTY FIVE

WEWELSBURG CASTLE

DECEMBER, 1942

Erich woke up and found himself fastened upright to a surgical table. His head was pounding with a splitting headache. The last thing he remembered was talking to Himmler, who then pulled out his pistol and shot him. He tried to look around the room, but he realized his head was strapped to the table along with his wrists and feet. He could tell this was a sort of examination room somewhere underneath the castle. The smell was a mixture of earthy mildew and chemicals such as formaldehyde and alcohol. A large bright medical light was positioned above his head. The intensity of the light was burning his eyes making it extremely hard for him to focus.

"He's awake, doctor," a voice said from across the lab.

Erich tried to squint to see who it was. He could only make out the silhouette of a man in a white lab coat.

"Perfect. Please do retrieve the Reichsführer at once," another voice said.

It wasn't long before Himmler entered the room as the two scientists saluted. "Heil Hitler!"

It felt like the Angel of Death himself had entered the room as he watched Himmler slowly stroll over to him and examine his face. The bullet wound had completely healed. As his body regenerated, it pushed the 9mm slug out of his forehead, then closed itself behind it.

"Fascinating," Himmler said curiously, looking over Erich's forehead.

"You… you shot me," Erich said.

"Yes. I had an itch that needed to be scratched. Mr. Kaiser, do you realize that in just under nine hours, you have completely healed from a fatal gunshot wound to the brain? So again I ask, how do you feel?"

"You shot me," Erich repeated.

"Yes, yes, we already know that. Please tell me, how do you feel?" Himmler asked matter-of-factly.

"I feel fine, other than a pounding headache. Oh, and I'm famished. I could use some food," he said.

The Reichsführer clapped his hands together in anticipation. "This is most excellent. Bring us the Zyklon B."

"What's Zyklon B?" Erich asked.

The man in the white lab coat wheeled over a large air tank contraption that had tubes coming out of it connected to what looked like an oxygen mask.

"Oh, it's a nasty little cocktail I had perfected. More or less cyanide gas and a few other things," Himmler said while waving his hand around like it was no big deal.

"Cyanide gas!" Erich yelled as one of the scientists strapped the mask over Erich's face and the other began to slowly turn the valve on the canister.

"I'm afraid this is going to be excruciatingly painful," Himmler said as he watched intently.

Erich tried to hold his breath as long as he could, but one of the men in lab coats punched him in the stomach, causing him to reflexively gasp for air. Shortly after the gas entered his lungs, he began to scream. Then he started to convulse uncontrollably. The straps on the examination table held him in place as the mask muffled his screams. It only took a few minutes for him to go into cardiac arrest. Shortly after that, he fell limp.

"Please come get me if and when he wakes up," Himmler said. Both scientists saluted him as he left the room.

The beast inside Erich was aware of everything being done to him. It was not yet strong enough to make the change at will or when Erich was under threat or duress. For now, it could only wait until the night of the full moon. In the meantime, its hatred for man festered deep inside its chest. It would heal Erich for its own self-preservation as it waited.

As long as they did not learn how to use silver or remove his head from his body, they would not do any real harm to Erich. The curse could regenerate a person's limbs but not a head if it was cut from the body. Silver hurt the beast and could end the curse as long as it was a fatal blow and was not removed. Something in the silver canceled out the regenerating effects of the curse.

Some cultures believed that silver was symbolic of the moon and sometimes referred to as "moon-metal" and since the werewolf was created by the light of the moon, the moon-metal was able to help destroy it. The beast knew Erich was special. The average life expectancy of a lycanthrope was not very long, for the cursed usually went insane after a month or two. Due to the mental state of the host, it made a young lycanthrope reckless and wild, which usually led to them being hunted down and destroyed. The ones that stayed sane usually committed suicide due to the guilt they would constantly struggle with.

Erich was too strong-willed and his drive to live was what made him perfect for Nikolia's gift. All but a small handful of lycanthropes still existed across the globe. They once roamed the countryside in packs, killing and taking what they wanted. During the Middle Ages, they were hunted down and destroyed, sending the stronger, smarter ones into hiding. Over the centuries, they learned that secrecy was their greatest asset and they eventually became just stories and folklore of days gone by. Soon Erich's captors would learn exactly what he was becoming.

Since Erich's body had already used up most of its energy to heal the gunshot to his brain, it took longer for his body to regenerate from the Zyklon B and the cellular damage it had caused. After about two hours, his heart began to beat again. Still unconscious, Himmler ordered his men to take Erich back to his cell where he remained under close watch for another forty-eight hours while still in a comatose state as his body slowly regenerated.

When Erich awoke on his cot, he was emaciated from the regeneration process. For his body to regenerate, it burned a lot of calories, which took a toll on his physical appearance and physique. He sat up and swung his legs over the edge of the cot to find himself back inside the small, musty cell. Himmler sat in his small wooden chair just outside the bars in his usual position with his legs crossed in front of him, smoking a cigarette. The Reichsführer marveled at the fact that Erich not only survived a headshot from his pistol but also had a heavy dosage of Zyklon B. He also took note of how gaunt Erich's face was now. He appeared to be just skin and bone as his clothes seemed to no longer fit and loosely hang off him like a prisoner of war.

"How are you feeling, Erich?" Himmler asked him with great curiosity. Erich rubbed his eyes with the heels of his palms and sat up straight.

"I'm starving and exhausted. I don't feel like I can even stand at the moment," he said.

Himmler took a drag off his cigarette. "I will have my cooks prepare a hearty meal for you so you can regain your strength. Then we will talk more because I have a lot of questions to ask you about your current condition." Then Himmler stood up, dropped his cigarette on the stone floor, crushed it out with the toe of his boot and turned and walked away. With his elbows on his knees, Erich buried his face in his hands and sobbed at the memories of everything he had been through over the last month and how there was no end in sight to this nightmare.

CHAPTER TWENTY SIX

MEMPHIS

APRIL, 1986

Tanaka went down to the police station first thing the next morning. His story was that he was at the drive-in the night before. He saw the double feature and fell asleep. He woke up in his truck that morning and had the ticket stub to prove it. They believed his statement and then introduced him to half the Memphis PD. The way the other officers were saluting him, it was like Tanaka was some war hero veteran. All the attention was hard, but he managed to get through it and be polite.

He was able to get into Samantha's loft that night and was relieved to find it untouched. The detectives had told him they only poked around to see if there was anything out of the ordinary. They didn't find any of his ammunition or his Remington 870. Tanaka packed up his things and went back to the Knights Inn. He couldn't bear staying at Samantha's place anymore. He had a ball of guilt festering in the pit of his stomach.

It took him another three weeks before he spotted Judy jogging around the river walk. The bracelets that Mato made were working. He was able to stay close, but not too close. It impressed him how well she was blending in with society. Not a soul around her had any idea of the monster that walked right past them.

She did not pick up on Tanaka's scent or his position as he carefully followed her down the banks of the Mississippi River. He noticed that she was wearing her left arm in a sling. This suggested to him that Samantha at least got a shot off. That made him smile. It also made him wonder if the slug was still lodged in her shoulder or if non-lethal blows with silver just took longer to heal. He enjoyed the thought of a piece of silver burning away at her from inside her shoulder.

He followed her back to a house that overlooked the river. It was a huge expensive home, easily 5000 square feet, with huge windows facing Mud Island. He watched her use the front door like she owned the place.

I'll see you soon... Âłeechaa'itsa'ii biyaazh, he thought in his native language as he walked back towards downtown.

Tanaka waited for her to leave that night. Then he carefully broke into the home. Upon gaining entrance, he could smell the odor of death wafting up at him. The Memphis heat and humidity had done its job. He had to cover his mouth and nose with his handkerchief to keep from gagging.

He quickly cleared the home to check for survivors or anything that would cause a threat. During his sweep, he came to the master bath which was located upstairs. He was horrified at what he found. This was the source of the stench.

In the master bath lay the bodies of the family that owned the house. Blood seemed to cover every inch of the large, luxurious bathroom. The massive mirror had smiley faces drawn all over in the family's fluids. What was left of two adults and three children were scattered all over the room. Parts of them were in the sink and the bathtub. Each piece of flesh had been gnawed on. As if it was placed there to munch on when

Judy got up to pee at night. Tanaka had to turn away and walk back downstairs to try and block the sight out of his mind.

Tanaka sat in the dark house and waited for Judy to return. As he sat, he spent the time remembering all those that he had lost as a result of Norman Thatch. His daughter Barbara was gone, his best friend Mark Winston was dead and now Samantha had been lost. Not to mention all the innocent lives that had been taken as a result of this Yee Naaldlooshii. This hatred that grew inside him now started to become all-consuming.

It had only been a couple of hours before he heard the front door start to unlock. He backed up just out of sight to the side of the kitchen and waited for her to enter. Trying not to make a sound and control his breathing so she wouldn't pick up on his presence.

Judy glided over the kitchen floor and went straight for the refrigerator. She opened the door and pulled out a bottle of water. Tanaka quietly stepped out behind her. Just as her head cocked to the sound of something, he fired his Glock. He sent a silver bullet into the small of her back. The silver 9mm round lodged itself in her spine, instantly paralyzing her and dropping her to the ground.

"Evening Judy," Tanaka said as he walked over to her as she thrashed about on the floor.

She paused when she realized who it was.

"You!" she spat as blood pooled from her lips.

"Surprised?" he asked sarcastically as he pulled a chair over to sit near her.

"How did you?" she asked as she writhed in pain.

"Wolfsbane," Tanaka answered and shot her again in the right shoulder.

She growled. He could see that she was starting to transform. It appeared the silver was not allowing her to make the change complete. Like Samantha's husband Ned, she lay there looking up at him as some kind of mutant half-creature. Her eyes flickered yellow and her teeth began to sprout as she tried to snap at the air. He found this interesting because it was not a full moon.

"I am going to kill you!" she said in a deep growl.

"There is nothing as eloquent as a Rattlesnake's tail," he responded to the helpless thing that flopped around on the floor in front of him.

Without giving it another thought, he shot her two times in the forehead.

Tanaka searched the garage for anything that would be useful. Saws or shovels would have come in handy. He had to dispose of the body and he didn't want to have to leave the house and come back and risk being seen by the neighbors. His eyes stopped on a can of gasoline that sat in the corner. After he checked to make sure it had gas in it, he paused to think it over for a minute.

"Fuck it," he said.

He found a pack of matches by some decorative candles on the kitchen table and walked over to Judy's body. Turning the can of gasoline upside down, he poured the entire contents all over her remains. It took a few tries, but eventually a match set the fuel on fire. Before leaving out the back door, he watched her body burn on the kitchen floor. He still felt guilty for all the lives lost, but he was going to make it right.

The next day, Tanaka checked in with Deputy McFerrin. They both agreed that as hard as it would be for him, he needed to stay till the next full moon had passed to make sure that all of Norman's creations had been destroyed. After that, he would make his way up to Columbus, Ohio and they would go from there.

Just as they both predicted, it seemed that once Memphis was in the clear, attacks started to happen in Columbus. It was like Thatch knew that Tanaka had succeeded. On his last day in Memphis, Deputy McFerrin called.

"Looks like Norman is at it again, boss," she said with a heavy sigh.

"What do you have for me?" he asked.

"A middle-aged couple had been brutally attacked a few nights ago in Goodale Park. They had been walking their dog when something attacked the man's wife," she said.

"Sounds like Norman," Tanaka responded.

"Wait, it gets better. The man told authorities that it was some kind of beast with demonic yellow eyes and stood about eight feet tall with the head of a wolf and the body of a large man. After it brutally attacked his wife, he said he blacked out. Then after that, he awoke the next morning to his wife, torn to pieces on the sidewalk next to him," the deputy said.

"That's not good," he replied.

"Still gets better. The man was placed under night watch once he was admitted to the hospital and before the Columbus Police Department could ask any more questions, the man escaped and never seemed to return home," she said. Then there was a long pause.

"Ch'iidii," Tanaka said.

"Yuuuuup," she replied.

After the phone call ended, Tanaka packed up his things and got ready to leave his motel room. Before he closed the door, he just stood there. All the thoughts of what had happened over the past couple of months went through his head. He was now a different person than when all this had begun. This seemed to bother him. Then, with one heavy sigh, he turned off the light and closed the door.

CHAPTER TWENTY SEVEN

COLUMBUS

OCTOBER, 1986

Robert Klein stepped out of his apartment in Columbus, Ohio, and made his way to his Toyota Corolla. He carried a thermos of coffee with him like he did every day. He started up his car and made his way to work.

Robert was one of the medical examiners for the Franklin County Coroner's office. His office handled the greater Columbus Metropolitan area. He had worked there for the past ten years and happened to like his job.

"Hey, Steve," he greeted the security guard as he walked into the building.

"Morning, Rob," the guard replied.

He continued down the hallway to the Coroner's office. Once inside he put on his white medical coat and poured himself a cup of coffee from his Thermos.

"Hey, Robert," another medical examiner said as he walked into the room.

He handed Robert a magazine board that had a John Doe listed on it.

"Thanks, Mike," he replied.

"John Doe came in last night. Looks like a clear-cut suicide. Gunshot to the head," Mike said.

Robert looked at the paperwork on the clipboard as he sipped his hot coffee. Nothing looked out of the ordinary. Man in his mid-40s, with no ID and no next of kin.

"Poor guy," Robert said. "Report here says he was found by a dumpster behind the Pizza Hut."

"Yeah, pretty sad," Mike replied.

"Hey, you start up those racquetball lessons with the Mrs.?" Robert asked.

Mike was putting his lab coat on and adjusting his clip-on tie.

"Yeah, actually. They are going great. You should come and play with us sometime," he replied.

"Yeah I will," Robert said. "Whelp, this John Doe isn't gonna autopsy himself."

"We gonna do lunch at Chi Chi's?" Mike asked.

"Oh yeah. See ya then, bud," Robert said as he left the office and headed to his examination room.

The naked body of a man of average height and build lay on the steel examination table in front of Robert. The man had short-cropped hair with gray streaks throughout. His face was covered with salt and pepper stubble and there was a bullet hole in his right temple.

Robert pulled a cassette tape out of his desk drawer and placed it in the tape recorder he used to document his autopsies. He turned back around to begin his work.

"Middle-aged John Doe. The cause of death appears to be a self-in-flicted gunshot to the head. Looks small caliber with no exit wound," he said into the small microphone.

Robert retrieved his microfracture awl and began to extract the bullet from the cadaver. To his surprise, he was able to remove what looked like the entire bullet.

"Removed an intact slug from John Doe's right temple. It appears to be a 9mm slug…" Robert paused as he looked at the bullet closely. "It also appears to be … silver?"

He placed the bullet into an evidence bag and wrote the proper information on the label. Then he reached for his bone saw. As the blade began to whir, Robert bent over to open the chest of the cadaver.

Robert's face went pale as the man's hand shot out and grabbed him by the throat. The bone saw ceased and fell to the floor.

"Please stop," Norman said politely as he looked up at the medical examiner with yellow eyes.

Columbus was a college town and this worried Tanaka. This meant it was a melting pot of inexperienced children. Quickly he began getting a lay of the land. He spent a lot of time walking around the historical district, parks and campus. The city was known for having one of the best zoos in America. So he also spent a lot of time there. He had also rented a room at the German Village Inn.

Tanaka purposely did not wear any wolfsbane. He wanted to make his presence known. He knew Norman was here and that he would find him soon enough.

With his hands in his pockets, he walked through Goodale Park. His cowboy hat was pulled down over his eyes and his black braids hung over his shoulders onto a red plaid shirt. This park was where the couple had been recently attacked.

Tanaka was trying to look for any clues or signs that it was, in fact, Norman. There had still been no signs of the man who survived and was possibly bitten. He was still missing.

How long are you going to drag this out, Norman? he thought to himself as he stopped to watch a few children feed some ducks.

They made him think of the little girl who was found with her parents back at the Oklahoma Zoo. It infuriated him that Thatch seemed to have no qualms about who he killed. He didn't seem to care.

I guess evil doesn't bother with honor, he thought while he shook his head.

Tanaka stopped at a hot dog vendor and ordered a Chicago-style dog.

"You hear about what happened yesterday?" the vendor said as he slathered mustard on Tanaka's order.

"No. What happened?" he asked.

"One of the medical examiners had his throat torn out yesterday down at the coroner's office," the vendor said as he handed him his hot dog.

"Are you kidding me?" Tanaka replied as he paid the man.

"Yeah… crazy, huh? He was examining a John Doe and things didn't work out so well," the man said, then closed his cash register.

Tanaka just listened to the man as he chewed on a mouthful of food.

"Yeah and the John Doe is now missing," he said.

Tanaka tried to act surprised, but by now nothing shocked him anymore. He complimented the man on his Chicago dog and continued his walk.

That had to be Thatch, he thought while finishing his lunch.

It was very unlikely that that was the missing man from the previous attack here in the park. Only Norman would have the self-assurance to kill someone in daylight and in public. But why was he there?

This perplexed Tanaka. This also complicated things. Now the authorities would be on the lookout for this John Doe. Tanaka had to check in with Deputy McFerrin as soon as possible. So he quickly made his way back to his motel room.

"What were you doing in the morgue, Norman?" he asked himself.

Norman had already picked up on Tanaka's scent soon after he left the morgue. This excited him to know that the sheriff had finally arrived. He fidgeted with his wardrobe. The Medical examiner's clothes didn't exactly fit him well, for the man was too short.

I look like a fool, he thought as he looked at himself in the reflection of a public bathroom in Goodale Park.

A young man walked into the bathroom and gave him a very odd look. Norman just smiled back at him as he watched the man walk over to the urinal.

"Say, buddy… you look like you have about a 32-inch waist. What's your inseam?" he asked with a malicious grin.

Back at the German Village Inn, Tanaka spoke with Deputy McFerrin while reviewing a stack of handwritten notes he had been keeping.

"Okay, so what I was able to find out is that a John Doe came into the Medical Examiner's office with a self-inflicted gunshot wound to the head," Deputy McFerrin said.

"Self-inflicted gunshot?" Tanaka asked.

"Yup. They think someone must have snuck in and killed the medical examiner, took his clothes and stole the body of the John Doe," she continued.

"Wait a minute? Who kills someone, steals their clothes and then steals a body?" Tanaka asked.

"Right? The police think the clothes were put on the body before it was taken," she said. "Between you, me, and the paint on the walls, I'd say that the John Doe was Norman."

"Were you able to get a description of John Doe?" he asked while jotting this all down in his notes.

"Nope. Just that he was a middle-aged man and prints that didn't match anything in the database," she replied.

"It's him for sure," he said.

What was Norman up to? he thought as that pit in his stomach rolled over again.

"You able to get the ballistics information?" he asked.

"Yup… take a guess," she said.

"Silver?" he quickly responded.

"Yuuup," she said.

"That's interesting," Tanaka said with intrigue.

"Why would Norman shoot himself?" she asked.

"He wouldn't," Tanaka said bluntly.

Norman stood on the sidewalk in front of Tanaka's motel room. He wore another man's clothes that were still a few sizes too small. He sniffed at the air and smiled.

"Hello, sheriff," he said while quietly clapping his hands.

Deep down, Tanaka had a feeling and from then on out, he would not go without his Wolfsbane. He knew Thatch was here and had a feeling that Norman already knew that.

He had started to form a plan: If he could somehow incapacitate Norman and take him to a safe isolated location. Then interrogate him before killing him. He figured he could use silver to make the man talk.

Barbara's memory was still weighing very heavily on him. What could he have done besides begging her not to go? If he were with her that night, he wouldn't be here today. Which he was beginning to believe was his purpose.

As horrible as the creator would be to do it to him, he believed it gave him purpose. Instead of mourning, he hunted. He was put here to stop this evil from continuing its slaughter of innocents. This belief gave him confidence and resilience. When in reality, he had not slowed down enough yet for everything to catch up to him. Once he ended Norman, he knew deep down that a freight train of emotions was headed his way.

Norman strolled along with confidence and bravado. His headphones from his Walkman played "Kodachrome" by Paul Simon. He swayed his hips back and forth as he walked. Stopping every few steps to dance with a lady and laugh and smile. The lady would blush and giggle and then go on her way.

He was ecstatic. Sheriff Tanaka Chee was finally here. His old friend Tanaka. Boy, was he looking forward to sitting down with him again. They had a lot of catching up to do.

For now, he was gonna snag a cab and head over to campus and check out the college girl situation. Nothing would rub the sheriff more than a few missing female students. He could imagine the look on his face and he relished it. He tossed his hand up to hail a taxi and before he knew it, his right hand exploded from a .357 bullet.

He jerked back and snarled. Holding the stub of a hand, he looked around as people ran. They scattered left and right, screaming for help.

"Sheriff," he said calmly.

Tanaka looked down at his hand holding the smoking revolver. He closed his eyes for a second as he couldn't believe what he had just done. People continued to scream and run in all directions.

He had been following Norman for about an hour now. The wolfsbane was working, and he was staying out of sight. When Norman used his hand up to hail a cab, he knee jerked and pulled. Firing one shot that went right through Norman's hand.

"Well hello, sheriff," he said as he attempted to clap his hands together.

There wasn't a right hand anymore and he managed to fling his blood in every direction.

Tanaka just aimed for his chest as he breathed slowly. Trying to keep his body calm so he would not miss. Thatch just smiled at him.

"Norman," Tanaka replied.

"I see you have discovered wolfsbane," Norman said. "Well played, sheriff."

The crowd was still hysterical. Norman could hear police sirens off in the faint distance.

"You look good. Find Barbara yet?" he said with a smile.

Without faltering, Tanaka fired two shots into his chest. The bullets hit their target and Thatch fell to the ground. Tanaka could now hear the sirens coming as they drew closer. So he turned and ran.

Tanaka sprinted as fast as he could back towards the German Village Inn. Then he quickly packed up and gathered his things. He made sure not to make a mess or leave it in any way that would be memorable. After he tossed the room keys on the bed, he closed the door and left in his truck.

Just north of Dayton, Ohio, Tanaka used the payphone at a rest stop.

Deputy McFerrin was telling him what she had heard about Columbus.

"What do you mean you may have shot him in a public area in broad daylight?!" McFerrin cursed.

"That wasn't part of the plan," Tanaka mumbled.

"At least the coroner gets his John Doe back," Deputy McFerrin said with a light heart.

"That's one way of putting it," Tanaka replied. "However, I probably just killed a man and possibly more by doing that."

Sensing the guilt in his voice, McFerrin cut in. "You can't look at it that way. Thatch would have killed tonight. Probably tomorrow too. He's gonna kill, regardless. You, however, just slowed him down."

"I'm going to head back out west where I know I can lie low for a while. I can stay hidden and we can stay connected. You can still keep an eye on what you can find and keep me up to date. When I feel it's safe, I'll come to him," Tanaka said and waited for a response.

"That sounds like a plan. How long?" she asked.

"Six months more than likely," he said, then thought for a second. "Depending on the area, I might be able to venture out sooner."

"Alright, reach me when you can," she replied and they both hung up.

Tanaka had to play this close to the chest. If he went back and waited for Norman to escape from the morgue again, he ran the risk of being seen or identified. This was not a risk he was able to take. If he went away, that would leave Norman out here, free to do as he pleased. It was something he had to live with. He was no good to anyone locked up or incapacitated. This wasn't over, but he had to play this smart and carefully.

CHAPTER TWENTY EIGHT

DETROIT

MAY, 1987

Daniel decided to walk home after the date with Cassy was a bust at Vince's Italian Restaurant. His date never returned from the bathroom and he wondered if she had crawled out a window. Was anything Stanley had told him true? What was going on lately? Did he have a brain tumor? All these thoughts worried Daniel and made him think something wasn't right.

He had a seven-and-a-half-mile walk to his apartment to reflect on what had happened earlier that night. The sidewalks were still damp from a light spring shower and the smell of petrichor was still in the air. Daniel walked past a few abandoned houses with overgrown lawns and graffiti marking gang territories all over them. With his hands in the front pockets of his jeans, he walked with his head down, deep in thought. Passing the occasional bum that asked for spare change or the scantily dressed hooker who asked if he needed a ride. He paid them no attention as he ruminated over the things Stanley had said.

Not real? Daniel thought to himself as he strolled.

Nothing made sense to him lately and he was starting to question the very essence of his humanity. Was he walking in and out of his dreams and nightmares? Were these things that happened to him real? He stepped over a bum that was snoring on the sidewalk and stunk like malt liquor and urine. Daniel snapped his fingers in a sort of "Aha!" moment and realized that's exactly what he needed on this walk. He saw the party store's lights flicker just ahead and knew that's exactly where he was headed.

The door to the party store was covered in beer ads showing what was on sale through spider-webbed glass. The door chimed as he entered. The young man who sat behind the counter looked up from his black-and-white TV and nodded. Daniel whistled his way down the half-empty aisles and went to the beer cooler in the back of the store.

"It works every time," he said to himself as he reached in and grabbed a forty-ounce bottle of Colt 45 malt liquor.

When he closed the door to the cooler, he was startled by a six-year-old girl who appeared out of nowhere and was looking up at him. He recognized this little blonde girl who was wearing a pink Hello Kitty raincoat and matching galoshes. He just couldn't place from where.

"Hey mister, whatcha doin'?" the little girl asked.

Daniel fumbled for his words. "Um, getting myself something to drink."

The girl gave him a puzzling look. "Why?"

"Because I'm very thirsty and depressed," Daniel said.

"Why?" the little girl asked again.

"Because I've been walking for a while and still have a few miles to walk till I get home," he stated.

The little girl paused as if to think about what he had just said and process it.

"Why?" she asked once more.

Daniel began to grow mildly irritated and just turned away and strolled back to the cash register.

"Because I'm an adult and well, just because okay," he said.

He placed his bottle of malt liquor on the counter and the man rang it up.

"Hey man, is that your kid? Or do you know who her parents are?" Daniel asked.

The man behind the counter just leaned to his left to see around Daniel, then leaned to his right to see around the other side of Daniel.

"Ehh, what kid?" the man asked.

"The one that was just right over by the…" Daniel said as he pointed back towards the beer coolers, realizing they were the only two in the store.

"Nevermind. I must be losing my shit. It's been an odd couple of weeks. What do I owe you?" Daniel asked.

"$1.50," the man replied.

Daniel pulled the exact change out of his pocket, paid the man, asked for a brown bag and took his purchase out the door. He took a moment to open his forty-ounce Colt 45 and take a long swig.

"Hi," the little girl said as if she had appeared from nowhere.

"Jesus Christ!" Daniel said as he almost dropped his bottle. "Stop doing that, kid. Where are your parents, and what are you doing out at this time of night? It's not exactly a safe area," he said in his best grown-up voice.

The girl just shrugged at him and said, "They died." Daniel was taken aback for a second. "Yeah mister. They died last year. It was a real mess," the girl said.

Daniel started to pick up his pace a bit as he was weirded out by this entire conversation he was having with a six-year-old girl. As small as she was, she was keeping up with him on his right side.

"Go home kid. This isn't funny and you shouldn't be out here," Daniel said.

"Why?" she asked.

"Oh, for fuck's sake, we are not starting this again," Daniel replied as he picked up his stride even more.

She clung to his side as they quickly walked down the poorly lit street, passing more burned-out homes, vacant lots and a few gang bangers who just looked at him oddly.

"Can I ask you something, mister?" the little girl said.

"I really don't have a choice, do I kid?" Daniel replied.

"No, not really," the girl said.

Daniel sighed and slowed down to a stroll while still sipping on his bottle of malt liquor.

"You think you can get it right this time?" she asked.

Daniel stopped mid-drink and just looked at her inquisitively.

"What are you talking about, kid? Get what right?" Daniel asked.

The little girl just sighed heavily, rolled her eyes and began to boil with aggravation.

"Suicide," the girl said in a very dark tone for a six-year-old.

Daniel closed his eyes, tilted his malt liquor back and began to chug all the while thinking to himself. *She's not real, she's not real, she's not real. Please go away.*

When the bottle was empty, he slowly opened his eyes. The little girl was gone without a trace or a sound. Daniel stood alone on the wet sidewalk listening to the wind whistle through the back alleys and burned-out buildings of Detroit, Michigan.

Daniel walked into Mac's at about noon the next day and took his usual seat at the bar. Mac just grunted at him and slid a can of Black Label his way. Then poured a shot of Kessler's for him. Daniel looked exhausted like he had not slept in weeks.

"Rough night?" he asked as Daniel slammed back the shot and took a sip from his beer.

"You could say that Mac. I didn't sleep a wink. Stanley's been filling my head full of all sorts of weird shit. Have you seen him yet today?" he asked.

Mac just shook his head no and went back to wiping down rocks glasses.

"So I was on this amazing date with this woman named Cassy. I met her over at Large Marge's. So I asked her out to Vince's Italian restaurant and we had dinner and drinks. The night was going great, then she got up to go to the bathroom," Daniel said. "Then out of nowhere, Stanley walks in and sits his ass right down."

He motioned for Mac to pour him another shot while he continued his story.

"Stanley then proceeds to tell me this deranged story about how Cassy isn't really there. That she's some kind of figment of my imagination. He points out that I've been sitting there all night talking to myself," Daniel said, as if overwhelmed.

Mac just looked at him, void of any emotion, while he did his usual prep work behind the bar. Daniel took another drink of beer and asked Mac for yet another shot.

"Yeah, did I mention he showed up at the hospital after I got hurt last week and then told me I have to come here to talk to him?" Daniel asked.

Daniel quickly tossed back his third shot and rubbed at his temples, letting out an enormous sigh.

"Mac, am I going insane? Weird shit has been happening and I don't know why?" he asked.

Mac just looked at him and shrugged.

"So here I fucking am. What does Stanley want to talk to me about? What's so important he couldn't do it last night?" he asked.

Mac just nodded. "I'm sure he will be here soon. He always is."

Without hearing him come in, Daniel was startled by Stanley when he pulled out the seat next to him.

"Christ! Are you trying to give me a heart attack?" Daniel spat.

"That really would solve a lot of people's problems if I did," Stanley muttered under his breath.

Mac served him his usual drink and went back to cleaning glasses.

With his elbows on the bar and his face resting in his palms, Daniel asked what was going on and why was it so urgent for him to meet him there. Stanley motioned for Mac for pour Daniel another drink because this was going to get complicated.

"You are cursed Daniel," Stanley flat out said.

Daniel turned to him with a look of disbelief, not understanding the words coming out of his mouth. He began to squirm in his seat. Deep down he thought he was going crazy but on the other hand, maybe Stanley had a point. The nightmares he was having. The giant wolf beast that seemed to stalk him in every corner of his mind. All of this was very hard to deal with and process.

"Yeah, buddy. Cursed with a capital C. Actually for some time now," Stanley said as he put his hand on Daniel's shoulder. "I don't know exactly when it happened or how, because it happened before my time."

Daniel ordered another beer from Mac and brought it to his lips with shaking hands.

"What do you mean cursed?" Daniel asked.

"Shiiiiit… I don't know how else to spell this out for you buddy." Stanley paused and looked at Mac.

"You are a werewolf, Daniel," Mac said with callousness.

PART IV

"I'M SO SORRY STANLEY..."

CHAPTER TWENTY NINE

WEWELSBURG CASTLE

JANUARY, 1943

Erich had been in the depths of Himmler's Temple of Doom for three weeks now. Every day was pretty much the same. He was fed first thing in the morning. Then, after that, he was taken to the laboratory to undergo various tests and experiments. Some days, he was hooked up to a metal contraption that allowed him to run in place for hours while they monitored his vitals. Then some days he was dumped in a vat of boiling water and submerged completely, causing his skin to painfully melt away.

Each day ended the same. He was killed in some painful manner, then they watched him regenerate. Once he seemed to be fully healed, he was taken back to his cell. There he was fed a large high-protein meal while he discussed things with Himmler himself.

Himmler had begun to like Erich because he was so strong-willed and had a drive to survive, which he respected as a soldier. On the other hand, Erich was beginning to despise Himmler more and more. Though he kept it to himself. Erich found the man arrogant, condescending, a sociopath and just flat-out insane. He knew Himmler was more of a monster than whatever it was Nikolia had turned him into.

In Himmler's warped mind, he truly thought what they were doing was for the good of man. The entire war was to make the world a better place in their image.

Today Erich had gotten off easy and was forced to inhale massive amounts of mustard gas which was not fatal but was extremely painful causing 3rd degree burns to the portions of his skin that were exposed. His burns and lungs had healed in a matter of hours and he now sat on his cot in his cell eating a plate of beef that Himmler had his chef make just for him.

There was a stack of books on the floor of his cell that included writings from Ernest Hemingway, Jack London and Karl Marx. These authors were seen as anti-German and banned or burned by the Nazi regime. Himmler was a well-educated man who had his own personal secret library which held plenty of banned titles. Sometimes the two of them would sit up late at night and discuss the works of Hemingway and other American authors.

This only made Erich dislike the Reichsführer more because it showed that he was a hypocrite on top of many other things. Until now, Himmler and his men did not know exactly what Erich was, nor did Erich for that matter. That would change soon.

Deep down, he could sense that tomorrow was the beginning of the full moon. He didn't know how he could sense it. Something stirred inside him and yearned to be let out. Himmler and his men were soon going to find out what exactly Erich was becoming.

The next day, they gave Erich a high-protein breakfast and took him down to the laboratory. His day was the usual endurance test of being tasked to run in place on the giant metal machine. It allowed him to run on a track that automatically moved under his feet at various speeds. What was different today was that they had brought in numerous large heat lamps that were all aimed at him. This brought the temperature of the room to well over 54 degrees Celsius.

They forced him to run nonstop for eight hours straight at a steady pace with no breaks or water. They kept a constant check of his vitals as he ran. His pulse rate never went above 62 bpm and his blood to oxygen levels never fluctuated from 95%. Even though he could regenerate and come back from the dead, the experiments the Nazi scientists performed on him were still excruciatingly unpleasant. But Erich never put up any resistance and did as he was told. For now.

Deep down underneath the castle, Erich never saw the light of day. Himmler made it so that he was unaware whether it was day or night. As the full moon began to rise above the pines of Wewelsburg village, Erich began to hear that familiar hum. He could sense the moon was calling out to him. His pulse began to rise rapidly which grabbed the scientists' attention.

Himmler just happened to be in the observation room when he witnessed Erich's first transformation from man to beast. He watched with great interest as Erich's heart rate increased as he went into some form of cardiac arrest. Erich eventually lost his footing and was thrown off the machine he had just spent the last eight hours running on without even breaking a sweat. Once he stopped rolling across the floor, Erich started to contort and scream in agony.

Himmler watched as the man's bones broke and painfully reshaped and his body mass tripled in size. His teeth became fangs and his jaw began to lengthen as his screams turned to growls. He tore off his clothes as his entire body sprouted gray hair.

The lycanthrope let out an explosive howl. The magnitude caused the scientists in the laboratory to cover their ears.

"A Werwölf. Oh, this is so magnificent. Finally, the Reich will have the perfect weapon," Himmler said to the four other SS officers in the room. "Can you imagine a legion of Werwölf Waffen-SS troops storming the streets of London?" he asked.

Overcome with aspiration, he paid no attention to the two scientists being brutally massacred on the other side of the observation glass.

Himmler casually pressed a button on the wall to the left of the glass window. With a whack of his palm, the room then filled with cyanide gas. The gas appeared to slow the beast down significantly. The Reichsführer then ordered a team of men to run in and sedate the beast in any way possible. He suggested they use tranquilizer rifles and to use their MP-40s if they needed to as a last resort.

Six SS soldiers ran to their doom. Even as subdued as the beast was, it could still dismantle this small squad of troops. Four of them were torn to pieces but it only managed to bite the remaining two. The beast roared, causing the observation glass to once again vibrate as Himmler looked on. He quickly ordered the two soldiers to be rescued and placed into quarantine immediately.

The massive beast that had once been Erich Kaiser just stood in the room and looked directly at Himmler in the observation room. Its chest heaved up and down as it focused its anger on the man behind the glass.

"Do you see that? It recognizes me," he said to his officers as he slowly clapped his hands.

The beast growled and curled its lips at the sound of Himmler's voice through the glass. Three more troops with gas masks barged into the room and opened fire with their MP-40s, driving the beast back as another set of soldiers shot the monster full of tranquilizer darts. The beast finally stopped fighting and just knelt on its haunches. It seemed to be submitting to the group of soldiers.

This tickled Himmler. He was in awe at the sight of the beast's ability to understand the situation and willingly submit. Finding a way to use this creature would guarantee a German victory over the West. This was what they needed to take the eastern front, then possibly the world. The reign of the 3rd Reich was about to come to fruition.

CHAPTER THIRTY

DETROIT

MAY, 1987

Daniel spat Black Label all over the bar and Mac. This wasn't quite where he thought Stanley was going with this. For some reason, he thought he meant cursed as a form of sarcasm. Since his life resembled Charlie Brown trying to kick the football, only to have it yanked out from under him at the last minute.

"Seriously?" Mac responded. He continued to grumble under his breath as he wiped down his bar yet again.

"Daniel, you are a werewolf. You just can't remember that you are. In fact, in about a week after the next full moon, you will probably forget all of this. Then some time will go by and then here we are having this conversation all over again," Stanley said.

"What do you mean again?" Daniel asked.

"It's what the man said, didn't he?" Mac snapped in annoyance as if he had seen this conversation play out more than once.

"Your memory issues were not because you hit your head at some point in your life. It's what the curse is doing to you," Stanley replied to Daniel's question.

"Doing to me? What?" Daniel asked as he motioned for Mac to pour another shot of whiskey.

Mac just flipped him off and continued to clean up the mess he had made.

Stanley went on to explain that at some point, he had been attacked and bitten by a werewolf and survived. This was the only way to transfer the curse from one person to another. Stanley couldn't offer any more details because, like he said before, it was before his time.

He did know, however, that the thing that bit him had been around for many centuries. Something that had lurked in the shadows since the Middle Ages. It had many names from other cultures. Loup-garou, Skinwalker, Yee Naaldlooshii, Rougarou, Vircolac and Lycanthrope were just some of the names. Stanley spared him the rhetoric.

"Come on guys, is this a joke? Am I on Candid Camera? Is Allen Funt gonna pop outta the back room with cameras?" Daniel asked in disbelief.

Stanley pointed out that's exactly what he said last time and continued.

"Don't you think it's odd that for as long as you can remember, you have been in your early 40s? You have no memory of your childhood, or even your parents for that matter. Do you hear a voice in your head? See people that aren't there?" Stanley asked as Mac topped off his gin and tonic. "Maaan… how do you explain getting run over by a garbage truck last week and sitting here right now?"

Daniel was at a loss for words. Stanley went on to point out that it was the curse that caused him his selective memory loss. Every twenty-nine days, in most cases there was a full moon. This caused him to change into an eight-foot beast that would kill with a ferocious appetite.

To make it even worse, he went on to explain that it was not just one night. The nights before and after the full moon, the curse would also take hold. With every transformation, the beast became stronger and fought to take full control until every last morsel of Daniel's humanity was gone and only evil remained.

In the beginning, the curse only caused him to change during the nights of the full moon. As the decades passed, the beast grew stronger and was no longer attached to the moon alone. It had the ability to change at will whenever Daniel was not in control.

"Like I already said, Daniel, eventually the world as you know it will be gone. You will be gone. All that will remain is this thing inside you. It's only a matter of time." Stanley said with empathy.

"So, what did you mean last night? About Cassy?" Daniel asked.

"It's all a product of your imagination, bud. What's happening is the last bits of your humanity are causing you to see the ones you have killed. It's what the curse does. The good in you is trying to send you messages subconsciously. It's like your soul knows deep down that evil is coming and doing everything possible to help you end the curse. More or less a Hail Mary of sorts," Stanley explained.

"Let me guess. You are going to tell me how I end this curse?" Daniel asked.

"There is only one way," Stanley responded.

"You have to die, Daniel," Mac quickly interrupted.

Stanley just glared at Mac, "Nice… real nice."

Mac just shrugged in response. "This is getting old, Stanley."

Daniel tried to steady his hand as he tried to take another drink. Everything that he was just told made sense now.

He didn't have a brain tumor or Alzheimer's. The pieces began to fall into place like giant boulders.

"So the only way to lift the curse is for me to die?" Daniel asked.

Stanley just nodded and said, "Yes. I hate telling you all this… again. I do, but here it goes. You murdered me back in 1971 when you were living in Albuquerque, New Mexico."

Daniel's jaw dropped.

"Oh, for fuck's sake, guys," Mac butted in. "Daniel, we aren't real. You're imagining all this. We aren't ghosts forced to roam the earth till the curse is lifted. It's not like some bullshit Hollywood movie. The curse is making you go insane. It's twisting you into a thing of evil. All these memory blackouts you have are because your other half was in control."

Daniel looked at Stanley, then looked back at Mac, then looked back at Stanley.

"How else can we put it?" Mac asked.

"MAAAAANNNN," Stanley replied while throwing his hands up in the air.

"What? The man's a fucking werewolf and has to die. What more do we need to say?" Mac said as he shrugged and went back to cleaning glasses.

It was like a mule had kicked Daniel in the chest.

Now, if there are no more interruptions." Stanley took another sip from his drink and waited for Mac to say something. Mac just nodded in response. So Stanley began his story.

"I had just closed my car dealership up for the night when I heard something strange coming from between the cars in the lot. It was like a scraping noise as if something was being dragged across metal. So I grabbed a flashlight and against my better judgment, I went to take a look. Well, that didn't end so well for me. That son of a bitch toyed with me for an hour like a cat with a mouse. Fucker pulled off one of my legs too. Made it pretty hard to run."

"So you're dead and have been dead all this time? All the times we have sat here and drank together? I've been drinking with a ghost?" Daniel asked as he buried his face in his palms.

"Not a ghost," Mac butted in again.

Stanley gave him a sharp glare. "Yes. Like Mac said, we are figments of your imagination. You widowed my wife and left behind my beautiful daughter."

"I'm so sorry Stanley," Daniel said empathetically.

"Meh, I'm kinda over it," Stanley said.

"Wait… did you say 'we'?" Daniel asked.

"Yup," Mac responded.

Mac slid Daniel another imaginary shot of whiskey and another Black Label because the look on his face said his brain needed it.

Daniel didn't know whether to scream or run. Something deep down inside of him was telling him this was all true. For God knows how long he had been roaming the country, murdering people.

"So. How do I end this curse again? I mean, I get it. I have to die, but how?" he asked.

"Well, that's the bad news, my man," Stanley said.

He explained once more that there was only one way to lift the curse, and that was for Daniel to die. That was not an easy feat because there wasn't much that could kill him. Only three things could end the curse: 1. Silver, but it had to be a fatal blow, and the silver had to stay in place. Once removed, he would just come back. 2. Decapitation, but you had to get close enough to do that. And finally, 3. When all else fails, kill it with fire. But the body had to be completely destroyed for it to work so it couldn't regenerate. The best way was to do all three.

"Can't I just kill myself?" Daniel asked.

"Funny you mention that. That's what we all have been trying to get you to do for some time now, but the beast either finds a way to stop you or you just fuck it up. Like with the garbage truck," Stanley said.

Daniel couldn't remember that he had previously tried to take his own life numerous times in the past. All in various ways, hoping someday he would get lucky.

He tried hanging himself, drowning, and drug overdoses. He also tried driving his car off a cliff one time on the West Coast. Each time, he would either wake up in a hospital or his bed with no memory of anything.

He got close once when he finally shot himself with a silver bullet. He even left a sticky note stuck to his forehead that said, Please do not remove the bullet, only to wake up mid-autopsy.

Daniel looked at Mac, who was standing there looking at him with his arms folded. He could tell the man had something to get off his chest.

"Go on Mac. Tell me what I did to you," he said.

"You killed me about six months ago. I was taking out the trash one night after closing when you crept up out of nowhere. Big smelly hairy bastard with yellow eyes and big teeth. So I hauled ass back inside and went for the shotgun that I kept behind the bar. Needless to say, I didn't make it. The next morning, you came back and burned my bar down. Apparently your other half is very clever with covering its tracks," Mac said.

"Wait? This bar?" Daniel asked.

Mac just shrugged and kept polishing glasses before putting them away.

"So that leaves us with the matter at hand," Stanley said. "You have seven more days till you are forced to make the change again. That is unless the beast decides to do it sooner. So you have to do your best to end this before the week is up."

Daniel stood up from his bar stool and backed away. "Wait a minute. It burned down this bar? The bar we are all sitting in right now?"

"He is coming, Daniel," Stanley said. "You need to take care of this before he gets back. Or more people are going to die like Mac and I."

"Who is coming?" Daniel pressed.

"Norman," Stanley responded.

Daniel could feel the panic attack starting to swell from deep inside his chest. He slowly backed away from the two men.

Mac and Stanley just looked at each other, then back at Daniel. Mac let out a heavy sigh of annoyance and snapped his fingers.

Just like that, Mac's bar was gone. Daniel was left standing by himself in the burned-out interior of a condemned building. He could tell by certain remaining details that it was once Mac's bar. None of this seemed real. With a few quick slaps to his face, he tried to wake up. From the stinging pain he felt in his face, he was awake. This was real. He climbed his way out of the usual empty hole of a shattered window and onto the sidewalk.

He stopped for a minute to let the sunlight warm his face. There was way too much for him to process at the moment. His brain was running at speeds he couldn't keep up with. Were all of his trips here to Mac's real or not? He spent a lot of time coming here. Was everyone that he saw at Mac's dead? All the time he spent and all the people he spoke to here. Daniel gave serious thought to checking himself straight into rehab or committing himself to an institution.

Just as he took a deep breath, he felt a pinprick from the syringe on his neck. A sense of euphoria came over him right before he blacked out.

CHAPTER THIRTY ONE

WEWELSBURG CASTLE

FEBRUARY, 1943

Now that Himmler knew exactly what Erich was, everything made sense to him. He had his men isolate the two SS soldiers who had been bitten by the beast. He wanted to do further tests on these men before the next full moon. This took Himmler's focus off Erich for the time being.

This made his life somewhat easier. The rigorous experiments had halted and he remained locked in his cell. They fed him twice a day and provided books to keep him entertained. Erich was quite content with this. In between his meals and reading, he kept himself busy with exercise. A daily routine of pushups, situps and stretches kept his mind focused on something besides his current situation. The only human contact he had was with the soldier who brought him his food and books. Even Himmler hadn't been by for at least two weeks after the incident.

When Himmler finally visited, he spoke of the two bitten soldiers. How each soldier was affected in completely different ways. Neither of them had any scars from being attacked. First, the men stated they felt great but complained of stiffness in the muscles where the bite occurred.

As time went on, the soldier's demeanor started to change drastically. One of them began to show signs of schizophrenia and paranoia. This soldier also developed a series of nervous tics and twitches and started complaining about hunger pains that seemed to never go away.

The other soldier went into a dark, demented state. He would violently lash out. Just like an animal, he would snarl and snip at anyone who got near. This soldier seemed to have gone completely mad. What humanity he had left was slowly dwindling the closer it got to the next full moon.

What both soldiers did have in common was aggression. Himmler asked Erich if he had experienced such changes in his behavior after he was bitten. Erich never spoke of being bitten or even brought up Nikolia.

"How did you know I was bitten?" Erich asked Himmler.

Himmler sat in his usual chair just outside of Erich's cell. Once again, cleaning off his small glasses with his handkerchief.

"Because you have been in a Panzer tank for the past three years and I figured we all would have found out about your little secret by now," he said.

"What am I?" Erich asked.

Himmler put his glasses back on and cleared his throat.

"You, my friend Erich, you are the Werwölf," he said while making quotation marks with his fingers.

Erich didn't know how to take that since he never actually remembered what happened during the nights of the full moon and he never remembered the transformation either. Himmler went on to explain about werewolf lore and how Erich turned into a terrible beast that was part wolf and part man.

Erich couldn't believe what he was hearing. Being a well-educated man, he was fully versed in the ancient folktales of Germany and the stories that had been passed down through the generations. None of which he thought were true. Then again, he was locked in a cell beneath Heinrich Himmler's own personal castle. He decided to tell Himmler everything that had happened to him since his Panzer exploded at the battle of Stalingrad.

"Fascinating," Himmler said. "So this Nikolia is the one that bit you?"

"I believe so, yes. Every time I close my eyes, I still see his face," he said, void of emotion.

"I wonder how old this… Nikolia is?" Himmler asked himself.

"If all of this is true, I believe he might be well over a century old," Erich stated. "Last I saw him, he had mentioned something that alluded to being around for centuries."

"Ahh yes, the small village you massacred. Tell me more about that," Himmler pressed.

"I've already told you everything I remember about that. I really would rather not repeat myself." Erich said firmly.

"Are you sure there were no survivors? You mentioned that you burned all the remains of the town folk you slaughtered. Yes?" the Reichsführer asked. He seemed to enjoy twisting the knife somewhat into Erich's conscience.

Erich took a moment and looked down at his hands, remembering that morning and all the blood. All the bodies and all the children whose lives ended that night. He wiped a tear from his cheek as he tried to collect himself.

"Yes, I am sure," Erich responded to the question with a coldness that Himmler had yet to see from the man.

"Good. That will be all for tonight. Please get some rest," Himmler said. The Reichsführer stood up and gave him a solemn nod and walked off down the corridor.

Erich lay down on his cot and stared at the ceiling. All these thoughts swam through his head like some form of torture.

So many children, he thought and sobbed.

Erich began to see things during the night. The people he killed started to haunt his dreams and reality. One night, he thought he heard General Hube wail and cry about the loss of his family. On other nights, he thought he saw the general pass his cell door rambling on about some horrible monster that was after him.

Some of it bothered him more than others. The faces of children he remembered from the small village back in Russia began to show up in his cell. Faces he could never forget, even after he had burned them. They always seemed to want to talk to him at night. Sometimes they asked him why he did the things he did for which he never had an answer. Even though Himmler had stopped his experiments on him, these nightly visits were becoming far worse.

By the next month's full moon, Himmler had constructed a special room for Erich that had him chained to the wall with heavy iron shackles. When they were first put on, they were far too big. It was obvious they were intended to keep the beast detained.

When the change started to take place, they pumped the room with a steady dose of Zyklon B, which sent the beast into a berserk rage.

The gas kept it just weak enough to be unable to break its bonds. Himmler kept it heavily sedated by continuously sending in his men and repeatedly shooting it with tranquilizer guns.

The beast was smart. It sensed what was going on and it somehow knew the man behind the glass was not trying to kill it. So far, the Nazis had not shown any knowledge of how to truly hurt a werewolf. So it stopped fighting. The beast never fought against its restraints again. Instead, it knelt and studied Himmler and his men. This excited the Reichsführer and showed him that this was a highly intelligent creature. More so than any other animal he had ever encountered or read about.

The curse seemed to affect every host differently. Most just turned into bloodthirsty beasts, hell-bent on murderous intent. They were smart, but in the end, they were still just animals. They were about the same level of intelligence as chimpanzees. However, these chimpanzees were seven-foot-tall killing machines.

Erich was different. Nikolia knew this and that was why he chose to pass the curse on to him. Himmler was also beginning to see this as well. No other test subjects ever came close to Erich. He was able to still maintain his humanity and never once gave up during his incarceration at Wewelsburg. He was too strong-willed. Or some might say he was too stubborn to die.

This only made the beast inside Erich grow stronger. The longer a werewolf's host lived, the more powerful it would become. It would evolve into a very malevolent and cunning killing machine. It knew Erich's current situation would only benefit it in the long run. His human form was fed, given shelter and most importantly, kept alive. Eventually, in time, it would take over. Then all of Erich's humanity would be gone. Even in human form, the beast would be able to take control and the man that was Erich Kaiser would be no more.

H·immler had ordered the commandant of Niederhagen to bring in three Russian POWs for testing on the night of the next full moon. They brought the three men into an observation room, where they sat tied to wooden chairs. On the far side of the room, they shackled the two infected soldiers against the wall. They connected the restraints to a mechanical device that could be operated from inside the protection of the viewing room. Here, Himmler could press a button and it would retract the chains into the wall.

Once the soldiers made their change, they would attack the three men offered up in front of them. Himmler would wait just long enough for a bite to be made, then he would quickly press the button. This worked in theory, however, it resulted in only one of the POWs surviving with just a bite. The other two were torn to pieces before the chains could be fully retracted. This is a process that the Reichsführer would have to work on over time until it was just right.

Himmler's men removed the lone survivor and then ordered the room doused with cyanide gas. This weakened the creatures but didn't fully sedate them. They relentlessly tried to escape their bonds. Like a wounded animal in a trap, they caused self-inflicted wounds trying to get out of their shackles. One of them chewed its own hand off and began smashing at the other shackle with its stump.

Himmler was greatly disappointed by this. Neither test subject showed any of the possibilities that Erich did. He repeated the process over the next two nights of the full moon. Once he had three new test subjects, he gave his men the order to torch the room on the third night. He was also very curious about how these beasts reacted to fire.

Like some medieval dragon, the SS soldier waved his flame thrower as it spewed molten fire. As if he were effortlessly painting a canvas the soldier worked the flame to and fro. It took a while, but the fire finally did its job. Leaving them as smoldering husks dangling from their shackles. They remained in a half-transformed state of half man and half beast. Himmler believed that the fire caused so much damage to a cellular structure that their bodies could not fully return to human form after death. He then had the skulls bleached and hung in his personal trophy room.

In time, Himmler began to worry about whether the beasts could be controlled. His end goal was to be able to use Erich's curse in his favor to bring waves of super SS soldiers to wreak havoc amongst the Allied armies. Himmler knew that without being able to control the beasts would deem them useless for what he had planned. He now believed that Erich held the key to this puzzle.

Soon the bitten soviets began to show similar symptoms of psychosis and increased aggression. They were put through the same tests as Erich was. However, they were much harder to deal with. The men had the same regenerative abilities that Erich had shown and required a lot of protein to keep their muscle mass up once their bodies healed. Himmler had brought in more POWs once again. He continued this process over and over in hopes that he would eventually find his own Erich.

Every time the soviet beasts showed the same uncontrollable rage. Clawing and gnawing at themselves to break free of their bonds in any way they could. It was time for a new test.

Himmler figured if he was going to have an army of these super soldiers at his command, he needed to see how they interacted with each other. Until now, the beasts didn't seem to be too concerned with each other and their only drive seemed to be self-preservation. Neither of the previous infected interacted with each other. So he decided to put one Soviet in with Erich to see what would happen. He hoped that they would show a pack mentality. He figured it might be possible that Erich would be seen as an alpha and the other beast might fall in line.

Erich was shackled to the wall per usual. A pair of men in white coats brought in one of the Soviet prisoners and shackled him to the wall next to him. Even though their shackles were too big for them, neither of them tried to slip them off.

"How's it going," Erich said in Russian. The Soviet just looked at him with a nervous twitch and emotionless eyes.

"Name's Erich, what's yours?" The man just blankly looked at him, then sat on the floor.

"My name? Dmitry." The man finally answered.

"Glad to meet you, Dmitry." Erich sat down as well. "Wish it was under better circumstances."

The man just looked at Erich and nervously scratched at his own skin and seemed to open and close his mouth as if to stretch his jaw.

"I told my wife I would be home soon. I hope she isn't worried. She gets upset if she has to worry. I hope they don't pour acid on me again. Shut up! I can't help you!" The man seemed to ramble and grow agitated at himself at the same time.

"Right," Erich said with a sprinkle of sarcasm.

They both looked off towards the observation glass, noticing that the Reichsführer was standing there watching them. "Whelp, that can't be a good sign," Erich mumbled.

"Ангел смерти! Ангел смерти!" the Soviet screamed.

He was pointing at Himmler and referring to him as the Angel Of Death. The Reichsführer just smiled through the glass at both men.

After Dmitry quieted down, Erich started to hear the humming noise in his ears as the full moon rose into the sky. He quickly wished he were back in his cell with his books. Whatever the Reichsführer was up to, he knew this was not going to end well.

Himmler watched with intrigue as both men began to contort and convulse as their bones broke and reshaped. He did take note that Erich's change was much faster than the Soviet. Erich's transformation had taken about thirty seconds, whereas the Soviet took just under two full minutes of agony. The gray beast that had once been Erich just stood and watched as the soviet prisoner turned into a similar, darker gray wolf.

"Aren't they beautiful?" Himmler asked.

"Yes they are, sir. We can see that Erich is a bit bigger than the newcomer," the man to his right said.

The larger beast turned and looked directly at Himmler with a glare of disgust as if insulted to be in the presence of the smaller Soviet beast. With incredible brute force, it lunged upon the Soviet, ripping and biting into the weaker beast. The smaller one tried to fight back but was easily overpowered by Erich's werewolf form.

In a fury of claws and teeth, the larger beast drove the smaller one to the ground and pinned it under his weight. It reached down and grabbed the Russian's head with both its hands. Then snapped his neck and wrenched back and forth until he pulled its head off in a spray of gore. The massive beast then stood up and threw the severed head at the observation glass. It hit with a wet thud. Then the massive monster just stood there with its chest heaving and glared straight at Himmler.

"Magnificent. Let's make note that Erich doesn't seem to play well with others," Himmler said as he pressed the button to douse the room with Zyklon B.

CHAPTER THIRTY TWO

DETROIT

MAY, 1987

Tanaka had spent the last six months up near Shiprock in northern New Mexico. This was part of the Navajo Nation and he did what he could around the reservation to help out. The news had quieted down from what had happened back in Columbus, Ohio. Luckily, the story did not make many waves on a national level.

The John Doe that was reportedly returned to the Coroner's office in Franklin County was once again reported missing. It just seemed to disappear overnight. This time, no one had been killed in the process which was a relief to Tanaka.

What he theorized was that the silver bullets he shot Norman with either passed through his body or had been removed. Thatch could have possibly played possum until the time was right and made his exit. His presence had now become too widely known in the area, and Tanaka figured that he would have gone into hiding just like he did.

The wolfsbane had allowed Tanaka to be able to get close to Norman without him knowing. This gave him the upper hand. It seemed that Thatch had put his little game on hold since someone had flipped his script. This made him smile because now he sensed that Norman was scared, or at least this put his ego in check. The big bad wolf just came up onto Tanaka's brick house and didn't know what to do.

It wasn't until May 1987 that Deputy McFerrin reached out with an update. There had been a possible Norman attack up in Detroit, Michigan during the night of the full moon. This had been the first reported attack that matched his MO in almost six months.

"What do you have for me?" Tanaka asked as he sat at the dining table in his small trailer.

"I have four people killed behind a RadioShack. Reports are of a large wild animal," she responded. "The coroner's report pointed out something very odd. It said that some of the remains had the initials NT gouged into them.

Tanaka paused for a minute. He knew this was Norman. It was a message. Norman's sign meant he was ready to resume their game.

"The report said whatever did this was huge. There were no eyewitnesses or survivors. There was a news broadcast interviewing an old lady who said that after the gunshots, she heard a howl. The woman looked pretty terrified during the interview," Deputy McFerrin explained.

"He's sending me a message. He wants me to come to Detroit and pick this game back up," Tanaka said.

"You know he's probably laying a trap for you," she quickly replied.

"I know," he said bluntly.

"So… You just gonna waltz up there and walk around all swinging dick until he tears your head off?" she asked curtly.

"I am going to lay a trap of my own," Tanaka responded. "I just have to get close enough to hit him with 20 cc's of fentanyl."

When he arrived in Detroit, he checked into a hotel as usual. He picked a place that wasn't far from the crime scene. From the moment he pulled into town, he was wearing the wolfsbane. Once in his room, he organized his things and read over some of the local newspapers. He had the information that McFerrin had given him, but he wanted to make sure he was up to date. Something caught his eye.

There was a small story about a man who was hit by a garbage truck over on the city's westside. They ruled it an accident. Some poor guy stepped out in front giving the driver no time to stop. The man miraculously survived.

What Tanaka found interesting was a week later, they found the man missing from his hospital room. They believed he jumped out his window and ran off. The article also pointed out that the room was on the second story of the hospital.

"Oozbą́." Tanaka said in Navajo as he snapped a finger.

It seemed like Norman might be having some kind of inner struggle. When the Elders of the Navajo Nation explained the legends of the Yee Naaldlooshii to him, they made sure to point out that once cursed, the host was driven mad. A mental battle would occur. This would usually result in a few suicide attempts within the first year.

Why would Thatch be attempting this now? He's okay with knowing what he is, he thought to himself.

Tanaka checked out the crime scene behind the RadioShack where the four people were murdered. It had been a week since the crime scene was wrapped up, but he still wanted to take a look. There was nothing out of the ordinary there. The victims were two younger couples who appeared to have cut through the alley. They were all torn to shreds and had their livers and hearts taken postmortem. One victim put up a fight and fired a few rounds into their attacker. It didn't help much because he got it the worst way and his head was never found. He ended up just a mangled corpse in a rain poncho.

The alley stank like garbage and wet rat piss as he looked for any clues that the police might have left behind. Tanaka figured Norman had jumped down from above and began to kill them one by one. It must have happened fast because the victims were all within a ten-yard radius of each other.

Tanaka didn't discover anything new from examining the old crime scene and he had nothing else to go on other than how Deputy McFerrin described the victims' bodies. Tanaka had theorized that, even though Norman was a predator and an extremely intelligent man, deep down he was still just an animal. An animal that had certain territorial habits. The beast seemed never to be too far from where it killed. He was willing to bet that Thatch was somewhere within a ten-mile radius of this RadioShack.

He's getting sloppy, Tanaka thought to himself as he drove back towards his hotel.

Afternoon, Mario," Tanaka greeted the old man as he walked through the door.

"Well, Mr. Chee. Great to see you today," the man said as he picked out expired citrus from a pile of oranges.

"What's good today?" he asked as he grabbed a handbasket and perused the apple bins.

"Oh, we have some great Asian pears in and the Gala apples are nice and sweet right now," Mario said.

"Perfect," Tanaka said, as he put a few of each in his basket.

Tanaka enjoyed Puzo's Market, and he thought the owner was quite a character. He had been searching the city for the past two weeks and couldn't find any sign of Thatch. He didn't know if this was a good thing or a bad thing.

"I'm sorry the place is such a mess, Tanaka. My only employee has been out for a few days," Mario said apologetically.

Tanaka knew he had a part-time employee, but he never saw him in the store. He figured Mario was helping someone who didn't have much going for him and needed the extra work. He knew that the old man put on a wise guy front, but deep down he was a good person who believed in community values.

"No worries at all Mario. The store looks fine as usual…" Tanaka trailed off.

He couldn't believe his eyes.

Right there in Puzo's Market, not more than ten yards in front of him stood none other than Norman Thatch. His heart started to pound as he gripped his basket tightly. Norman looked right at him.

"My employee Daniel here hasn't been here in a few days. So the store has somewhat gone to shit," he said. Putting his hands on his hips, he scowled at Daniel.

"Has he ever done this before?" Tanaka asked.

Norman just walked right past him, carrying a wooden crate of grapes. He politely excused himself as he walked past. It was like Norman had never seen him before. Tanaka was taken aback because he excused himself. This was something that was totally beneath Thatch's character.

"Yes, a few times here and there, but never for this long," Mr. Puzo said as he furrowed his brow.

Tanaka just watched the interaction between the two of them. Norman blushed and apologized to the old man for missing so much work. Norman then smiled once again at Tanaka and went into the back of the store.

Without taking his eyes off the direction that Thatch was going, he inquired to Mr. Puzo. "What did he say happened to him?"

"He was in the hospital for about a week. He had some kind of traffic accident after leaving his favorite hole in the wall, Mac's, which is a few blocks over," the man replied.

"You don't say?" Tanaka asked.

"Yeah… weirdest thing, too. The only Macs I know about was burned down about six months ago. Old Mac died in the fire as well. Real sad story. Bar had been in the family for years," Mario said while shaking his head.

"You don't say?" Tanaka repeated. Still keeping his eyes trained towards the back room.

"Daniel doesn't have a phone. So there isn't any way to get a hold of him unless you run into him on the street or at work here. My wife has taken a real liking to him. He's a good worker, just not all right in the head," said Mario with empathy.

"I need to get going. I forgot I had something very important to do," Tanaka said, bringing his attention back to the old man.

Tanaka handed the old man his basket and hurried out the door. "I'll see you soon Mario."

"Have a good day, Mr. Chee," he replied.

Tanaka sat in his truck outside Puzo's market for another two hours, waiting for Norman to leave. Impatiently tapping his fingers on the steering wheel.

What the actual fuck just happened? he thought.

He was very glad he didn't repeat what happened in Columbus again. That would have seriously made things worse.

Who the hell is Daniel? Why did Norman just look at me and walk past me? Why was he so polite to me? And why the fuck is he working at a produce market? Tanaka tried to slow his brain down and catch up with the situation.

He checked his duffle bag and made sure he had what he needed to make his plan work. He was going to wait for Thatch to leave and follow him to see what he was up to. Tanaka didn't want to rush this. He already screwed that up in Ohio. Tanaka knew he had to keep a low profile and see what was going on here before he made his move.

Tanaka tailed Norman all over the west side of Detroit. The man never used a car and seemed to walk everywhere. He thought his behavior was very odd at times. Thatch appeared to stop from time to time and talk to himself at great length. Then continue like nothing happened. He either went to work at the market, stopped by a diner, or stayed at his apartment. This was very strange behavior for the killer he first met back in the Coconino National Forest.

Most days, Thatch would visit a rundown building that looked like it had once been a local tavern. He would crawl in through a busted-out window. Then he would stay there for hours and just sit inside on a scorched barstool and have long conversations with himself.

One night after Thatch left, he decided to climb inside and take a look around. What was so special about this place? Why was he coming here almost every day? Questions he hoped to answer by getting a closer look inside.

The inside looked like it was your average tavern that had probably been in the city for some time. Not much was left since it was burned down. He noticed a charred plaque above the bar that read "Mac's Bar". This was the place Puzo had mentioned. He shined his light around the barstools and the top of the bar. He could see huge gouges carved into the burnt wood. Gouges similar to what he has seen before.

Something happened here, he thought as he shined his light around.

The gouges in the wood were clear claw marks. He could tell that they had happened before the bar had caught fire. This means something happened before it was burnt down. He remembered what Mario said about the owner being killed in the fire.

Tanaka highly doubted that the fire was what killed the owner. Quickly, he wrapped up his search and went back to watching Norman's apartment.

He wasn't there very long before he saw him leave again. Norman had changed his clothes and walked seven miles to an Italian restaurant named Vince's. Outside, he watched Norman talk to himself once again, then entered the restaurant. After a couple of hours, Norman left and began to walk back to his apartment. He just made one small stop at a convenience store and bought something to drink out of a paper bag.

Tanaka slowly crept behind him. Keeping his distance, but still staying close enough to see what he was doing. Every so often Norman would stop and have a complete conversation, take a swig from his brown bag and continue his walk. He did this quite a few times before reaching his apartment.

Tanaka debated on whether to just kick in the door and take him out. He figured it would be best to check in with McFerrin first and follow the plan. He had to find out what happened to Barbara.

This was not just about stopping Norman, it was about getting closure for himself.

Later that night, Tanaka sat in his hotel room and spoke with Deputy McFerrin on the phone.

"Are you 100% sure this is Norman?" she pressed.

"As sure as I'm standing here," Tanaka responded.

"The plan still the same?" she asked.

"Yes. This changes nothing," he responded.

"How long are you going to drag this out?" she asked.

"Tomorrow is go time. We have seven more days till the next full moon and we both know he will for sure make the change then. My goal is to get to him before that," he explained.

Around noon the next day, he followed Norman out of his apartment. He made his way over to what was left of Mac's Bar and he climbed in through the window as usual. He seemed to sit and talk to himself like he always did. However, this time, he seemed a little more flustered and animated than usual.

"Well, this is different," Tanaka muttered.

Norman seemed to be arguing with himself. He was being very erratic and even flailing his arms up in the air. Once he stood up, he backed away from the bar with his hands up and seemed to be repeating himself. Then he quickly climbed back out through the window and stood there, staring up at the sun.

This was Tanaka's opportunity. He had already been waiting outside for Norman to come out. Once he came out and seemed distracted, Tanaka quickly came up behind him and jabbed him with a hypodermic needle, injecting him with 20 cc's of fentanyl.

It didn't take long for Norman to collapse dead on the ground.

He placed zip ties around his hands and feet, binding him in case he woke up. Tanaka dragged his limp, lifeless body across the street and back over to his truck. He smiled at a few bums that shambled by and seemed not to want to bother the man. Then he opened the tailgate and heaved his body up into the back of his Blazer and slammed it closed. He quickly hurried around the side and jumped into the driver's seat.

So far, so good, Tanaka thought as he fired up his truck and drove off.

It was about a twenty-minute drive across town where Tanaka pulled his Blazer up to a locked gate with a sign that read "Sgt. Rock's Storage Emporium". He stepped out of the truck, unlocked the gate and pulled his truck around to a side entrance. He left his truck in a position to make a fast getaway if he needed to.

Tanaka waited a while, so he was sure no one was around before he got out and retrieved the body. Luckily, this part of the city was mostly light industrial and old abandoned factories. There wasn't a soul around. Not even the bums and vagrants would come down here. He specifically picked this location for that reason. There was going to be a lot of noise later tonight.

"In ya go," he said as he held open the door with one arm and pulled the body through.

Once inside, Tanaka dragged Thatch's body down a hallway that was flanked by closed storage units. When he got to the one he rented, he opened it, pulled Norman in and closed the door behind him. He figured Thatch would regenerate eventually and when he did, Tanaka would be waiting with questions. Once all his questions were answered he was going to dispose of Norman Thatch once and for all.

CHAPTER THIRTY THREE

WEWELSBURG CASTLE

MARCH, 1943

Erich sat in his cell per usual reading Jack London. He was trying to make the best of a horrible situation. He could feel something inside him growing. It started to give him a sense of serenity. He couldn't explain it or why. It felt like he was where he was supposed to be for the time being.

"So what do you think is going to happen next?" Petrov said in Russian.

"Please be quiet Petrov. I am trying to read," Erich replied without looking up from his book.

"Oh, pardon me. I am so sorry to inconvenience you," the dead man responded.

Erich paused to rub the bridge of his nose with his thumb and forefinger. Trying to clear his head, he wished this apparition that constantly haunted him would just go away.

"You know that wasn't me. Why don't you just move on?" Erich sighed. "Don't you have someplace to be like with angels and puffy clouds?"

"Sorry Erich. It doesn't work that way. I am only in your mind. Kill yourself and end this," Petrov said coldly.

Erich just ignored him and turned to the next page in his book. He was getting annoyed with this man. He was truly sorry for what had happened. However, it wasn't his fault it was that damn gypsy's. Why didn't this man haunt him instead?

"I know you can feel Nikolia's gift growing inside you. Eventually, it is going to push you out of your own mind. Erich Kaiser will be no more and only the beast will remain," Petrov said as he paced back and forth inside Erich's cell.

"Look, I'm sorry I murdered your family. I'm sorry I killed your entire village," he said with remorse. "That wasn't really me, though. I have to live with this for the rest of my life. You think I enjoy being tortured by you and all the others?"

"It doesn't matter what you think, Erich," Petrov hissed.

"Just leave me alone. Let me read my book in peace. One of two things is going to happen. I am either going to die in here or I am going to get out, eventually. If I get out, I can spend the rest of my life looking for a cure for this curse and atone for what has happened," he said as he tried to return to his book.

"There is no cure, Erich. Your death can only lift the curse," Petrov said.

"THAT'S ENOUGH!" Erich shouted.

He then stood up and threw his book across his cell at the dead man with unhinged anger.

"Leave me alone! Let me be! There is nothing I can do!" His voice almost turned into a growl as the anger built up inside him.

"You will eventually regret this, Erich. Once the beast pushes you out, many people will die," Petrov replied.

"I Don't Care!" He spat once more.

"Umm… Here is your food, Mr. Kaiser," a guard said from just outside the cell doors.

Erich didn't realize he was standing there the entire time watching him scream at someone who wasn't there.

Himmler sat in his chair outside of Erich's cell and drank a cup of warm tea. He was interested in how Erich was progressing. The guards had informed him of his outbursts and his sudden increase in mood swings.

"Do you hear voices, Erich?" Himmler asked.

"Well, not exactly," he replied.

"Please explain," Himmler inquired.

"Well, I don't hear voices as much as I see people. People I think the beast killed," he said as his voice seemed to quiver. "I think the people the beast murdered are haunting me. Trying to convince me to kill myself and end this curse."

"I wouldn't call this a curse, Erich. I would call it a gift," Himmler said proudly.

"How so? I mean, I think I have killed a lot of people that did not deserve to die. I murdered them and I have to live with that," he replied.

"They were all collateral damage in the name of evolution and science. You have been bestowed with something great. Something we need to learn to control. Something that will serve the greater good of man in the long run," Himmler said as he drank from his teacup.

We? Erich thought to himself.

"You have no idea how much I wish to be given such a gift. However, with the inconsistency of the other test subjects, we just don't understand enough at the moment," he said.

Understand? I wish I could just reach through these bars and tear out your throat, you pompous ass, he thought as he balled his hands into fists.

Relax... a voice inside his head said.

While Himmler kept rambling on, Erich's attention went elsewhere.

I'm sure his time will come soon enough. The voice continued. *I am not strong enough yet, but in time I will be. So just bide our time and do as this fool asks of you.*

Erich grinned slightly as he listened to whatever the Reichsführer was going on about. He knew deep down inside this chapter of his life would eventually be over and he would move on to greater things.

CHAPTER THIRTY FOUR

DETROIT

MAY, 1987

When Daniel awoke, he found he was bound with zip ties to a chair in the middle of a 12x12 storage unit. There was a shop light to his right that blazed away at his eyes. A short Native American man with a hard, stern face stood in front of him.

"Hey," Daniel said and tried to smile.

The Native American just stood there looking at him. After a long awkward silence, the man finally spoke.

"That's it? No diatribe?" Tanaka asked.

"Where the heck am I? What's going on?" Daniel asked as he began to panic. "Why am I tied up?!"

Daniel rocked back and forth at his bindings. Trying to see if he could get loose.

Tanaka was taken aback by this. This was nothing like Norman, who was someone who loved to talk. Thatch should have blabbered on and on about how he's going to slowly kill him. He wondered if Norman had finally lost it or if he was playing some kind of game.

"Look Norman, you're going to give me some answers... Now!" Tanaka said with clarity.

"Norman? Who the fuck is Norman?!" Daniel spat, still trying to wiggle free.

Then Daniel briefly paused for a second. He remembered Stanley had mentioned a man named Norman, but he still had no idea what was going on.

"Enough of this shit. Tell me what happened to Barbara," Tanaka ordered.

Daniel had a panicked look in his eyes as he peered up at the unknown assailant. He recognized him from Puzo's Market.

"You were at Mario's the other day. Yeah, I know you. He called you Mr. Chee," Daniel said.

Tanaka just glared at him, wondering how long this charade would last. Was Daniel more or less the man that became Norman Thatch?

"I have no idea who this Barbara is. I have no idea what is going on. Most importantly, why am I here?!" Daniel asked frantically.

"Look, I need to know what happened to Barbara…" He paused and thought for a minute and rephrased the question. "Tell me what Norman did to Barbara."

"WHO IS NORMAN!" Daniel screamed with so much intensity it caused his veins to bulge.

"Are we still doing this?" Tanaka asked.

He then put a silver bullet into Daniel's right upper thigh. He screamed in pain and tried harder to shake himself loose of his bindings.

"Jesus Christ! Please don't kill me! Please don't kill me!" Daniel repeated and begged as he tried not to pass out from the pain and the sight of so much blood. His heart began to race and he could feel a panic attack coming on. Then he was suddenly calm. Tanaka instantly noticed the shift in behavior.

"Well hello there, Sheriff Chee," Norman Thatch said as he looked at his situation and surroundings. "How delightful. I see you have met Daniel."

"There you are, Norman," Tanaka said.

"Oh look. You shot me, sheriff," he said. "With silver … again."

Norman looked down at his right thigh as blood began to drip onto the floor. The wound seemed to boil.

"Looks like it hurts. Now tell me. What happened to Barbara?" Tanaka demanded.

"Barbara?" Norman asked as he played coy. "Oh, That Barbara."

Norman paused for dramatic effect. He could see Tanaka's anger starting to fester.

"I tore her apart and then I devoured her liver," he said with a playful smile.

Then in a flash, Norman broke his bonds and shot up out of the chair. He swatted the gun out of Tanaka's hand and lifted him up off the floor by his throat.

"So good to see you, Sheriff," Norman said.

Tanaka's face began to turn red as Norman had pinned him securely to the wall of the storage unit. Norman's eyes were now yellow and rimmed with red veins.

"You look well," Tanaka said as he gasped for air.

"What should I do with you, sheriff? I've enjoyed our little game of cat and mouse, but I'm afraid it's time to wrap things up," he said while increasing pressure on Tanaka's windpipe.

Tanaka remembered he still had his revolver in the small of his back.

"How about letting me go? So I can kill you?" Tanaka responded with what little air he could squeak out of his throat.

Slowly, he inched his right hand towards his revolver.

"Why would I want to do that?" Norman asked with a smile. He revealed a mouth full of sharp teeth. "I really should just kill you and get it over with, but I think I owe you for Columbus. For that, I am going to kill you slowly. First, I'm going to rip out your tongue and eat it."

Tanaka reached for his Smith and Wesson and carefully slipped it from behind him.

"You really would drive a wooden Indian crazy with all your talking," Tanaka said.

Slowly, he cocked the hammer back on the revolver while he tried to keep him distracted.

"I'm sorry you feel that way, Sheriff. I've been nothing but polite to you from the start."

Tanaka cut him off by pulling the trigger, hitting the man in his left hip bone. The discharge of the firearm was deafening in the tight space. Norman dropped Tanaka to the floor as he reeled back in pain, holding his left hip as blood began to pour out of the gaping hole.

Tanaka grasped at his throat, trying to regain his breath, and hoped his ears would stop ringing soon. Norman calmly limped back to the chair he had been tied to and sat down. The rounds that were now embedded in his thigh and hip bone burned him from the inside as the silver began to poison his blood. Using his now talon-like nails, he began to dig the bullet out of his hip. Tanaka was still trying not to lose consciousness with the sudden rush of oxygen to his brain.

Look at you, sheriff… I love how much of a fight you always seem to put up when adversity is not in your favor," Norman said as he dropped the bullet he just dug out of himself.

It made a clinking noise as it bounced on the floor.

Tanaka scrambled to get the storage door open. Norman continued to dig into his right thigh and removed the second bullet. He then looked at the silver he extracted in his blood-soaked hand. Shaking his head, he looked over at Tanaka and frowned.

"You know, when I change, these wounds are just going to heal," Norman said matter-of-factly.

Tanaka got the storage door open. It retracted into the ceiling with a loud bang. He scrambled to his feet and took off in a run down the hallway, past the other units. Tanaka knew he didn't have time to grab his other pistol, and he cursed under his breath at the thought of the Detroit PD possibly finding it. From there, they would trace the gun back to multiple homicides between Texas and Memphis. He could not worry about that right now. His only worry was survival. Tanaka would not be able to put an end to this if he were dead.

Norman laughed as he began to change into the Yee Naaldlooshii. Tanaka ran as hard as he could down the hallway towards the flickering exit sign. The entire time thinking to himself that all this could have been avoided if he just accepted the fact his daughter was gone and would have just killed Norman without hesitation. This was all a moot point now.

The beast howled from inside the unit. It slowly exited the 12 x 12 box and looked to its left and right till it saw Tanaka running for the exit. Norman's beast chuffed and gave chase, galloping down the hallway on all fours toward the former sheriff. With his shoulder, Tanaka bashed his way through the door.

The lot was barely lit by a small handful of street lights. Tanaka made the twenty-yard dash to his truck just as the massive gray and silver beast crashed through the exit. What remained of the steel door slid across the parking lot as the beast stood heaving his chest in and out. Tanaka made it to his truck and quickly dropped the tailgate, then pulled out his Remington 870. He retrieved a box of slugs from his bag and dumped the contents out on his tailgate. Just as the beast began to gallop towards him, he racked the pump action and began firing. With inhuman speed, the beast zig-zagged and dodged the slugs as fast as Tanaka could fire them.

"Shit!" Tanaka spat as his gun clicked empty.

The beast stopped about ten yards from him. It stood up on its hind legs to its full eight feet, and they locked eyes. Like a modern version of David and Goliath, they stood silently facing each other. The werewolf began to chuff as it showed its teeth to Tanaka. He knew the monster was laughing at him because he didn't have any other place to go. It then, to Tanaka's surprise, motioned to his truck with its snout, still giving its wicked grin.

"You wanna chase me, don't you Norman?" he said while slowly taking a few steps back.

The beast chuffed again and nodded. Tanaka didn't waste any time. Tanaka threw his shotgun in the back of his truck and slammed the tailgate without taking his eyes off the beast. Quickly, he sprinted around to the driver's side of his Blazer and opened the door. He climbed up into the driver's seat and fired up the Chevy. His heart began to race even harder as he heard the Yee Naaldlooshii howl in what sounded like excitement. Pulling the gearshift on the steering column towards him and down, he put the truck in drive and floored it.

CHAPTER THIRTY FIVE

WEWELSBURG CASTLE

MARCH, 1945

Erich was locked away underneath the Reichsführer's castle for a little over two years. Considering his situation, he found that he wasn't treated badly for being incarcerated in a secret Nazi dungeon. All the tests and experiments had stopped. Himmler would let Erich out into the courtyard of the castle every so often to get some fresh air and sun. He had plenty of books and food brought to him every day.

The people he had killed still haunted him when he slept. The children would ask him why he took their lives away. This was a very hard pill to swallow for Erich. Himmler came to visit him one last time in March of 1945.

"The Fuhrer has gone completely mad, Erich," Himmler said as he smoked a cigarette and sat in his usual spot. "The war is coming to an end soon. All because of his impatience. Sadly, Germany has all but already lost."

He slowly exhaled a cloud of smoke.

"What are you going to do, Heinrich?" Erich asked.

The Reichsführer took a second to ponder the answer to that question.

"I have plans to speak with leaders of the Allied armies in hopes of making a deal," Himmler said.

Erich was stunned to hear this. He always thought that Himmler would go down with the ship in a blaze of glory. He didn't figure the Reichsführer was a traitor.

"So you're going to commit treason? What about the Fuhrer?" Erich asked.

Himmler took another drag off his cigarette and blew the smoke out his nose.

"To hell with the Fuhrer! If he wasn't so impatient, the Reich could have taken over the world," Himmler said.

Himmler then explained to Erich all about his other experiments with other bitten POWs. None of them were usable. Nor controllable. The infected person either went insane or became too deranged in a matter of a month. Some of them were completely incapable of even having a simple conversation or expressing a complete thought. When they were beasts, they showed no signs of memory or cognitive thinking. Only rage.

They appeared to have just three interests in their minds: killing, feeding and self-preservation. Himmler learned that fire did kill them. The Nazis also discovered the correct way to use silver to kill the beasts. One thing they all seemed to have in common was the loss of memory. None of them would have any memories of what happened to them after they changed or regenerated.

"Why are you telling me this, Heinrich?" Erich asked.

"Because I want you to know how to protect yourself," he said with a sneer.

Erich's skin crawled whenever Himmler spoke this way. He knew he had something in store for him and that could not be good. Anything that this man had planned would eventually lead to death.

"I have a mission for you, Erich," Himmler said bluntly.

"A what?" Erich responded.

"You heard me," Himmler answered as his face darkened.

Erich began to fidget on his cot as the Reichsführer continued.

"In the next day or two, some of my men will escort you to the border. They will be poised as British soldiers," Himmler said. "My plan originally was to unlock your secret and use it to create the perfect Waffen Werwölf" SS squad. This plan was to create a turning point with the war and eventually overthrow the Führer himself."

Himmler dug out a fresh cigarette and lit it taking a slow arrogant drag.

"But I've come to realize that was never the universe's actual plan. You, Erich. You are the plan. I believe it was fate that we met," Himmler said with pride.

Erich wasn't feeling any better about what Himmler was saying.

"You ARE the squad, Erich. It was always you. Because you're special. You are the only one who has been able to retain his humanity and your beast shows the highest cognitive brain activity. Which leads me to your mission," Himmler said.

"What is this mission you have planned for me?" Erich asked as he stood up from his cot and looked at the Reichsführer.

He wondered what fresh hell he was about to embark on now. How many more people were going to die because of this madman's ideology or at the hands of the monster he was cursed to change into?

"Once you meet my men, they will provide you with credentials that show you are a Czech immigrant fleeing the War. You will leave from Southampton by boat. I have already purchased a first-class ticket for you aboard the RMS Aquitania, which will take you over to the United States. They will provide you with enough money to start a new life in the Americas. There will be nothing else the Reich will ask of you. You will not have to report to anyone anymore after that," Himmler said.

"So correct me if I'm wrong. You're going to go through all this trouble to smuggle me out of the eastern front right under the Allies' noses. Just to have me shipped off to America to become a citizen of the United States?" Erich asked.

He wondered if he was about to become a free man.

"You are correct. I will ask nothing else from you. I want you to live a very long and happy life there, Erich," he responded like a Cheshire Cat.

The Reichsführer knew exactly what he was doing. What better way to get back at the Allies than to attack those pigs in their own homes? Himmler was going to unleash the ultimate hunter-killer on American soil. This is what Heinrich Himmler thought his destiny was. He was going to be the man who unleashed the real "Project Werwölf" and go down in history as the greatest Reichsführer that ever lived.

That would be the last time Erich ever saw Himmler.

CHAPTER SIX

DETROIT

MAY, 1987

Tanaka's Blue, 1984 Chevy Blazer raced across the parking lot of the self-storage warehouse with an eight-foot werewolf right behind it. He floored it and bashed through the wrought-iron gate in a shower of sparks and iron. He cut hard to the left and pressed the accelerator to the floor. Checking the rear-view mirror, he saw the gray beast slide across the street, then barel rolled into a parked car as it failed to make the sharp turn.

"Shit, shit, shit," Tanaka said as he white-knuckled his steering wheel.

Seeing how this was not part of his plan, he figured he would just improvise and drive like hell. Luckily, there were not many people on the road at this time of night. A few bums and prostitutes dove out of his way when he barreled past as the 700-pound beast ran after him.

The beast was enjoying this way too much. It had been a while since it was able to run like this. Tanaka quickly turned a corner and it leaped on top of a parked car with such force that it caused the side windows to blow out under its weight. It used its momentum to catapult itself towards Tanaka's truck. He watched his rearview mirrors and slammed on his brakes, causing the beast to smack into the back of his truck, shattering the rear window.

Tanaka once again stomped on the gas. The beast was stunned a bit as the Chevy tore off, spitting gravel and dirt in its face. Burned-out buildings and blight began flying past his windows as he reached sixty miles per hour. He checked the rear-view mirror and saw that the beast was no longer behind him.

He let off the accelerator so he had better control of his truck and dug into the center console for a spare box of silver bullets. While holding the steering wheel with his left hand, he retrieved his Smith and Wesson from the back of his jeans. Tanaka cracked open the cylinder wheel with a flip of one hand and ejected the empty shells. Laying the gun on his lap, he started loading six silver bullets into the cylinder as he swerved to miss road debris.

The beast got up after rear-ending the late-model Blazer. Then it darted off and climbed onto the nearest building, taking to the rooftops out of Tanaka's sight. It chased alongside the speeding truck, leaping between buildings as it galloped.

"Where are you, you bastard?" Tanaka said as he slowed his truck down and flipped his freshly loaded pistol closed. Scanning to his left and right, he wasn't able to locate the beast anywhere. In a sudden crash, it landed on his roof and began to drive its claws through the sheet metal.

"Shit shit shit shit," Tanaka said again as he pointed his pistol towards the roof and fired three times. The beast roared in rage.

As the beast expressed its frustration, Tanaka hammered on the accelerator. When he reached fifty-five miles per hour, he buckled his seat belt.

"Alright, shit-ass. Let's get this over with," Tanaka said.

The beast roared again and began to peel the top of his truck open like a tin can. He saved his bullets and concentrated on the road. As street lamps blurred by, he started to develop somewhat of a plan.

He slammed on the brakes, nearly t-boning a city bus. The werewolf was tossed from the top of his truck. The beast hit the bus like a meteor, causing the bus to rock back and forth on its shocks.

"Not quite what I had in mind," Tanaka said.

Grabbing his revolver, Tanaka ran around to the back of his Blazer and dropped the tailgate.

Jesus H Christ!" the bus driver screamed as the massive werewolf crashed through the side of his bus. The driver was the only other occupant at that time of night.

The beast gave a low growl as it tried to right itself. The bus driver was already bolting for the door when the beast roared. Tanaka pulled out his Remington and began jamming shells into the magazine port.

The beast still struggled to get free of the bus. The bent steel had punctured the beast's hide in multiple places, pinning it inside for the moment. Tanaka snatched up an ammo belt full of silver slugs. He tossed it over his left shoulder and ran.

Tanaka quietly muttered something his grandfather would always say: "The spirits of our ancestors guide us through life."

Across the street from the twisted bus was an abandoned church. Its single steeple leaning off center from years of neglect. Boarded-up windows now stood where intricate stained glass designs once were. Tanaka smashed through the plywood that blocked the front door and scrambled inside among the dirt and dust-covered pews.

"The spirits of our ancestors guide us through life," Tanaka said to himself once again as he prepared himself mentally.

The mangled skeleton of the bus began to rock back and forth as the interior lights flickered on and off. The werewolf went berserk as it tried to free itself. It kicked and bent steel as it pulled shards of metal out of its limbs. Savagely, it clawed and bashed its way through the side of the bus as it stepped out into the street and howled.

"Spirits…guide us through… life," Tanaka panted as he reached the pulpit.

Placing his shotgun across the podium, he pulled out his wheel gun and opened the cylinder. He pulled out the three spent casings and reloaded it with three fresh rounds. He quickly smacked it closed. With new confidence, he looked up towards the door and saw it standing just outside the threshold.

The beast hesitated. It did not like the scent of hallowed ground. To the werewolf, it always smelled tainted or soured. It snarled at the sheriff inside as it looked directly at him. Tanaka quickly grabbed his Remington from the podium and aimed. The beast was gone.

"Great. Now what?" he mumbled.

Taking his ammo belt, he pulled it over his head so it draped from the opposite shoulder like a bandoleer. After he tucked his pistol away, he raised the shotgun towards the boarded-up windows. He stepped down from the pulpit, keeping his eyes trained in front of his barrel as he cautiously aimed it in all directions.

"Through life…and they will continue to guide us in the next world," Tanaka whispered to himself.

Everything was silent. Nothing made a sound, not inside or outside. He figured after his epic drag race down Cass Avenue with an eight-foot werewolf running after him, someone must have dialed 911 by now. If the police arrived and Norman was still full-on Lon Chaney Jr, it would not end well for the Detroit Police Department. Lives would be lost and families would be ruined. Tanaka figured he had better kill this thing fast, or die trying.

As more perspiration began to drip down his forehead, he wiped his palm on his jeans to clean off the sweat. Just as he returned his grip to the Remington, he felt a heavy thud. The sound came from the floor under his boots. Followed by the floorboards slowly beginning to creak.

"What are you up to?" he asked to himself.

The floor behind Tanaka exploded, sending dirt and old, rotten wood through the air. The beast burst through the floor underneath the pulpit, causing the podium to fall to its side. It roared as it flung itself at Tanaka. He was able to spin his gun around just in time to pump two slugs into the beast's midsection. The beast went down, but its momentum made it tumble past Tanaka and slide to a stop.

With the gun still trained on the beast, he removed two shells from his ammo belt and thumbed them into the magazine port. He raked the pump once more and thumbed in a third shell so he had six rounds in total. Before he knew what was happening, the beast stood up and grabbed him by his face. It hurled Tanaka across the church and over the tops of empty pews. The werewolf steadied itself as it fell to one knee in pain from the silver in its gut. Then the beast looked down at its blood and it began to chuff at the situation.

"The spirits of our ancestors guide us through life…" Tanaka slurred before he blacked out.

The werewolf dug out the two burning silver slugs from its body and dropped them on the floor as it growled in pain. It stood up and began to slow down its breathing as it looked at Tanaka lying unconscious against the wall. The beast began to twist and deform as Norman Thatch started to regain his shape in human form. Once he transformed back, his wounds regenerated and healed. Now naked, covered in blood and grime, he walked over to Tanaka lying lifeless on the floor.

"Good God. Now that was fun," Norman said while he slowly clapped.

He could hear the sirens of the Detroit Police and Emergency vehicles far off in the distance. It would be just a matter of time before this area would be crawling with police and Norman had more pressing matters to deal with.

"Let's go, sheriff. The night's not over yet." Norman leaned down, grabbed Tanaka by his left pant leg and dragged him out of the church and over to his Blazer.

"99 Luftballons. Auf ihrem Weg zum Horizont," Norman sang.

The naked man dragged the sheriff across the street and placed him in the back of his truck as he continued to sing.

He opened the driver's door and then paused. Before getting in he looked around as if to survey the scene. Norman nodded in approval at all the chaos the last fifteen minutes had brought. The moment actually almost made him sad because it was time to leave this place behind.

"I hear North Carolina's nice this time of year. How does that sound, sheriff?" Norman said as he adjusted the rear-view mirror and started Tanaka's truck.

Tanaka awoke in the back of his Blazer. Wind and small fragments of glass swirled around his face as he bounced along to every bump Norman hit.

It took him a few seconds to figure out what was going on and get his bearings. He quickly noticed the duffle bag by his head.

"I can hear you moving around back there sheriff," Norman said while looking in the rear-view mirror. "We are not done just yet. Oh, no… There is much more fun to be had."

Tanaka launched himself over the back seat as he brought down a second syringe filled with fentanyl towards the back of Norman's shoulder.

"God, I'll miss this," Thatch said as he spun and caught Tanaka's wrist before he could drive the needle home.

The truck careened and side-swiped a parked sedan. Metal screeched and bent as the truck bounced like a pinball across the street and into the side of another parked car. Norman crushed Tanaka's wrist, shattering the bones. His Blazer continued to barrel down the city street, leaving a wake of scratched and mangled cars behind it.

"I have to admit. You are seriously not one to be taken lightly," Norman complimented. "As much as I don't want this to end, I believe you have overstayed your welcome."

Tanaka quickly saw his chance. In one fluid motion, he let go of the syringe in his right hand. When it dropped, he snatched it with his left hand, drove it into the side of Norman's neck and pressed the plunger. Just as Thatch let his wrist go, Tanaka pushed himself off and dove behind the seats. Bracing himself for the impact.

The blue Blazer veered off into a telephone pole. The impact hit the front passenger side. It crumbled like an accordion, causing Norman to sail from the driver's seat and through the windshield. His naked body slid and rolled down the sidewalk, leaving patches of his skin behind.

The sirens approaching from the distance brought Tanaka out of his daze. He quickly learned his wrist was broken as well as a few ribs. He could tell he had also dislocated his left shoulder. The grogginess he was feeling was probably due to a concussion from the impact.

"Damn it. Where are you?" Tanaka spat as he tried to look around.

Norman ripped the driver's side door off with intense anger. He tossed the entire door aside and staggered back and forth as the effects of the fentanyl ran through his veins.

Tanaka noticed that Norman looked a lot thinner than when the night started. He speculated this had to be from all the healing he had been doing and he was possibly growing weaker the longer this went on.

"Okay… I think… it's about time we wrap this up, Sheriff," Norman said as his speech started to slur.

The sounds of police sirens now filled the air. He also could hear the officers scream at Norman.

"Freeze!" multiple officers yelled out as they all began to aim their weapons towards Norman.

Right there, Tanaka saw the change from Norman back into Daniel. The fentanyl was causing Norman to short-circuit in this high-pressure situation.

"Holy Shit!" Daniel yelled and looked around at what was going on. He was naked, high as a kite and had no idea where he was or why there was a wall of police pointing guns at him. With panic in his eyes, he looked at Tanaka sprawled over the front seat of his truck.

Tanaka just watched him. In a way he felt sorry for Daniel. He didn't ask for any of this. He was sure that Daniel never wanted to be a bloodthirsty monster who slaughtered hundreds of people over the last few decades.

Daniel was just one more life the curse of the Yee Naaldlooshii ruined.

"Freeze!" the officers repeated. "Hands up and get on your knees!"

Daniel just looked around wildly. He was not sure what he was going to do. He couldn't think clearly due to the opioid in his bloodstream. His limbs were weak, and he was having a hard time keeping his balance.

"It's okay Daniel," Tabitha said.

Daniel looked down to find her standing there next to him, still wearing her Hello Kitty poncho.

"What are you doing here?" he asked.

Time seemed to slow down for him.

"Down on your knees! Now!" the cops belted.

"Let's see if we can get it right this time, okay?" she said as she took hold of his hand.

Noooo! Norman screamed from inside his head as the lights from the police cars danced up and down the sides of the buildings.

"Is this gonna hurt?" Daniel asked Tabitha while he stared at the wall of uniforms in front of him.

"Probably," she responded.

Right before Tanaka lost consciousness, he watched Daniel roar and charge at the line of the police officers. They were left with no choice but to open fire on him. Bullets tore through his body as the fentanyl did its job. Daniel fell to his knees and his momentum caused him to slide along the concrete and topple forward onto his face and chest.

Daniel watched Tabitha look at him as he lay there. He finally felt at peace as everything went to black.

CHAPTER THIRTY SEVEN

NEW YORK

APRIL, 1945

Erich Kaiser stepped off the boat at Ellis Island in April of 1945. Himmler had somehow arranged and funded for him to be expedited right away out of Czechoslovakia in first class. He was posing as a Jewish business owner by the name of Albert Metrik who was a wealthy merchant fleeing from the war that had ravaged Europe and his homeland.

Being a first-class passenger, he was able to bypass being detained and avoided any hassle from immigration. Once they got a clean bill of health, they took him to another ship that was allowed to dock and enter America. If you could afford a first-class ticket, the United States didn't feel as if you were going to be a bane of society. They processed you through pretty quickly so you could go spend your money on American soil as fast as possible. When they processed his paperwork, they misspelled his last name and it now read Methric instead of Metrik.

As Erich stepped off the dock, he looked at a small handwritten piece of paper. During his boat ride, he had compiled a list of names for aliases. The names Norman Thatch and Daniel Metrik were circled at the top of that list. He knew he was more than likely going to be living the life of a gypsy and wouldn't be staying in one place too long. So he figured that changing his name was going to be a frequent occurrence.

With this whole new world at his fingertips, he pondered on where he would end up. Erich had seen photos of the western United States as well as the West Coast. He thought it would be nice to see that someday. Or maybe he would go visit New Orleans and finally listen to some real jazz music. He daydreamed about all the different mixtures of culture he was going to take in while he was in this unfamiliar country. He even thought about growing a beard, which seemed to be a very Western thing to do.

For the first time in a few years, he was free. Other than being cursed with lycanthropy, he could come and go as he pleased. Soon he was growing excited at the thought of starting a fresh new life. Himmler had provided him with more than enough money to get by on his own.

"My God, these motor cars are huge," he said in broken English as a late model Cadillac Fleetwood drove past.

He took in all the awe and wonder as he looked up at the skyscrapers that made up Times Square. Everywhere he turned, his optical senses continued to be overloaded.

New York City was like nothing he had ever seen before. Everything was so big and loud. Giant buildings of steel and glass towered over the city like colossal titans of architecture. He noticed right away that people were not as welcoming as they were back home. This he attributed to America still being a young country full of inexperience and self-determination.

"Good lord. This place is magnificent," he said to himself.

Erich continued to walk along the sidewalks of the city until he found a sign that said "Room For Rent".

Thank you Himmler was something he never thought he would ever say after all those years in that megalomaniac's dungeon.

A month later, Erich read a New York Times article that informed him that Himmler took his own life at the end of the War in May of 1945 by swallowing a cyanide capsule.

For the next couple of years, he would stay in New York City. He found a way to isolate himself on the nights of the full moon. He would just take himself far into the wilderness of upstate New York and let the beast roam free. He was still haunted by apparitions of those lives he had taken as the beast. This constant persecution of his mind would kick-start the cracking of his sanity.

By the early 1950s, he would make his way south in hopes of finding less populated areas for him to reside. At first, he tried very hard not to allow his curse to hurt anyone else. Soon, he would discover the swamps of southern Florida. It didn't take him long to become a hermit who spent the next decade in isolation. He eventually changed his name to Daniel Methric, taking up the identity of Albert's son.

As time went by, the beast grew stronger and the death toll rose, unbeknownst to Erich. It became smarter and learned to kill secretly during the nights of the full moon, with Erich having no knowledge of what he had done. As a result, Norman Thatch was born. Norman was the wolf in sheep's clothing. He was evil incarnate. With Norman, the beast was in complete control and could walk among men like an average person. The curse had begun to push Erich out of his own body and mind. Once a month for three days, Norman came out. For those three days, Erich would have no memory of anything that had occurred.

Soon Norman was pushing himself to the surface more and more.

Still, he was limited and could only change on the nights of the full moon. Erich would, however, find himself blacking out when he found himself in distress, which caused Norman to come out. What started as only three days a month grew into weeks. Erich began waking up in strange places surrounded by death and carnage that was brought on by Norman's sadistic appetite.

In August of 1965, after the full moon, Erich would commit himself to a mental institution in Baton Rouge, Louisiana. At Saint Marie Richards' hospital, he checked in under his new identity as Daniel Methric. Here, he learned that sedation might help keep Norman at bay. So he'd hoped.

It wouldn't take long for the doctors to see the transformation from Erich to Norman. They began treating him for a personality disorder with electroshock therapy. It was like he was in Wewelsburg all over again. With every electro-shock session, the adrenaline and punishment on his body pushed Norman further and further into the foreground of Erich's mind. Shortly after that, the man known as Erich Kaiser was no more.

Norman was now the dominant personality. His psych evaluation labeled him as deceptive, manipulative, callous and arrogant. He was also prone to bouts of violence and rage. Yet he managed to remain very engaging; assertive yet polite. It didn't take him long to befriend one of the nurses at Saint Marie Richards which allowed him to get close enough to strangle her with his bare hands. This would lead to Norman being placed in isolation away from the general population. Here he was now under twenty-hour surveillance.

The only thing that Norman was able to do was read. Like Erich, he shared a similar love for the arts. Music, food, and literature were all he wanted to talk about while he sat in his cell. He considered and presented himself as somewhat of a renaissance man, or at least he liked to think he was.

Norman wouldn't learn of his full potential until a week before September's full moon in 1965. He waited until the time was right, snuck out of his cell and proceeded to go on a killing spree and murder the nurses, doctors and guards. One by one, using his bare hands and the new gifts the curse bestowed upon him, he became the perfect killer, even in human form.

Once he had neutralized the threats, he made the change for the first time without the control of the full moon. From there, the werewolf went from room to room. Slowly and quietly, he visited each patient. It crept through the hallways on all fours like a family dog making its nightly rounds, checking on its pack. It watched each one with cold curiosity as they slept before ending their lives. The only sounds it made were the crunching of bones and the smacking of its lips as it tore the patients of Saint Marie Richards apart.

Nobody made a sound. Not one person screamed. Most of the patients were lucky enough to die in their sleep. For the ones that did not, all they could do was lie in their beds frozen in horror as the beast made its way to them. Once Norman finished his massacre, he made the change back to human form. He would end his night of terror by setting fire to the hospital and erasing any trace that Daniel Methric or Erich Kaiser were ever there.

From Baton Rouge, Norman went to New Orleans and took advantage of the city's mysterious nightlife. Even though Norman was in control, Erich's will, however, was too strong for the beast to take over completely. A new personality would awaken from time to time as Erich's soul tried to fight back against the curse. Daniel was the result of this.

His Norman persona and his Daniel persona would fight for dominance on the battlefield of Erich's mind, causing a sort of "Hyde Effect" to develop. Daniel was the complete polar opposite of Norman. He was a kind and soft-spoken person who cared about people's well-being. In the beginning, he was well aware of what he was. He just couldn't remember who he was. He would go to great lengths to keep away from innocent people. Leading him to become isolated and alone. He eventually turned to alcohol and drugs to help sedate his other half to keep him suppressed as long as he could. This would eventually turn into a physical addiction that Daniel would never remember how, when, or why it started.

While Daniel was in the driver's seat, he tried to live a quiet, normal life. Norman hated this. He saw himself as perfection and Daniel as his major weakness. Daniel began to hear Norman's voice inside his head as he tried to badger him into giving up complete control of Erich's body.

As Himmler discovered in his experiments, lycanthropy tried to mold the host's body and mind into submission. It was quite common for those with the curse to hear the voice of the beast calling to them as it grew stronger over time. Himmler was never able to witness this with Erich Kaiser. Due to him being unlike the others.

The fact that Erich was bitten by Nikolia himself made him different from many of the other lycanthropes before or after him. Nikolia was currently the oldest living werewolf in existence. With that came certain benefits. Erich's beast was much larger, stronger, and smarter than any other after him. With Erich's strong will to live and stubbornness to not die came patience. The beast knew that, in due course, Daniel would just be a memory of Norman's past.

After a series of murders in New Orleans, Daniel packed up and moved out west by 1970. This enraged Norman when he awoke one afternoon to find himself in Albuquerque, New Mexico. Daniel had created a new life for himself. He even registered with the DMV and obtained a driver's license. As revenge and to show his dominance, he took it all away from Daniel. Norman killed everyone Daniel cared about in this new life he created. This led to the murder of Stanley Hawkins.

When Daniel finally reemerged in Portland, Oregon, he had no knowledge of how he got there or even any recollection of Norman. His memories were all but gone. All that was left were small blotches of Erich Kaiser's life from once he came to the United States. This made Daniel's alcohol addiction spiral. He would sink into a deep depression and further isolation.

What little remnants that remained of Erich's mind continued to create hallucinations of the people that Norman had murdered. Just like his mind did back in the bowels of Wewelsburg Castle. Each manifestation would haunt Daniel in hopes that it would drive him to end this torment on his own. This and Norman's constant henpecking inside Daniel's mind drove him to multiple failed attempts at suicide.

By 1980, Norman made his way to Seattle. There he spent years out in the Baker-Snoqualmie National Forest. He preyed on unsuspecting campers and hikers. This lasted a few years until Daniel once again emerged. His subconscious was doing its best to push him in the right direction to stop Norman once and for all. Stanley began to show up whenever Daniel found himself alone or drunk, constantly pestering him to "get it right" and doing his best to coach him into taking his own life. But Norman would consistently find a way to thwart Daniel's attempts.

1985 found Norman heading southeast to northern Arizona. Here he discovered the vast Coconino National Forest. The population of Coconino County was a quarter of what the Seattle area was. It was the perfect area for Norman.

Norman Thatch leaned against the base of a Ponderosa Pine in the Coconino National Forest. He had been playfully watching two women argue over tent stakes as they set up their campsite. He had noticed their scent as soon as they entered his forest. It impressed him that these two women were even out here so far in the woods alone. Especially after all the latest news reports highlighted some of Norman's work over the past month. Since he arrived in Arizona, his death toll there had already reached the number fifteen.

"This happens every time!" The blonde woman spat at the dark-skinned woman.

"What?" the other replied. "I'll just go find some sticks and whittle them down and we can use them for stakes. I mean, we only need four more."

Norman watched the blonde pace back and forth in annoyance. He could tell she was growing increasingly frustrated at what he sensed was her mate.

"Arrrgggghhh!" the blonde called out and stormed off to tend to the fire pit.

"Love you!" the other called out in response to her tantrum.

Norman found himself fascinated. A smile began to crack on his face at the thought of tearing these two apart. He hoped they would put up a fight. He assumed they would because they were brave enough to camp out here alone on the night of a full moon no less.

"Which one of you will I take first?" he said to himself as he watched them from a distance.

The two women were not aware of Norman's presence. They just went about their business setting up the campsite as he watched. That's when he was able to hear another vehicle making its way towards them. He took cover as the Jeep Scrambler approached.

It was coming in fast as it darted across the forest floor. With it came two new players to his game. One male and one female. The female's scent was different. He couldn't figure out why or put his finger on it. She gave off a sort of aura. He wondered if this was what Nikolia saw in Erich.

"Well well. What do we have here?" Norman whispered.

The Jeep tore through the landscape as a woman leaned out of the side.

"WOOOOOOO! YEAAAAHHHH! Looking good MAMA!" Barbara called out from the passenger window.

EPILOGUE

Tanaka lay in his hospital bed wrapped up in multiple bandages for broken bones and torn ligaments from his battle with Norman. His long black hair had almost turned completely gray since that summer in Flagstaff, 1985. He sipped on a small carton of orange juice through a straw while the TV in the corner played the evening news. Bill Bonds shared a story of a Satanic cult that was stopped by the Detroit Police Department after going on a bloody rampage across the United States.

"Satanic cult, now is it?" Tanaka said and chuckled, causing him to wince in pain.

"Hello, sweetheart! My name is Nurse Evans and I'll be your nurse for the rest of your stay here," a robust, overly animated woman said as she sprang into the room.

"Please tell me you have green Jello," Tanaka said

"I'll see what I can do, sugar," the nurse said with a wink, then scurried off to fetch him some Jello.

The story that Tanaka spun to the Detroit Police Department and FBI was that Norman Thatch, aka Daniel Methric, was the last of the cult that attacked the Sheriff's Department in Flagstaff in 1985. This wasn't exactly far from the truth, but he wasn't about to bring up the Yee Naaldlooshii or even say the word werewolf. They more than likely would have locked him up and thrown away the key.

On the other hand, he told them that he tracked Norman here across the country to Detroit, Michigan. He told them that one of Norman's MOs was to murder people by shooting them with silver bullets and then decapitating his victims. The FBI didn't flinch at the opportunity to wrap up the case and call it a day.

Tanaka couldn't tell if they were lazy or knew more than they were letting on. Regardless, he didn't care because they bought his story and, for now, he could rest. It had all gone by so seamlessly. Even Deputy McFerrin and the detectives in Memphis who worked Samantha's case vouched for him. Tanaka, however, kept waiting for the other shoe to drop. But it never did.

He started to wonder if he would go back to Flagstaff and try to get his old job back. With the loss of his wife and daughter, he felt that there was nothing left there for him. It was probably time for a change. Maybe he would head out to Montana and look for law enforcement work. He relaxed at the thought of slowing down for a while. Even just taking a job as a simple patrolman made him smile.

He was finally able to realize how tired he was. There had been so much death. Some of which were by his hands. Tanaka was afraid he was no longer the man he was two years ago. He worried about what his future would bring with what he now knew existed in the world.

"You have a visitor, honey," Nurse Evans said.

Tanaka nodded. A tall skinny man in a cheap suit and glasses walked into the room. He smelled like stale cigarette smoke.

"Hello. Tanaka Chee is it? My name is Special Agent Miers, and I work for a certain department of the government that deals in the sort of things like we just had here last week."

"What can I do for you, Agent… Miers?" he asked.

"I'd like to talk to you about what you saw or thought you saw the other night. Or any other night, for that matter. Was there anything out of the ordinary about this Norman Thatch? Or was it Daniel Methric?" Agent Miers asked.

"I have no idea what you are getting at, Agent Miers. I didn't see anything out of the ordinary. If you don't count the lunatic I tracked across a few states that was cutting people's heads off," Tanaka said.

"Right. So he was just a man, then?" Agent Miers asked.

"Yup. What else would he be?" Tanaka responded.

The agent furrowed his brow and then smiled at Tanaka lying there in the hospital bed.

"Tell ya what. Here's my card. If you ever need a job, contact me at the number there. I could use a man like you." Agent Miers handed Tanaka his card turned around and began to leave.

"What happened to Norman's body?" Tanaka asked before the agent could leave.

"I'm handling that personally," Agent Miers said without turning around and left.

He figured that Norman was probably going to be dissected and experimented on at the cost of taxpayers' money. Tanaka chuckled to himself at the thought of some special branch of the government tasked with hunting werewolves.

After he left Detroit, Tanaka found himself up in Livingston, Montana. There he worked with the Crow Nation tribal police offering his assistance in whatever ways he could. He never remarried and stopped his search for his daughter. In time, he accepted the fact that she was gone. He never received the closure that he had hoped for, but he had to move on. Like his grandfather used to say, "One cannot see the future with tears in your eyes."

His luck would change before long when something began murdering people in Yellowstone National Park. But that is a story for another time.

NORTH CAROLINA JULY, 1990:

Daniel sat at a table in the center of a white padded room 200 feet below Fort Bragg in North Carolina. They had handcuffed his hands to the center of the table. Across from him sat a young lady in a lab coat with a stack of files in front of her. As she reviewed the notes within the file, Daniel noticed Stanley was leaning against the wall behind her.

"Hate seeing you like this, buddy," he said.

"I miss Mac's," Daniel said, causing the interviewer across from him to look up from her papers.

"Come again?" she asked.

"I miss Mac's. It was a bar on the west side of Detroit. Mac was cool. I liked Mac," he said lowering his head in shame.

"What happened to Mac?" she asked.

"I killed him," Daniel said without making eye contact. He oozed melancholy.

He kept his head down and started to sob. The doctor knew exactly what Daniel was. He had been here for three years now. They brought him straight there from Detroit after he opened his eyes during an autopsy. He had been dead for forty-eight hours and was on a slab in the morgue. Just before the coroner started his autopsy, Daniel opened his eyes and began screaming.

While locked away under Fort Bragg, just like Erich was back in Nazi Germany, he was studied, poked and prodded. On the nights of the full moon, they locked him in a reinforced bank vault of a cell. Three-foot-thick walls of steel kept him from escaping and causing anyone any more harm. Daniel could remember just about all of his time while they incarcerated him. It was just the nights of the full moon that he could never remember. The days and nights in between the lunar phases, he remembered very well. It was as if Norman was gone.

The tests, the food, the smells, the people, all of it. Of course, Daniel made a few new friends while he was there, but he was forever hesitant to believe whether they were actually real or just ghosts from his past.

"You know, maybe if you blew yourself up, you might be able to end all this," Stanley said and chuckled.

"Shut up, Stanley," Daniel whispered beneath his breath.

"Excuse me, Daniel. Did you say something?" the doctor asked.

"Or maybe just set fire to this place and let you burn. Not sure how we can do that. Still, I think the idea holds some water," Stanley said.

"SHUT UP STANLEY!" Daniel yelled hysterically.

The Doctor jumped out of her seat and placed her hand near the alarm button on the wall. Nervously, she watched Daniel. He had always been so polite and docile until now.

"You okay there Daniel?" she asked while trembling

"I am so very sorry about that, Ms.?" Norman asked empathetically.

"S... Ss... Smith. Dr. Smith," she responded.

"Please, Doctor Smith, would you sit back down so we can talk some more?" Norman asked politely with a tender smile.

Realizing that he was still chained securely to the table, she relaxed a bit and sat back down. She smiled nervously and pulled out her pen and opened her notepad.

"What would you like to talk about this week, Daniel?" she asked, trying to hide the fact she was terrified in his sudden change of behavior.

"Well, I'm afraid to inform you that Daniel is no longer here. It's just me now," Norman said with a smile and a wink.

"And who are you?" the Doctor asked.

"My real name once was Erich Kaiser. Born in 1902, just outside of Berlin, Germany. I was an adept student who learned very quickly and later became what you would refer to as a scholarly man. In 1940, they drafted me into the 3rd Reich and they tossed me into a Panzer Division. My tank was destroyed at the battle of Stalingrad and I survived by running into the woods. Well, let's just say while in the forest I was given this…" Norman paused and looked at the doctor across from him. She reeked of fear. "Wonderful gift…" he continued.

The doctor frantically scribbled on her notepad. "Okay, if your name is no longer Daniel, then what is it?"

"Mein name is Norman Thatch. It is fery nice to make your acquaintance." His accent changed as he answered the doctor's question.

"Do you have a German accent now?" she asked.

"Do you know vhy Adolf Hitler lost ze Great Var? It's because he vas fery lacking in ein machor schtrategy," Norman said as he smiled devilishly.

The doctor started to tense up as her heart rate increased. He could sense this, and it brought him such joy and it had been some time since he felt this.

Norman effortlessly broke his handcuffs and chains and lunged for the doctor. He grabbed her around her mouth before she could scream. His eyes turned yellow and he started to grow new teeth. Very long sharp teeth.

"Ze Führer lacked Die Ausdauer," Norman whispered in a thick German accent as his bones began to crack.

The guards outside heard the doctor's screams as they saw the blood creeping out from under the door. Just as they were about to swipe their key card to gain access, the steel door jolted from the impact of something huge trying to get through.

RIAZA SPAIN JULY, 2024:

Nikolia Sergeev sat at a small bistro table in Riaza, Spain. He had a meticulously trimmed beard and medium-length hair that was slicked back on his head. Slowly clanking his spoon, he stirred his cafe con leches while reading the afternoon's paper. Riaza was about an hour north of Madrid in the province of Segovia. The modest village circled a town square and only had a population of around 2,000 people. A young woman with long black hair and Native American features sat down at the table across from him.

"Hello Barbara, I was expecting you to show up at some point in my life," Nikolia said.

"Nikolia Sergeev I presume?" Barbara asked.

He just looked at her for a minute, as if trying to decide whether to kill her right now or hear what she had to say first. He took a long slow sip from his cup.

"Da, that is correct," he politely nodded.

"You are not an easy man to find, Nikolia," she said.

It was the tenth anniversary of her father's death. She had never seen Tanaka again after Norman Thatch destroyed her world. Once her father died, she took up the task of ending the man who started all of this. Over the years, she had learned to hide her gift, at the same time researching everything she could. With the current use of the internet and social media, the modern age made it much easier than what her father had to go through.

Sergeev quietly stared at her from across the bistro table. A cool breeze blew by them both as time seemed to stand still.

"Da," he finally replied.

"I want to learn from you. I want you to teach me your ways," Barbara said.

Nikolia raised an eyebrow and took another sip from his cup. He didn't speak until he set the cup back down on its saucer.

"I have some potential. I've lived this long and haven't been killed yet or turned into a lunatic," she whispered while leaning into the table.

"Okay, I'll bite, little one. What would you like me to teach you? True, you have survived this long, so my interest has peaked," Nikolia asked with amusement.

"Everything. I want to know everything," she demanded.

Nikolia just smiled and stared at her for a minute. Tilting his head back and forth, studying her.

"Da," he said, as he nodded.

Barbara smiled back at him.

"Da!" he said louder with a grin and slapped his right hand on the top of the table.

He signaled to fetch the camarero. The server rushed right over to take his order.

"Please get whatever my young guest here would like," the Russian said in Spanish.

"I'll take whatever he is having," Barbara responded in the regional dialect.

The man nodded and quickly spun around to retrieve the woman her beverage.

She took a satisfying drink of the sweet, warm coffee mixed with milk and sugar. She looked directly into Nikolia's eyes. He seemed very pleased at the fact of taking on a protegee.

Barbara just smiled to herself and thought,

Patience…

THE END???